Battle
in the Avenue

Sean McCutchen

Published by Lake Time Books, Inc.

ISBN 979-8-9854131-0-6

Cover and Interior design by www.ebooklaunch.com

For Dad.

"Let's be clear. The planet is not in jeopardy. We are in jeopardy. We haven't got the power to destroy the planet—or to save it. But we might have the power to save ourselves."

- Michael Crichton, Jurassic Park

CHAPTER 1

Owen Bradley made broad strokes as he erased the chalkboard. The University of Chicago, where Owen was a postgraduate student, had managed to gather the swamp-green colored boards from shuttered schools in and around the city. Every time Owen worked with them, the dust tickled his nose and made him long for the days of dry erase markers.

"Excuse me, Professor Bradley?" Came a voice at his back. "What you talked about in class, the SOR supply chain problem, can it be fixed?"

Owen turned from the board, leaving half of the subject in discussion still visible.

"I don't think so. The problem with anything we make is that it requires raw materials. These calculations are based on real data that shows the yield per acre declining rapidly for the primary material needed to make Synthetic Oil Replacement—sugar. I'm afraid it's the beginning of the end for SOR."

The pair of undergraduate students looked at each other with wide eyes. They were two of only thirteen students enrolled in the spring semester of Physics 101. Going to college had become the exception to the rule, instead of the norm, over the last decade.

"Are we headed for another collapse?" the first student asked.

"Yeah, another Fuel Wars?" the second added.

Owen raised his hands with palms open and looked at each of their questioning faces. He could only imagine what their parents went through raising babies as the Fuel Wars ravaged civilization. Owen himself had been only five years old at the time. The moment in history was shortly after his parents had passed, and the beginning of his long road of loneliness that had led him here. His eyes cast down on the table between them. "I don't think so. The Fuel Wars were a dark time for the world, but I think we can keep from going there again."

"How?"

"Throughout history, society had lifted itself up by the bootstraps and when innovation was needed, it was delivered," Owen said, giving precisely the reason why he studied alternative fuels. All he had ever known of a connection to humanity, was hope. This led him to want to solve the SOR crisis and deliver a future that could unite them all. Owen had to cling on to the hope, because there hadn't been a breakthrough in years—the outlook among his academic circles far bleaker than he let on.

He continued. "Well, for one, we know what the Fuel Wars were like and I want to believe we'll avoid that at all costs. And two, the best minds at this University and around the world are working on a solution. Trust me, we aren't the only ones that know that the sugar required to produce SOR isn't keeping up. There are daily yield reports and governments are constantly debating clearing more and more land to grow on. Only society can tell us if there will be another Fuel Wars, but I'm not overly worried about it."

Owen turned back to the board and continued erasing. He always had a hard time maintaining eye contact when he was lying, so he took it out of the equation.

"Won't an alternative take time? How much time do we have?"

"There's no way to accurately predict how fast the supply will dwindle. The same sort of thing happened for the end of natural oil. Everything from demand fluctuations and line breaks, to weather and storms—they all impact the supply and that has to be modeled globally. There are just too many variables. The calculations we worked today are a simple example of a complex real-world application for statistics and predictive modeling."

A fresh cloud of dust erupted from the end of a swipe. "I'm looking for Owen Bradley," came an unfamiliar voice from the back of the room.

"I'm Owen," he said, as he finished cleaning the chalkboard. Satisfied, he turned to find a courier quickly moving towards him. Owen could only watch in amazement as the matching purple shorts, shirt, and hat came to stand next to him. Before he knew what was happening, Owen found himself holding a package.

"I didn't order anything." Owen said. "Who is it from?"

"I just deliver, man." The courier replied. "And I get paid by the delivery."

"Ah, okay." Owen said to the man's back. He could only watch in awe as long strides took the purple swiftly out of the room. Owen muttered to himself, "I wonder what it is?"

He found in his hands a plain brown cardboard box with no identifying marks on it except for the courier's label. Owen turned it over and over on all sides, surprised at how light it was despite being slightly bigger than a ream of paper.

Owen realized the two students were still looking at him, their faces as forlorn as if they had lost a pet.

"I know it's tough," Owen said. "But SOR isn't going to collapse overnight. We've already seen the price climb and climb. At some point, people won't be able to afford it anymore. It will still exist though, and maybe even come down a little in price. SOR won't be like the collapse of oil, where suddenly there wasn't any more and we couldn't make it. Don't worry, something else will have to meet the demand—it always does."

The student's eyes went from loss of a beloved dog to first time goldfish. Satisfied they weren't overly distraught, Owen dismissed them. The next class would be arriving soon. A course in statistical analysis was an appropriate session for their conversation, but the first years weren't ready for it and Owen needed a few minutes to prep. He was subbing in due to the declining numbers in academia and he took the job seriously. Setting the box on the edge of the desk, Owen began to add notes to the freshly blank board.

The class proceeded smoothly with many hands scratching notes to the rhythm of Owen's voice. When they concluded, Owen was done for the day. As the final remnants of the nine students in the class filed out, Owen gathered up his tattered bag and wrapped the package under his arm. He decided to wait and open it when he got back to his apartment.

The late-afternoon sun was shining bright and added to the warm, early May weather. Like the majority of people,

Owen had grown accustomed to his body's temperature being left to the whims of nature. He didn't mind, and any thought of discomfort was absent as the intertwining sidewalks of the University campus led him home.

The buildings were a portal in time, standing almost as they had been since before the Fuel Wars. What little money the University could spare went towards upkeep and their task as landlord. A majority of universities had shut down and those that remained open were usually in a major city. This allowed them to use their once sprawling campuses to house students, teachers, plumbers, and everything in-between. The offset in rental income went towards keeping the lights on, something that wasn't a guarantee in the age of SOR.

Owen lived on campus in one of the last University acquisitions before the Fuel Wars. An old canning factory had been converted into student housing but kept most of its previous charm. Owen saw it as he rounded a corner and by force of habit, found his window on the second floor. He had left it closed with the black-out curtains drawn. Good, he thought, not long now before the sun would start to set and he could open it up to let in a nice breeze.

Entering the apartment, Owen set his bag and the package next to his keys on the discolored dining table. He brushed past one of the four mismatched chairs as he made his way to the kitchenette and got a glass of water. Owen looked beyond the rim as he drank.

The walls were mostly exposed brick wall with industrial style panes for windows. Owen really enjoyed it and it was a good thing, because the walls were mostly bare. He was supposed to have a roommate, but they left a few months before to seek a more stable economic situation. Owen understood. Having spent a majority of his life in boarding school, he was used to the coming and going of people. Owen was happy to commandeer the spare bed as a place to spread out notes and school work. The setup made everything easy to see all at once.

Academic work made sense to him. He had grown up living in the endless silence of contemplation. Owen knew that was why he continued at university when everyone he knew came and went like the changing of seasons. He understood that he was in the right place, doing the work that needed to be done. He knew that was why he had lied to those undergrads about his true fear for the end of SOR. Somewhere, deep down, Owen still held on to hope.

Trading his empty glass for the package, Owen was ready to find out what lay behind the mystery. With a little bit of effort, he managed to tear open one side of the box.

He peered inside. A dark void of brown greeted him.

Tilting the box for better light didn't help. There was nothing in it but walls, four brown corners, and a packing slip.

"Wow," Owen said. "I can't believe I got an actual package of nothing but air. This is a first."

Curious as to what was supposed to be in the box, Owen dug out the paper. The act was surprisingly difficult as the paper clung onto the wall of the box with an invisible static force. Prying it off, Owen brought it up to read. He looked at it, blinked a few times, then looked at it with furrowed brows.

His eyes saw what they saw but his mind did not comprehend. On the paper was a single line. The sight of it sent Owen's heart pounding as his feet sank into the floor. He turned the sheet over—nothing. He had just been sent a package with a line that read:

Celestial bodies abound in close family heirlooms found.

Celestial bodies? Family heirlooms? Found? Owen's mind swam with fractional thoughts and a thousand questions. He tried to focus and gravitated to the one word he knew nothing about—*family.*

As far as Owen knew, his entire family had died suddenly when he was four years old and he hadn't been able to find any trace or history of them since. Looking up from the paper held clutched with both hands, Owen's gaze found the lone item hanging on the wall—a framed sketch from a cartoon. The show had been his favorite growing up and it was the only thing he had from his childhood. There weren't any pictures, no hand-me-downs, and certainly no heirlooms. And now he held a piece of paper in his hand that, with a simple phrase, turned his world upside down.

*****

The air was heating up quickly on that quiet Friday afternoon, and Clare welcomed it. The sweat running down her cheeks and beading across her neck made her appear vulnerable—adding exactly the element she needed to complete her desired look.

Keeping an eye on the clock, Clare smiled in revered silence as she ran her hand across the dash of her 1967 Chevy Nova. The car was the only thing her biological father had left to her, and thinking about it always struck sentiment in her heart. She didn't really know the man, only a handful of faint memories. She liked to believe that he was as beautiful as the car he loved. This was the reason she had decided to add the SOR convertor to the classic Nova, because the machine needed to live on despite what the world tried to take away.

Clare hadn't seen a single car in the ten minutes she spent pulled over to the side of the road. Her research showed that County Road 513 was rarely used. The lone stretch of road was the perfect place for her to set up. Clare watched as the clock rolled over a new minute; it was time. Flipping a switch below the ignition to disconnect the battery from the starter, Clare looked to the rearview mirror and kept an eye on what was behind her as she adjusted the two braids hanging to either side of her head. She needed to look as young as possible, and just as naïve. While getting out of the strikingly polished car, she unbuttoned the top three buttons of her blouse for good measure.

Clare knew every inch of the car and casually propped opened the hood in the same way she had done many times before. Positioning herself bent over the driver's side headlight, Clare shifted her hips to expose her long, toned legs to the road. The sun's powerful energy quickly warmed her newly exposed skin. Now transformed into a hot and stranded country girl… she waited.

Sometime within the next few minutes Clare knew that the county sheriff would be passing by. Her target kept a strict routine, but life was inevitably variable despite the best made plans, so Clare was ready and waiting.

Only a gentle breeze stirred as Clare took a deep breath to focus on what she knew. The Hancock County sheriff had an impeccable service record, with over thirty years on the force. He was friends with congressmen, union leaders, and community standouts all over West Virginia. But Clare knew the truth, and so did her client.

Hiding behind his badge and a flawless public persona, the sheriff was untouchable from within the system. Clare, however, took the liberty to operate outside the law. She believed some things weren't meant to be judged in polished mahogany courts of law run by corrupt men. There were some things that needed the swift decision of unrelenting justice.

Her process required that she had proof of the target's crimes before she committed to a contract. The client knew exactly where to look and provided Clare with the info. Only a week before, Clare had snuck into the man's house to find proof of his crimes. The images of what she had seen were gut-wrenching and flooded her thoughts now as her sweat dropped onto the engine with a brief sizzle.

As she recalled each one of the horrific scenes she had discovered, it made her boil with rage. The experience focused her and was the jolt she needed as her target's large SUV made its way around the bend.

She worked to steady her breathing.

The law enforcement vehicle—outfitted in the same way as her car to operate on SOR—slowed as it passed her then pulled over to the shoulder. The sheriff climbed out. The sight of him caused Clare's heart to beat steady. Her nerves retreated. She was in control.

"Oh, thank you, thank you!" she said in her best country drawl. "I haven't seen anyone pass by in an hour. Thank you so much, officer!"

The man had a thirteen-inch height advantage plus a solid hundred and twenty-five pounds on her. Still, she held her ground, confident in her ability.

"What seems to be the trouble, miss?" the sheriff asked, just touching the brim of his hat, his eyes hidden behind thick sunglasses. He had the look and the walk of a man with nothing to hide.

"I'm not sure, officer. I'm just on my way to see my aunt and Betsy here died. Now my cell phone doesn't work and if I'm not there by supper, then my aunt will call in the cavalry. Which I guess is you. I'm just having a terrible time today. But, now that you're here, I feel a lot better." She opened her stance and placed both hands on her hips to pull her shirt tight across her chest.

"Well, ma'am, these classics running a SOR convertor can be fickle," the sheriff said, his neck staying still as Clare felt his eyes scanning her body. "I'm surprised you could find a SOR convertor for her. Seems you can't find any quality classics anymore, most left to the scrap yards since the collapse."

"Well, I've always admired muscle," Clare said, biting her bottom lip.

The sheriff's left eyebrow rose above his sunglasses. A few moments passed as his mind caught up with his lust, and he moved to stand in front of the exposed engine body. "Betsy looks finely taken care of though. Maybe we can get her up and running again."

Clare moved closer to him, brushing her hand on his shoulder and taking note that he wore his uniform collar loose. She spoke lightly, "I would be much obliged."

"Well, I'm no mechanic, but I would be remiss if I didn't take the opportunity to get my hands on a '67 Nova." He pushed his sunglasses down his nose to reveal the brown eyes of a heartless bastard. He turned from the engine compartment to look at Clare. She met his gaze, putting on doe eyes as best as she could.

"Oh officer, you know your cars!" Clare said with a forced giggle. "That's about the only thing I know about this one. I just love the color."

The sheriff's lips curved into a primitive smile, thinking all that stood between him and getting lucky was probably a loose electrical wire. He was full of what stereotypes were based on. She had him and it was almost too easy.

"Well, ma'am, why don't you try it and we'll see what we're dealing with."

Clare slid back into the car and tried the ignition. Nothing happened—the car played dead.

"Could be an electrical problem," he shouted from under the hood.

She observed him with disgust through the slit under the open hood. He was looking around and jiggling a few wires, completely clueless. For some reason, men that didn't know any better thought a couple tugs would be enough to fix a complicated machine. The sheriff's hands passed over the engine compartment, hoping to get the bad karma out of it. In no time at all, he asked her what she knew was coming.

"Let's give it another try."

Clare smiled, a genuine smile this time—everything had gone according to plan. She flipped the ignition kill switch back and tried the key. The two-hundred-and-seventy-five-horsepower engine roared to life as perfectly tuned as it had been when it rolled off the factory line almost three-quarters of a century before.

Clare pulled out what looked like a makeup case and covered her left index finger thoroughly with the gooey substance inside of it. Satisfied she had enough on her finger, she stepped out of the car, leaving the door open.

Skipping over to the sheriff, she said, "Oh, thank you, thank you! My big, strong hero!" Without hesitation, she threw her arms around the sheriff's neck. The gesture didn't bother the man. Instead, he leaned heavily into her advance, despite being thirty years her senior.

Her skin crawled, breaking her concentration for a moment, as what she found at his house flashed once again before her eyes. Clare had gone in search of proof for her client's claims and what she came away with was worse than she had imagined.

In what Clare perceived to be the man's office, she found several boxes piled on the closet floor. Inside them were rows and rows of folders containing photos of young women tied up to the same dirty, cinderblock walls. The photos weren't enough for her to be convinced. The sheriff could have some sick perversion to the images that, although disgusting, was not the type of target she sought. So, Clare continued to look, pressed forward by her client's testimony. It wasn't long before she found the stairs leading down.

The walls of the basement were cinderblock, the same as those in the photos, but instead of one large room, it was divided into five partitions. Each area was bare except for a set of hooks driven into the wall and shackles ready to restrain. The stench of urine and feces had made Clare's eyes water. How many women had come through here? The thought of it had caused Clare to search frantically only to find that none of the holding cells were occupied. She had been relieved. She hadn't known what she would have done if she had found someone.

The dungeon at the sheriff's house was enough to prove his guilt. The man had been running a sex trafficking operation right from the inside of his house and the soulless piece of shit had been at it for decades. It took all of Clare's tenacity not to vomit while standing there among cages meant to hold women that were no different than herself. Recalling those feelings solidified Clare's resolve. The seemingly naïve young country girl had come for him to hasten his judgement—the man deserved to die.

She slid backward, letting her left index finger glide across the exposed skin of his neck. Clare made sure all of the substance she had taken from the case was transferred there.

She glanced at his badge, though she already knew his name. "Well, Sheriff Miller, you are my hero." Taking a step back, she pivoted sheepishly on the spot, hiding the fact that her left index finger was now in her shorts pocket, submerged in a solution to render any leftover acting agent inert. "I am terribly late, but I don't suppose…" she started, playing up the part and keeping his mind away from his oily neck. "I don't suppose I could bring some fresh-baked cookies by the station on my way back through town on Sundee," she said, putting a little too much emphasis on the accent. "I would like to show my appreciation, and maybe we could get a bite to eat. You know, when I'm not expected anywhere until… the next day."

"That sounds like a mighty fine invitation," the sheriff responded. "I wouldn't be a gentleman if I turned down such a generous offer from a pretty young lady like yourself."

Clare turned and walked back to stand behind her open driver's side door. "Well, 'til Sunday then—and bring your appetite." She winked in his direction.

The sheriff could only tip his hat to her as she put the car in gear and drove off. Glancing in the rearview mirror, she could still see his dumbfounded expression as he watched her go. Clare knew that a small rash would start to appear on his neck. The slight discoloration would be the only indication of the chemical agent entering the man's bloodstream. From there, it was only a matter of time until the sheriff suffered cardiac arrest and the world was rid of another parasite.

Clare let out a deep sigh. "Rot in hell, you bastard."

County Road 513 wound around a hill and she was on her own again. Clare opened and closed her fists to loosen her grip on the steering wheel. The job was done for now; she could relax. The steady sound of the Nova's engine settled her mind. She let out a long, deep breath. Driving in the quiet car allowed her past to creep into her thoughts. The screams were faint at the back of her mind, like far off birds forever fighting over scraps. The memory of it too far in the past to know what was real and what was only her mind's fiction.

She knew there had been a car wreck when she was young. The circumstances and facts surrounding that day she had tried to piece together with gut feelings and whatever she could find. Clare had lost her parents in that wreck and with it, they seemed to vanish from existence. Her memory was all that seemed to be left of them. Over the years, her memory had twisted and tangled itself in doubt, but it was all she had.

If she closed her eyes, crimson flashes of fire lit up her vision as the scarred image of her mother slumped over the steering wheel came forth. Clare believed the image to be true. Maybe the screams of pain were her own, the sound of her soul bellowing unrecognizable to her own ears. She could never fully comprehend it and had spent the last seventeen years searching for some form of closure. The pain of it caused her to remember what had happened while the belief that it hadn't been an accident drove her to a life of vigilante justice.

The life she had chosen was how she came to be on the side of County Road 513 that day. The sheriff was the next contract, one in a long line of her quest against the powerful. Clare sought to rid the earth of every bit of evil that crossed her path. Each contract she executed was an attempt to quell the screams plaguing the quiet recesses of her mind, but the shrill pitch of her memories remained. So, she continued to search for retribution, refusing to believe that the truth was out of reach.

CHAPTER 2

Three decades before the Fuel Wars would even occur, James Stevenson, at age 10, was already quite the extraordinary young lad. Not amounting to much in stature, James stood taller than his physical presence with his big heart and insatiable appetite to learn.

The son of a mathematics professor at the local city college, James had more friends with the title of librarian than that of classmate. He didn't notice, or really care; to him it was how things should be. His developing mind constantly created vast new narratives full of robots, monsters, and exploits of saving the world. James was always happiest with a book and the limitless expanse of his own imagination.

Or at least… so he thought.

A Friday afternoon in the fall before the start of the 21st century found young James coming home from school along his usual route down West Webster Avenue. His footsteps were on autopilot as his thoughts drifted to sounds of metal crunching and scraping as large robots battled among the swaying trees above his head. The size of the battle as limitless in his mind as the sky was vast. The brilliant blue peeking through the foliage brought on whistling from his lips in a joyful tune. His father had promised to take him star-gazing the following evening at Chicago's brand new Doane Observatory. James' mind already dwelled in the cosmos. Now, he would actually get to see it and he stood as gleeful as a kid in a candy store holding a crisp ten-dollar bill.

Coming to the corner of West Webster and North Cleveland Avenues, James was suddenly brought back to reality. His merry tune carried off into the breeze with what his eyes couldn't pull away from. Frozen in place, his feet firmly rooted, James couldn't help but gasp at the scene unfolding across the street from him.

Another young boy, appearing to be the same age and stature as James himself, stood surrounded by three older and considerably larger boys. James didn't recognize any of them but the intersection was near a boundary between school zones.

"What's wrong kid?" the older boys joked, swarming around the younger lad. "Heard your old man likes to pick up trash. Is that why he picked your mom?"

The largest of the bullies was the one running his mouth but that didn't appear to provide the desired result. So, he stepped forward and shoved the kid to the ground. The three burst out in laughter as their victim simply stood back up and planted his feet defiantly in the same spot.

"You being funny?" The kingpin of the lesser humans asked. "I think he wants some more." With that witty remark, he shoved the kid once again to the same outcome—back up the boy rose.

"You think you're being smart or something?" The main bully asked sarcastically. "I think this tough guy needs a lesson." And with that, he threw a right cross that landed square on the kid's chin. The boy went down hard but that didn't stop the three of them from proceeding to kick his small body from every possible angle.

James' heart pounded in his chest with every blow he saw. He wasn't sure what to do or what he could do as a heavy pressure grew inside him along with the baseball sized lump stuck in his throat.

"HEY!" James yelled, surprised to hear his own voice.

The kicks stopped as the three boy's heads snapped to look in his direction. James was certain now that he had not planned for the outcome of his outburst. But, in what was his most stupid and most daring act in his ten years on the planet so far… James gathered every nerve of his sixty-seven pounds and flipped them the bird.

The stunned looks from the bullies only confirmed their stupidity. And with one finger already raised, James dramatically brought the other hand alongside it—full double bird. The reaction was almost instantaneous as the older boys forgot about their downed prey and took flight after a new one. James smiled his broadest smile as he turned on his heel and ran. He couldn't outrun them, but he had a fifty-foot lead and his mind had taken the slight delay as an opportunity to catch up; his destination was close.

He could sense them closing in and fast, but he wasn't worried. Reaching the handle, James arrived at the convenience store he frequented often and opened the door quickly. Once inside, he hurried to the counter where the familiar clerk looked at him confused and a bit concerned that James was out of breath. Only moments later however, the clerk got his answer as the three brutes skid to a stop in front of the shop. They threw their hands up in disgust, then awkwardly began to wait around for him to come out.

James' big smile never faded as his mind began to work a new problem. He knew that he would have to come up with a better plan for next time. He wouldn't be able to outrun them forever.

*****

Clare made it back to the city late on Friday night. She needed to gather wood for the next day's classes, which was no easy task. She put the car away in her storage garage and retrieved her knife from the glove compartment. The knife was the only weapon she ever carried despite being adept in several. She turned it over in her hand for a moment as she sat there. The blade was the first thing Mr. Furmore had given her upon her arrival to the farm. He had taught her every possible use for it, including the skill of throwing it. He said that if she got good enough to hit a rabbit, then she'd never go hungry. Clare wasn't sure if that moment was exactly the reason, but the thought of eating a bunny to a seven-year-old girl was enough to convince her to be a vegetarian. Clare smiled, thinking about all the memories she associated with that simple gift. The act of spending time together. The passing of knowledge and skills down to her. She understood that it was the simplest gifts that were the most meaningful.

Exiting the car, Clare returned the knife to its resting place at the small of her back. The small comfort of it returned to its proper place gave her footsteps confidence as she walked the three blocks to her apartment. Her building wasn't in one of the nice neighborhoods of South Chicago, but the rent was what she could afford and she didn't mind the petty crime.

Clare's walk was lined with unused electric streetlamps that the city no longer deemed a necessary expense. Instead, people gathered on sidewalks and stoops, burning garbage and anything else they could. The dancing light transported the street to another time, before TV had enticed everyone inside their own homes.

Keeping her eyes peeled for anything remotely resembling a solid piece of wood, Clare turned into an alley she knew held a dumpster. She had her first bit of luck and found the rusted garbage receptacle with both of its large flaps already open. Clare walked up next to it and peered over the side. There was nothing but darkness. She held up her phone to confirm but her initial finding was correct—no wood there.

Clare could remember when things were easier and SOR was abundant, but she was a lot younger then. In the years since, the price of manufacturing SOR kept climbing. The higher cost of energy drove the cost of everything else. Soon, more and more people moved into the city and learned to live on less. They shared rooms, appliances, anything and everything they could just to survive on what money they could manage to earn. Clare enjoyed the sense of community the coziness brought. Evenings were now spent outside, gathered around in groups that could be heard laughing and singing down every block.

Clare made it to her own block and went around back to check out the two dumpsters there. These were a bit more difficult as their lids sat closed. She managed to hold the lids open and get a good look inside. The first had some bits of trash, but nothing useful. The second was more of the same. Clare's frown was as bold as the stench now surrounding her.

She would have to start early in the morning to find what she needed. She could of course buy some boards, but even the most diehard hobbyists had left their woodworking tools to collect dust. She could delay the board breaking lesson if she needed to, but it was one of her favorites.

With the soft tune of a single trumpet's melody at her back, Clare unlocked the door to her building. There may have been a renewed sense of community, but criminals still lurked in the shadows. People were forced to extremes with every uptick in the price of a kilowatt.

Passing the chained elevator doors, Clare made her way up the stairs. She lived on the fourth floor, which gave her enough time to check her bank account. She pulled out her phone and dialed the bank's number. She had heard stories of smartphones and mobile banking applications, but she had never experience them herself. The advancements of technology and convenience were seemingly starting to reverse themselves everywhere she looked. The automated voice reported that the latest transaction in her alias account had posted for two thousand dollars. The amount covered her expenses for the county sheriff cleanup job, which was what she and her client had agreed upon. That was all this client could afford and Clare wasn't in it for the money. Crimes against women got a discount and one fewer scumbag on earth was enough of a payment for her.

Putting her phone away as she reached the final step, Clare began down the hallway toward her door. She moved slowly, listening. Her eyes stared forward, allowing her ears to pick up the slightest sounds. There was music down the hall. The floor creaked under her weight. There were hearts beating, their eerie connection to her separated only by paper-thin walls.

She focused. Her left hand lightly touched the hilt of her knife. Her right hand turned the key in the door. The single-room loft apartment was pitch black. Clare stepped over the threshold and turned to face the door as it shut. The door clicked home in the latch.

She spun rapidly. Her knife flew out of her hand and landed directly at its target.

Thud.

The knife struck perfectly horizontal, buried an inch into the mounted board she used for target practice.

Clare approached slowly, keeping her eyes locked on it as the tattered face underneath took form. Grasping the hilt, she pulled the blade out and slid it methodically back into its sheath on her back.

Lingering there, she took in the remains of the relic: an old magazine cover, one of the last issues of *Forbes* before the demand for print magazines ran out. The cover a relic from the first few days of the Fuel Wars. The article speculated the impact of losing a global staple such as oil and its effects on the future. But with this resource gone, entrepreneurs had seized opportunity in the aftermath. The man portrayed on the front was one such person—a ruthless businessman, stopping at nothing for the next great conquest. Seventeen years later, he had continued ascension beyond comprehension, the *Forbes* reporter unable to predict his unparalleled success at the time of the article.

Clare had grown up with a sense of justice. She knew the man eliminated anyone that dared to stand in his way. Yet, he seemed untouchable. The police, the FBI, they all steered clear of him. The cracks in the system had splintered in all directions, in her opinion, and she was there to fill them.

He was local, living on her home turf of Chicago. And

over the years she had led herself to believe he was involved in the loss of her parents. She couldn't exactly place why. The circumstances of his rise to power. The lack of information regarding the loss of her family. Her ideas on the personal connection may have all been misplaced, but she was certain the man was a criminal that needed to die.

As she studied the jagged edges of the shreds on the board, her blue eyes turned steely gray with resolve, and she knew it was only a matter of time. He was the elusive, high-profile target. The man constantly surrounded by body guards and security. If she could take him out, then maybe she could quiet the screams with real justice.

She thought, *I'm coming for you Vigo.*

*****

Climbing into their 1967 Chevrolet Nova after an evening filled with astronomical wonders of the eye, James let out a long sigh.

"You didn't like the observatory?" his father asked, sliding the keys into the ignition and starting up the beautifully shined Tahoe Turquoise automobile.

"No, no, it was great," James responded, less than convincingly.

His father, ever the astute observer asked, "You know, despite my rugged looks, I was your age once. Perhaps I could help?"

"Dad," James started. "I saw a kid getting beat up yesterday and it's been on my mind."

"Oh," his father replied, taken aback. "Did you know the kid?"

"Nah, never seen him before. But he got ganged up on by three older kids." James cast his gaze out the window into the cloudless night.

"Well, what do you think about that?"

"It sucks. Not only were they bigger, but there were three of them. He didn't stand a chance."

"So, what did you do?"

"I yelled at them from across the street. It got them to stop and come after me. Luckily, I ran fast enough to make it into Ed's shop before they caught me. I had to hide out for almost an hour."

"That was good thinking. I am proud of you, son. It takes real guts to stand up for what is right."

"Thanks, but now I have this problem." James turned to look at his father. The math lecturer looked especially esteemed that evening, sitting behind the wheel.

"What to do when you see them again?" his father asked.

"Yeah, they are bigger and faster which means that even though I'm smarter, they will catch me at some point."

"True, very true," his father said. "James, if there wasn't an engine in this car, what would happen?"

"There would be no power. It wouldn't go anywhere."

"Right, and when you stand outside the car and look at it, can you tell if it has an engine or not?"

James thought for a moment. "No, I guess not."

"There is more to power than can be seen with both eyes open."

His father's words swam in James' thoughts as the street lights' glow danced off the polished hood of their ride. James watched the brightness come and go as he thought about the engine beyond the paneling in front of him. His young mind jumped to the things that he loved: robots, monsters, and sci-fi, the villains of which were constantly being outsmarted to their own demise. James wasn't sure if the old man would approve, but he had an idea.

CHAPTER 3

A paltry breeze passed over his warm skin from the small fan on Owen's desk. He hadn't slept much. Now, he was struggling as he sat over a pile of papers that needed to be graded. Owen's eyes looked at the Newtonian physics in front of him, but his thoughts were on only one thing.

Celestial bodies abound in close family heirlooms found.

Owen was a physicist, grounded in science. He believed everything had a logical explanation. So, Owen tried to focus on the facts.

The package had been sent to him. There wasn't another Bradley or even another Owen at the University, so a delivery mix-up was improbable. Maybe the source of the package was the key? Owen tried to determine where the package came from. He had contacted the courier company, but they could not give out information that wasn't already provided on the sender unless directed by a court order. The path was a dead end.

Next, he understood the package was meant to get him to do something. The note had a purpose and it was his job to figure it out. That was as far as he had gotten and didn't have a clue where to go from there. His mind had raced down so many rabbit holes while lying in bed, keeping sleep at bay, but each fragmented clue ended up in the same place: was it possible some piece of his family was still out there?

Owen had tried to find them multiple times over the years. All of his research into the Bradley name had turned up nothing. As he matured, he began to understand that the years he'd spent without answers had created so many narratives that he couldn't know what to truly believe.

Everything he knew for certain he had gleaned from facts. When he went to boarding school: age four. Where he was originally from: Chicago. What had happened to his parents: unknown. All he had was a trust fund to get him through a charter school education. There weren't any pictures, no heirlooms, no memories of family exploits or traditions; there was only him and his school.

And that's where he had been, in the halls of scholarly pursuit for as long as he could remember. And that was where he would turn now. Owen checked the time—his next class was in for a surprise exercise.

*****

James cleverly spent two weeks avoiding any possible interaction with the older boys. But, having exhausted all possible routes home, James found himself once again strolling down West Webster Avenue. This time however, he was ready. The comforting stories of battling robots were long from his thoughts. He was prepared. He was determined. He was focused.

Through the trees lining the street, James saw Cleveland Avenue approaching. He paused, slowly letting his breath settle as he removed the plug from his pocket. He knew that today he wouldn't be able to run. Today, he was loaded down with a pack equal to almost half his body weight.

Stretching the plug's cord away from the backpack, he connected it to the glove on his right hand. He knew he would only have one shot at this; he had to make it count. He wiggled his fingers and once again tested his ability to move his arm freely. He was ready.

The intersection looked almost as it had before. James saw the three older boys were there and they appeared to be keeping the younger boy from passing by. The boy moved right, the three shuffled left. James couldn't hear if anything was being said but the awkward dance spoke volumes—the kid just wanted a break.

Catching sight of James, the ring leader wasted no time changing his focus.

"Well, well, look what we have here. Thought we'd never see you again, since you lucked out last time and slipped away. And what is that? Big man wears a glove now?" He said to a chorus of laughter from his compatriots.

James knew that he was committed to this now. There was no turning back, he mustered up all of his courage. "You guys sure are tough, aren't you? Teaming up three to one on a kid half your size. Or are we comparing brain size? In that case, I have the advantage." James continued to walk towards them, entering the street.

"I'll teach you, you little skid mark." The taller of the three said, forgetting all about the other kid as he headed directly for James.

Stopping in the middle of the intersection, James placed his feet in a ready stance. Use their force against them, he thought to himself, quoting a martial arts book he had studied since their last encounter.

The large blonde-headed boy huffed towards James in large strides and as soon as he was within reach, took a big right-handed swing at him. James had seen him do this to the other kid and thus predicted that he favored the punch. James easily ducked the blow and with all of his grip strength, grabbed onto the elder boy's opposite wrist with his gloved hand, clamping down. Power surged out of the series of 6-volt lantern batteries he had chained together in his back-pack. The power coursed out as his hand became a taser. The elder boy's look of shock said it all. As electricity ran through his veins it took control of his muscles and the larger kid sunk to the ground. Now, James stood over him, but still he held on. He knew how much the boy could take, having carefully tested the device on himself several times to get the charge right. When he knew he had the boy where he wanted, he finally spoke.

"Now, you are going to leave us alone, you hear? In fact, you are going to give up this bullying business altogether. Why don't you try making the world a better place instead of tearing it down?" James said through gritted teeth.

The other two boys could only watch in complete shock as their buddy lay incapacitated on the ground, his every muscle rigid. As the ground began to soak with urine, James let go. Stepping over the once proud bully, James completed his crossing of the intersection of West Webster and North Cleveland Avenues to meet his fellow victor.

"I like the way you stood up to them." James said as he arrived next to the kid who wore an expression of amazement on his face. "It gave me the idea to create this." He added gesturing to his glove.

"How does it work?" The kid asked.

"I'll show you." James said, pulling the plug and holding it up proudly. "Do you like robots?"

The kid smiled; the first sign of emotion James had seen from him. "I love robots as much as I love monsters! My name's Walter."

"I'm James."

"Want to come over and play robot-monster space battles?" Walter asked.

They walked away from the scene behind them talking as rapidly as excited ten-year-old boys do. James' smile was wider than his face could physically represent. He had thought that he was the happiest when he was left alone with his stories and vivid imagination, but now that he had someone to share it with—he knew he couldn't have been more wrong.

*****

The familiar scent of chalk brought a smile to Owen's face—this was going to work. As the handful of students filed in for his only class on Saturday, Owen wrote out the riddle on the board.

"We are getting close to the end of semester, so I thought we'd have a little fun," Owen said. "Anyone here like riddles?"

A curly haired kid named Tommy sat in front and was the only one to raise his hand. Owen's eyes squinted at the lackluster enthusiasm. "Well, we will give this a try anyway.

This here is a riddle that I need help solving. Tommy, care to get us started?"

Tommy's chair creaked as he sat up. "I usually start by breaking it down into piece parts and making a list of things I associate with those parts."

"Great idea!" Owen said. He turned to the board and held up the chalk. "Break it down for us, Tommy."

"Well, celestial bodies." Tommy said as Owen drew a line to separate the section. "Then abound in and I guess, close, by itself. Then family heirlooms found."

"Okay, so we have four sections to start. You said make a list of associations?"

"Yeah, that's what I do."

Owen stepped back from the board. He tapped his lips with the end of the chalk as the class sat in silence behind him. After a moment, he said, "Anyone besides Tommy have any ideas?"

A female voice piped up, "Close, could mean near but could also mean almost."

"What about a generational thing because of its reference to family?" Tommy asked.

"Oh yeah." The female voice replied. "Close as in, only one generation between, like father and son or mother and daughter."

Owen swayed slightly to the right. His concentration trailed into what she had just said: father and son. The small ember of hope that his parents were out there began to burn a little bit brighter. He had to concentrate to perform the small task of adding notes to the board.

"Abound means a lot or in a great amount." Tommy offered.

"Good, good," Owen said, his head bobbing as he wrote.

"Celestial bodies could be angels or the heavens." The female voice said. Owen was about as religious as any other orphan that had spent years searching for a place to belong. He knew all the stories but they didn't feel right for this.

He wrote it down before adding, "Or it could be actual bodies, like the moon, planets, or the sun."

"Don't forget the stars." A new voice piped up.

"Stars, yup, very good." Owen said. "How about family heirlooms? What are some things you guys think of with that?"

"Pictures. Photo albums."

"Jewelry. Watches. A piece of furniture."

"Items that only have significance to the family like a love letter from a great-grandmother or a painting."

Owen wrote frantically to capture all of their ideas. The class continued the discussion, throwing out possible meanings left and right. Owen let the roar grow, not quite hearing the details of what they were saying. The sensation was refreshing and his heart leapt with every new suggestion.

"It doesn't seem right," the female voice said, pulling Owen right back into the thick of it. "It seems to me that the riddle is trying to say that a large number of celestial bodies are found in a family heirloom. That somehow the heirloom contains them."

"Oh, like a starry night snow globe or something."

The class continued on for a few minutes as Owen's attention waned once again. How could something contain the moon and stars? The phrasing didn't make sense to Owen logically, but something about the expression stuck with him.

"So, what does it mean?" Tommy asked, after the class had quieted for a bit.

All eyes were on Owen for an answer. The exercise hadn't given him the complete results but it had verified all of the ideas that he already been considering. Owen knew there had to be something missing, some kind of key to unlock the intent of the message. He told the truth. "I don't know yet."

Some brows furrowed, some eyes lit up, and others simply shrugged, chalking this up to another of life's little disappointments. Owen nodded his head. "I'll let you know when I find out."

The class generally accepted this arrangement and they moved on to the lesson of the day. The riddle was left to hang around on the board while they worked.

CHAPTER 4

Years passed and the duo of James and Walter grew inseparable. The pair never attended the same school but as soon as the bell rang, they were side by side on another adventure. Whether it was drafting up their own comic books, sneaking into a movie, or discussing the unknown extents of the universe, the weekends were always too short. Before they knew it, the young boys had grown into young men. The daydreams of heroic tales changed in tone and feats of valor, but the theme was always the same. One day they would save the world. In some versions, they would win the admiration of whichever girl they had a crush on at the moment despite neither one of them being at the front of the line to draw feminine attention. But in all versions, their lofty goals were bigger than themselves.

As they reached the end of their high school careers, their stories matured and left the world of daring heroics saving the planet from alien invasions, to starting a company and inventing a product to improve the world. What kind of product that would be, they didn't know, but their imaginations always ran faster than their current abilities. The practicality of it wasn't going to stop them though, together, they knew they would make a difference.

In the weeks approaching graduation, James could tell that something was off with Walter. His best friend seemed distant and was easily annoyed.

"What's going on with you, man?" James finally had to ask.

"Nothing much."

"Cool, cool," James said, unconvinced. "You want to head down to Ed's and grab some drinks?"

"Nah, I'm good."

"Cool, cool. Want to hit up Zach's comics and see they've got anything new in? Maybe spark some creative juices for our company?"

"There isn't going to be a company."

In all their years, this was a first. They had always been believers. James wasn't sure how to proceed. Walter's sullen tone and sudden disbelief had James' jaw slack and eyes aghast.

"What do you mean? What happened?"

"I'm not going to college. I didn't get in." Walter turned to hide his face from his best friend's gaze. "No college, no company."

"What?" James replied in shock. "Dude, you don't have to go to college to start a company. Think about all the greats that started in their garage, it just takes hard work and having something the world needs."

"You're going to college."

"Well yeah. I'm going to study engineering. That's what I need. I have to learn the basics and what others have done so that I can build upon it. You don't need that; you need more real-world experience. Besides, you don't care about the technical side and you have always been a leader. You have the makings of a great businessman."

"Thanks," Walter half choked out, still wading in his funk. "Seems like everyone else got in and I'm just being left behind."

James thought about it, weighing the infinite paths their lives could take. He knew that Walter was self-conscious about his situation and would get into fights because of his short temper. His best friend had the occasional bruise or black eye and James knew that it must have something to do with their family living on the lower end of middle class. Walter's father worked hard, long hours to provide for his family, but James never knew a moment when the man wasn't smiling. It must have been difficult for Walter to see his father work so hard and come away with so little. Maybe Walter felt the world owed the old man more for his day in and day out efforts, or maybe it was just the testosterone of coming into manhood that bolstered his aggressiveness. Either way, James hated to see his friend down on himself. Their future was bright and James knew it, but it was going to be a difficult road to get there, as with all things worth doing.

"Well," James said. "I guess we will just have to show them then, won't we?"

Walter looked up to meet James' gaze. James saw the fading of Walter's eyes, from boyhood sparkle to something new, something cold yet on fire.

"Let's hit up the comic book shop. It's Thursday and Anna is working, she always flirts with you." James said, encouraged to see the corner of his best friend's lips turn up slightly.

The young men headed off down the path they had traveled a thousand times before, not knowing that this time would be their last. Graduation would come and go, as would summer along with it. The pair would laugh and joke just as they always had but the chip on Walter's shoulder was still there, lingering in the background and growing in size.

*****

Clare held the board securely with her hands clasping each end. She had managed to find five pieces of various lengths and widths discarded outside a construction site. They were a little warped and splintered in places but perfect for what she needed.

"Deep breath." Clare said. "Don't see the wood, see past the wood."

The student, Sophie, stood in her fighting stance. She was only a year older than Clare was when she started. Seeing Sophie always filled Clare's heart with nostalgia. The pony tail slightly askew, the smell of freshly chewed bubble gum, and the precious shout Sophie made with every effort; it was like looking into a mirror for Clare.

Seeing herself in Sophie reminded her of one of her most cherished memories. A time at the beginning of her martial arts training. A special Saturday when her sensei had put together a demonstration in order to promote the dojo and get more people to join. Clare had only been to a few classes and was still undecided on whether or not martial arts were right for her.

She clearly remembered her biological father standing hand-in-hand with her as they watched. Now, his face was hidden in the shadows of time but she could still feel the warmth of his smile. Clare had watched in amazement as the sensei stacked board after board then struck them cleanly in half. Finally, the stack stood half the size of Clare. She remembered thinking that it couldn't be possible. There was no way that anyone could break sixteen boards at once.

The sensei delivered a blow that went fourteen deep but stood just shy of his goal. The man showed no sign of pain or discouragement, he simply bowed to the stack and then waved to the crowd. Clare was in awe of the power but most importantly, she was mesmerized by the control. Even she felt frustrated that the sensei hadn't met his goal and she couldn't comprehend why he wasn't as well.

As everyone clapped and thanked the sensei for the display, Clare turned to her father.

"I want to learn how to do that," Clare had said.

Her father knelt down beside her so that his eyes would be level with hers. He smelt of pencil graphite and stale coffee but his presence was as bright as fireworks. "One day," he said. "One day you'll break them all."

He believed in her and nothing else mattered.

"Hiya!" Sophie called, bringing her fist up then straight down onto the board Clare held.

Clare flexed her wrists inward at the precise moment of the strike. The two-foot-long piece of 1x4 split in two.

Sophie's mouth stood wide open, her eyes sparkling with amazement. Clare stood from her kneeling position and brought her hands to her side. Sophie understood and immediately snapped to attention as well. The pair exchanged bows.

"Discipline," Clare said.

"Confidence," Sophie replied.

"Respect," Clare said, before her lips turned upward in

a huge smile. "Great job, Sophie." Clare turned to the class gathered in her small dojo and held up the split boards for them all to see. The small group of students, in various ages from five to fifteen, stood in revered silence.

"Class," Clare said, repeating the words her sensei had spoken to her. "As we have seen here today, strength comes in all forms and from all places. You will learn this and embody it in your everyday life. The practice we learn here is more than physical, it is a state of mind. Discipline. Confidence. Respect."

"Discipline. Confidence. Respect," the class repeated.

"That's all for today," Clare said, bowing to the group. They returned the gesture, then swarmed around Sophie.

Clare grabbed a towel and took a huge swig from her water bottle in an attempt to cool off from the intense heat. Even with all of the windows open, there was very little breeze on that late spring day.

The space was partitioned off on the first floor of an older building. The mortar had cracks and pipes occasionally leaked, but that kept the rent down. Clare's goal was to help make the classes easily affordable to people from many walks of life. She felt that martial arts belonged to anyone with the discipline to study them, regardless of their financial standing—but the philosophy meant there was little left in the budget for air conditioning. She didn't care, preferring instead the purifying nature of being covered head to toe in sweat.

Wiping her face with a small towel, Clare noticed she had a message on her phone. No doubt it was her oldest and only friend, Malcom. A respected cyber engineer by day and crawler of internet remnants at night, he was her partner and the only one who knew of her role as a vigilante assassin. He handled all of her research, correspondence, alias accounts, and getting supplies. He was smart enough to never leave a trail and she trusted him completely. As a man with a wife and two young kids, he had more to lose than she did.

She opened the message to find exactly what she expected.

MTRex: Life finds a way.

Clare rolled her eyes as she grinned. Malcom was an avid Michael Crichton fan and likened himself to a young Ian Malcom. The only connection in reality was that he had black hair, loved Jurassic Park, and his middle name was Malcom. The lack of resemblance didn't stop him from embracing his love and he even adopted the moniker: MalcomTRex.

The message was actually a code. It meant that he had made a drop of the acting agent she used in her non-dojo-owning job. They had set up multiple drop boxes across Chicago and the "Life finds a way" location was in Terminal 2 at Chicago O'Hare International Airport. Even though the Fuel Wars had drastically cut air traffic, the terminals were still busy as the space had been repurposed for all types of activities. One terminal had even been converted to apartments to provide proximity to those that worked there. The amount of foot traffic meant Clare didn't like to leave it sitting for long. She made a mental note to pick it up after she locked up for the evening.

The acting agent was a compound that Malcom had stumbled upon while practicing his computer skills. He was deep into his third read of *The Andromeda Strain* at the time and obsessed with biological warfare. So, he went looking in the vaults of the government research and development projects to see what was out there. What he found was astounding and caused him to rethink his position on trusting the government. He wasn't a full-on throw the tea in the bay person but had come to realize that the government was a simple institution made up of people no different than himself. There had to be checks and balances, and Malcom had provided several over the years. His favorite tactic was leaking information so that the public would know the truth. What they did with it, he couldn't control.

So, when Clare approached him for help, he knew exactly where to find what they needed. Unfortunately for several rats and one very old cat, it took Malcom many iterations to perfect manufacturing the government's formula.

Completely untraceable except for a light rash at the absorption site, the agent took ten minutes to enter the body and between five to ten before heart attack symptoms manifested. Clare had used it on several occasions and usually wore gloves or used some other benign object to transfer the agent onto her target's skin. For flexibility however, Malcom had developed the neutralizing agent as well and Clare kept plenty of it on her when going on a job.

Her phone lit up again.

MTRex: Got a new job, big payout, looks like a protection gig. No details yet. Interested?

She replied: *Big payout? Sounds suspicious, find out more before we commit.*

Protection was hard because it required a lot of time and the lines between right and wrong were vague. A stalker, cousin who was owed some money, or just the random creep showing up oddly at the same place on a young lady's walk home every night; all things Clare had been contacted for before. Clare didn't usually take those kinds of contracts, even though she had one coming up.

Clare glanced around the room. A few students were still chatting but most had left. The place needed work. They needed new mats and it would be nice to just buy boards to break instead of hunting greater Chicago for scraps. A big payout could be the tipping factor on whether or not she took the job.

Malcom responded with more info.

> MTRex: Owen Bradley, UChicago PhD student in the physics department. Academic grant for alternative energy solutions. A few scientific papers co-authored, lives in an apartment on campus. Single, no criminal record.

Did he mention what was going on? Why does he need me? Clare replied.

> MTRex: He didn't send the request. Just a name and address from what looks like an anonymous third party.

Since when was someone online anonymous to you?

> MTRex: I know, I won't sleep til I find the source. But Clare, I got a bad feeling about this.

Because he seems like a normal dude that has no need for black market protection?

> MTRex: Yeah. Alt energy is big money and whoever wants to hire us is shelling out 100k.

100K? You think this Owen guy discovered something and it's about to get out?

> MTRex: I don't know or why he would wait. Maybe trying to sell it? That'll attract attention.

Not the kind he signed up for but if he did find some-thing, I think we have to see if we can help.

MTRex: Still trying to save the world, are we?

Feeling upbeat, Clare responded with her favorite quote: *Hold on to your butts.* The phrase was a joke they had used time and time again. She smiled at the thought of Malcom's laugh in response. They had been friends for a long time and occasionally still got to see each other. Still, even after months or even years of physical absence, they had a bond that would last forever.

Clare glanced at the clock on her phone; she had time. If she was going to accept this job and protect Owen, then she needed to find out more. She decided to start with his apartment.

Chapter 5

James took a bite of his sandwich. The lettuce was crisp, bacon perfectly cooked, bread was fluffy and fresh, but the tomato was the star. The slice of bright red fruit was plump and ripe, the juices dribbling out onto his chin as he chewed. Today is the day, James thought to himself as he swiped a napkin across his chin. I am going to talk to her.

The chatter of a busy University of Chicago campus surrounded him as he cleaned up his solitary picnic lunch. Was he really going to? He had this pep-talk almost every day now, endlessly psyching himself up only to let his nerves get the better of him. He needed reassurance. He needed a familiar voice.

They hadn't spoken in a few months, but James knew exactly who to call. He dialed the number and brought the phone up to his ear.

The line rang once before a terse voice answered.

"Walter."

"Hey man, how's it going?"

"James?"

He chuckled. "Glad you still recognize my voice even though you are apparently too busy to check your caller ID."

"I've basically got this thing glued to my ears," Walter said. "If it wasn't for these headphones, holding the phone would be the only thing I ever did."

"Wow, pretty busy?"

"Yeah, this gig with Congressman Bowler's office is really opening some doors. But its 24/7 if you want to get ahead."

"Nice," James offered. "Same here, I'm volunteering in the university lab. I like it." He knew it wasn't the same but they were both where they needed to be. Walter's Dad had worked in the local office for the Congressman so when it came time, he called in a favor. The result was an internship that Walter took to like a man who had dreamed of being in politics his whole life.

"Awesome, man. Good to hear," Walter replied. James could hear it, the subtle tone of someone who wanted to be somewhere else. The calls between them were getting further and further apart.

"You still liking DC? Any girls I should know about?"

"They are everywhere around here. Smart girls, dumb girls, driven girls, but I'm so busy, I don't really have time for any of them."

"You got to take a break for the ladies," James said, knowing full well that he didn't subscribe to his own advice. He was thriving in the self-driven learning atmosphere of higher education and soaked up everything he could. There just wasn't time to date, not that he had many opportunities.

"Once I'm on top, there will be plenty of time for that,"

Walter said. "How about you? Got a special lady I should know about?"

"Well actually, there is this girl that works at the library."

"Library? You always had a thing for books."

"Yeah, I guess so. Thing is, I haven't actually spoken…" James started before he was interrupted.

"Listen James, I've got a big tag-up with some people that have ins with the Senate Armed Services committee. I need to run."

"Oh okay, no problem. Give a call when…"

Click.

James brought the phone out in front of him to stare at it—that was a new development. Why did he even ask if he didn't care to hear the response? James could only wonder in shocked disbelief at what had happened to his best friend. As he did, the device seemed to weigh a little bit more than usual.

"I guess, I'll talk to you later," James said, resolving to himself that their friendship was a thing of the past.

James ran his fingers along the seam of his bookbag. The edge was beginning to fray. Not today I'm afraid, James thought. He slid the bag over his shoulder and set out on a diagonal towards the library entrance.

The doors parted and James moved along his worn path through the stacks and stacks of books. The columns passed by without being given so much as a glance. He knew the locations of what he needed from memory. James would pick up the books he needed, then return them to the shelves when he was done. He didn't check them out because then he would never have an excuse to come to the library. Plus, she worked the checkout desk and who knows what gibberish he would have said to her in that situation.

The checkout desk was tucked against a wall and faced outward over a sea of tables. Spots were sporadically occupied by students filling their brains with everything from Hannibal's passage through the Alps, to Laissez-Faire Capitalism theory, and endless theories about the fate of Schrödinger's cat. Not for James; it was all advanced control algorithms and practical application of robotics for him.

James wisely picked a chair facing perpendicular to the checkout desk. That way, as he wrote with his left hand, he could slightly turn his head and catch a glimpse of the librarian.

James laid out his notebook and lined up his pens perfectly parallel across the top. He stacked the books neatly, making sure the spines faced the same way and were lined up along the edge. He sat down for what was going to be a multi-hour study session.

Pulling *Multivariable Mathematics* from the top of the stack, he placed it in front of him. The book fell open. A crisply folded, white sheet of paper stuck out from the pages.

James jerked back, sitting up perfectly straight with a dumbfounded expression slapped on his face. He had used this book only yesterday and it wasn't like him to leave things behind. He paused. The room was a low murmur of pens writing and pages turning. Finally, convincing himself it wasn't a government conspiracy or some James Bond note to meet by a bridge at midnight, he opened it.

> *You know, if you asked me out, I'd probably say yes.*
> *Mairéad*

Mairéad? He thought. He didn't know a Mairéad. Was this meant for him? His eyes darted around the room, bouncing from table to table in search of a clue. James scanned the room. The pattern grew larger and larger until his eyes found their target.

She sat at the librarian's desk, twenty yards away, past a handful of other students. Her chin was in her hand and she stared directly at him… at him! Mairéad, a name to match the perfect curls of red hair. Their eyes locked and the room melted away around them.

The heat on his cheeks boiled like the surface of a supernova. The jig was up. He had to talk to her or make it awkward forever. She had put herself out there for him. If only he could remember how to make his legs work.

He rose to his feet. Since when were his shoes made of iron? The most basic of tasks seemed insurmountable. James' mind was going close to the speed of light. All of the pretend conversations he had with her welled in his consciousness, flooding his focus. His favorite books, movies, where he grew up, equations for finding the distance of an unknown side of a triangle? The whole time he was failing to figure out what he would say the distance grew shorter and shorter.

Then he was there. Standing in front of her with only the countertop of the checkout desk to separate the two of them. He must have looked like a fool, with bright lights beaming into his nervous, wide eyes.

"Uhh… hi," he managed, the feat so momentous, yet so simple.

"Hi," she replied, her voice melting his heart.

"I umm… got this note…" he started, stumbling to find any sort of confidence. He blurted out the first words in English he could find. "Do you like stars?"

Her head tilted slightly to the side in consideration of the question.

"Umm, and food? Do you like food?"

A corner of her lips turned up; her right hand moved gracefully to tuck a lock of hair behind her ear.

"I like food, many types in fact," she said, a gleam in her eye.

He chuckled, the ease of her patience allowing him to catch up.

"Well, I would like to take you for some food and to the observatory. There's a meteor shower this weekend, it's kind of cool… plus it's a great place to talk. Really… I just think it would make me very happy to hear anything you have to say."

It was her turn to blush as her face broke into a brilliant smile. "I'd like that… Friday?"

Studies were no longer top priority in James' heart after that moment. He had to make room for a new love, a different love—one that was intoxicating, wonderous, and pushed him to experience life outside his comfort zone.

*****

The seasons changed and their relationship grew. James worked odd jobs for date money while he studied towards a PhD. The effort and struggle felt like a dream come true for the young man. He got to learn and explore the things that he loved and found a partner that encouraged him—it was more than he ever thought possible.

A year turned into eighteen months and then, two days after successfully defending his dissertation, James turned into that nervous guy at the library once again as he fumbled a ring from his pocket. Mairéad stood before him, silhouette dancing on the wall from the stage lights at their feet; she didn't even have to look at the ring. Tears of joy ran down her cheeks as she mouthed the word, "Yes." The moment, the music, her eyes would be forever frozen in James' memory—a time in his life when he had felt totally complete.

With a bit of secrecy, James had managed to turn his doctoral celebration into a surprise engagement party. The overlapping events were the simplest excuse for all of their friends to be in one place and to talk openly about the event. All James had to do was extend invitations to a few special guests and the evening was a success.

They laughed and danced, celebrating late into the night. The basement pub that had been one of their favorite hangouts became a boisterous place, full of joy and merriment.

Then, the door opened to a sharply dressed young man. His jawline strong to match the large, imposing strength of his frame. James instantly recognized him from across the room. It had been five years since they last saw each other and three since they last spoke, but the friendship had never truly left James.

"I can't believe it," James cried out, stunned. The night of their engagement had been full of surprises, but none more so than who had just walked in the door.

"What is it?" his newly betrothed replied. James didn't turn to acknowledge her, instead his eyes remained dead set on the newcomer. Mairéad followed his gaze through the crowd and noticed the man standing just inside the door. The stranger's face searched the room for a familiar face but had the sly confidence of someone never out of place.

"It's Walter," James struggled to say, as if pronouncing his name might make the man turn and flee.

"Walter… the Walter?" Mairéad asked. James had shared countless stories of his best friend from growing up, but she had never actually met the man.

James brushed past the other party goers, indifferent to any disturbance he might have caused. Crossing the floor in mere moments, James wrapped up his old friend in a hug. The two slapping each other's backs like brothers reunited after war.

Catching sight of his fiancé, James broke the embrace but kept his arm around the man.

"Walter, there's someone I'd like you to meet. This is my darling bride to be, Mairéad."

"Walter? The Walter?" she said, extending her hand. "I've heard so much about you!"

The blast from the past took her hand in both of his. "It is a pleasure to meet you and congratulations," he offered with a charming smile. "You can call me Vigo."

"Vigo?" James blurted out as he shuffled them to seats around a small bar table. "You're using your grandfather's name?"

"Good memory," Vigo responded as he waved down the waiter. "I share my middle name with my grandfather, so legally I haven't changed anything."

"Ah, but I do love the name Walter," Mairéad said.

"That name was given to me as a way for me to fit into western society. My parents had big plans for me. They longed for me to be a part of a social system that wouldn't dare acknowledge the importance of a humble man's work. My grandfather knew hard work, as well as my father. Work is all the society I need. So, when I left, I knew if I pushed hard enough, nobody would dare laugh at me. I won't go by that name ever again." He smiled. "But you get a pass, for old times' sake."

"Well please, have a drink with us," Mairéad offered, her eyes sparkling with meeting the man that her soon-to-be husband talked about so fondly.

"I do appreciate the offer," Vigo said, smiling at them

both. "There are certainly many things we need to catch up on, but please, enjoy your celebration and come see me tomorrow, anytime." A card emerged from the man's jacket, James took it out of instinct and shock.

"Please, stay awhile," James said. "Have a drink with us."

"I don't want to take you away from your party. There is lots to do." Vigo turned to look fully into his old friend's eye. "It's time James. I have been very busy. I've made connections in Washington. I have investors lined up and contracts in the works; I just need a Chief of Technology."

The room shifted cataclysmically for the young doctor; he hadn't thought about their company in years. He had chalked it up to the dreams of adolescent boys, but now he was here, the same boys grown into men, learning that the dreamed lived on.

Vigo smiled. "We can talk specifics another time, for now, enjoy your evening... Dr. Stevenson." Vigo nodded his head slightly in Mairéad's direction. "Ma'am."

And just as abruptly as he arrived, Vigo Amarth disappeared into the night. James was left with his mind swimming, the visit transporting him back in time and flooding him with lost ideals. He wasn't sure what he would do, but his heart told him this was the right way to start.

A kiss on his cheek brought the room back around him. He smiled and turned to her; he could see in her eyes the wheels turning from behind his own.

"That was odd," she said, giving voice to the event. "I don't know about him, not really how you described him... gives me a weird feeling."

"Walter's had a rough life, but he's a good man."

"Don't you mean Vigo?"

"Yeah," James said, hesitating. "Yeah, I guess I do." The

encounter weighed heavily on his thoughts as the evening rolled on. James spun his grandfather's ring around his right ring finger, still getting used to its weight. His father had bestowed it to him earlier that evening, saying that he was proud.

If the newly mysterious Vigo, had an idea for a company and they could really work together to make a difference just like they had dreamed they would all those years ago, well, James owed himself that much and had to take the chance.

Chapter 6

Owen had the rest of the afternoon free from anything. The time each week was usually spent decompressing but the single sheet of paper on his desk indicated otherwise. The mysterious correspondence occupied his thoughts, even as he lectured that morning. Every word of the riddle, the associations they had come up with in class, it all floated in and out of focus for him.

His mind tried to analyze the message while his heart just kept leaping to tiny possibilities of being reunited with his parents or anyone who might have known him. He was lost, getting tripped up on the secrecy of it all. Why the note? If it was from his family and they knew where he was, why didn't they just come get him or contact him directly? Why the convoluted message? The whole thing just wasn't adding up. He made notes, he paced around the room, he even tried hanging upside down off the edge of his bed; nothing was shaking loose.

To solve this one, Owen Bradley was going to need help.

An hour passed. Owen sat diligently making a list of Saturn's moons when there was a succinct knock at the door. Owen's heart leapt into his throat. He really hoped it was another piece of this puzzle and not some ancillary thing related to school or his dismal social life.

Owen, now leery and hopeful at the same time, peered into the peephole.

In the hall stood a man wearing a solid-colored shirt, khaki pants, and athletic shoes. Owen didn't recognize the man but found it odd that he was still wearing his sunglasses. Nothing in his gut told him there was any immediate threat though, so Owen cracked the door. "Owen Bradley, my name is Walt," the man said, with only a curt nod, his hand not even hinting at a customary handshake. "I have been sent here to help you."

Owen studied the man. There was nothing distinct about him: tan Caucasian skin, dark brown hair, clean shaven, mid-thirties if Owen had to guess; it was as if it wouldn't be a challenge for the man to run a 5K while doing his taxes and no one even noticing him as he did it.

"Well, Walt, it's a pleasure to meet you. Now what do you mean by help me?"

Walt's lips stayed pressed together. His right hand rose slowly to chest height. Owen's reaction was instinct as his knuckles turned white, bracing behind the door.

Walt's fist rotated palm up and opened, revealing a large silver ring that bore marks from years of wear and tear. Owen looked at Walt then back at the ring, waiting for an explanation. "I'm sorry, I'm confused. Is this for me?"

This seemed to trigger Walt from his stoic stance. "Owen, this is yours. It was your father's and his father's and his father's before him. It is time you had it."

His father's? Owen thought to himself. He shook his head slowly in denial of the man and object in front of him. He had hoped for a moment like this. All the years spent alone while the rest of the boarding school kids were on holiday break thumped in his chest. He would stay up late, with the candlelight, staring at the door to his room, hoping for a moment like this. Now, a man stood before him, telling him that this ring, this family heirloom; could it be possible? Owen's thoughts shot to the paper lying flat on his desk— the riddle. His eyes unconsciously darted back towards his room. Was this the clue he needed? It couldn't be a coincidence, or could it? Was his misplaced childhood hope playing him for a fool?

Owen moved slowly out from behind the door. He looked from the ring, to the man, searching for any hint of deception, but Walt stood silently, holding the ring aloft. The man appeared to treat the object with the reverence it deserved.

Owen moved forward and carefully picked up the ring like a scientist discovering a new species. He held it up so the light from the far hallway window could illuminate its features. On the outside, he could see the remnants of the words *Illinois State Championship — Wrestling, 1941*. Turning it every which way in his fingers, he was mesmerized by it. The ring certainly seemed of that era, with all the dings and scratches left over three generations of owners, but Owen just wasn't sure what it meant. What did a wrestling championship have to do with him? The weight of it in his hand felt right and some deep, dormant instinct that told him: Yes, all this is true, you know this ring. Or possibly it was only a tiny ember of hope in his heart growing brighter and brighter with every turn of the silver band.

"I'm not sure…" Owen mumbled.

"It is yours," Walt stated matter-of-factly. "Owen, I have been sent here by your father. You are in great danger. All things will be explained in time, but please, we must go."

The succinct utterance from the ordinary man took Owen by surprise. "Is my father alive?" His very breath held in anticipation of the words that followed.

"All will be explained," the man simply stated. "You received a package two days ago?"

Owen nodded.

"The package was sent by your father. There is no time to explain, we must go. They are coming. This place is unsafe. Gather only what you can carry."

The words Walt used were alarming, yet his delivery had barely the emotional inflection Owen felt the situation warranted. So, he pressed.

"Here? Someone's coming here? Can you take me to my father?"

"There is no time to explain. We must go," Walt repeated.

Owen hesitated, backing up against the door to his apartment to get space between him and the mysterious Walt. He had to go with him, right? He had spent his entire life wondering what had happened to his parents. Countless hours researching, only to turn up zero leads, the Bradley namesake dead-ending before it even began. He had no choice but to go; he wouldn't be able to live with himself if he didn't.

"Give me two minutes."

Owen couldn't think straight, let alone imagine what he might need or how long he would be gone. Why would he, a simple academic with only a few research papers to his name, be in danger? And danger from whom? Owen moved quickly about the apartment, grabbing his wallet, keys, and cell phone. Seeing the single sheet on his desk, he folded it and stuffed it into his pocket as well.

Owen reemerged to find Walt in the exact same spot, holding his right hand out once again.

"Cell phone," Walt stated plainly.

"Why?"

"They can track it."

"It isn't a fancy phone with GPS," Owen argued.

"Cellular tower triangulation," Walt said.

Really? Owen thought. It made sense in theory but he didn't know anyone had the equipment or access to do it. "Who can do that?"

Walt didn't budge and his non-response was all Owen needed. The kinds of people that could do that were probably very powerful. Owen shook his head as he handed the phone over, his sense of preservation overcome by his need to see this through.

With phone in hand, Walt moved with exceptional speed. Brushing past Owen, he entered the apartment and advanced to the sloppily made bed. With no apparent effort at all, he hoisted the mattress up, put the cell phone on the box spring, and placed the mattress on top of it. Walt turned and exited the apartment. "They can track it."

"Again, who's 'they?'" Owen insisted as he hurried to catch up to Walt, who was cruising down the hall. Walt quickly exited and turned left. Own trailed behind as he burst out of the door, ignoring the young woman reaching the handle.

Once outside, Walt's pace slowed and they casually walked away from the building. The pair looked like two ordinary college guys headed across campus. Suddenly, Walt made an abrupt left and quickened his pace again, alarming Owen. But curiosity drove him to follow the man even if he did not understand the stakes.

They kept the pace with long, swift strides until just beyond a grove of trees, a vibrant location always occupied by students enjoying the shade and an occasional refreshing breeze. Walt moved gracefully among the books and sprawled undergrads before he turned around to wait for Owen.

Owen looked at Walt. The man was frozen in place, studying something at a distance. Owen moved alongside Walt and peered in the same direction.

They were at least three hundred feet away, but the car was unmistakable as it pulled in the lot adjacent to Owen's apartment. It stood out on a university campus or even a city street. Matte black and big, the car was a rare gem in the dying world of SOR. The size alone screamed money and power. Its dark tinted windows were probably bulletproof. Owen couldn't take his eyes off it. What was he involved in? His head swam in disbelief as the car parked in a front row spot and the driver's door opened. The largest man Owen had ever seen stepped out. The wad of towering muscle straightened his business suit that was worn almost like a uniform, the formal façade for something sinister lurking underneath. Looking around until he was satisfied, the large man walked directly into Owen's apartment building and out of sight. The young academic could finally breathe normally again.

"What? Who?" Owen stammered. "Who was that?"

Walt declined to answer, but Owen had seen him before, hadn't he? The growing dread of the last few minutes mixed with the thought of recognition. There was no way he could forget a man of such proportions, but he just couldn't place when or where he had seen him.

Owen felt more confused than when he first cracked a quantum physics textbook for fun at eight years old. Taking the ring from his clenched fist, he slid it onto his right ring finger. It fit perfectly. A deep connection to it began to grow in his chest, extending out into the past through the never-ending circle now snug on his finger.

He knew two things for sure: he was suddenly involved in something big, and he had to trust that Walt could help see him through.

The pair walked six blocks until Owen steered them to a coffee shop he knew. The shop was sandwiched between two large buildings and the squeezed effect brought a sense of security to Owen. The place was where an old girlfriend had used to work. Owen spent a bit of time there before long lab shifts and lack of economic prospects drove her into the arms of a businessman and suburbia. He stuck to cheap campus coffee after that. Now, Owen needed familiarity to help calm his nerves and since the university was out of the question, here they were. Owen ordered a cup of coffee before they found a seat in the back corner.

"Walt," Owen said, once the waitress had delivered his drink. "Who was that guy from the black car?"

"I have never met him."

"But you know who he is?"

"Your father informed me of other interested parties in ascertaining your location."

"Ascertaining my location? Walt, am I in danger?"

"Not presently."

Not presently? Owen thought. Who is this guy? Owen tried to focus on what he knew, taking stock of the situation.

"Why do they want me? Does it have something to do

with my father?"

"I do not know," Walt replied.

"He didn't tell you what kind of trouble we might be in?"

"He said to follow the plan."

"Great," Owen said. "Let's hear it."

Walt sat in silence. Owen waited until impatience burned into his skull. "Well, what is the plan, Walt?"

"The package that your father sent, that is the plan."

"The riddle?" Owen turned to his coffee. That wasn't a plan, he thought, that was a game. The man Owen saw outside his apartment, that certainly wasn't a game. How could a single riddle measure up to the enormity of power behind the black car? Owen looked across the table, the stakes of his situation becoming real. Could he trust Walt? The questions raised faster than Owen's mind had places to file them. He needed answers. He needed facts.

"Walt, you know my father?"

"Yes."

Owen looked at Walt with his vague eyes and taught jaw. The man's expression changed very little and showed no signs of stress or trauma when Owen mentioned his father.

"He sent you to help me?"

"Correct."

Owen kept looking for signs of any hint of an emotional trigger in Walt as he fought off the welling of his own. My father is alive, Owen thought. How is that possible?

"What about this ring? Did he tell you anything about it?"

"It belongs to you. It was your father's and his before him," Walt replied.

"Anything else?" Owen pressed. "Nothing of its meaning?"

"Only that I make sure to deliver it to you."

This guy is so infuriatingly blunt, Owen thought. He wanted to believe the ring was of his lineage but there were too many reasons not to believe it. The biggest one that had plagued him for so long, he asked Walt about next.

"Walt, where has my father been my whole life?"

Walt didn't move, instead he sat as casually as if they were discussing the weather. Owen stared daggers as he thought he could see the gears turning behind Walt's eyes. Owen pressed, "He didn't explain to you why he abandoned his son for almost two decades?"

Walt's body bobbed forward slightly before snapping back up to seated straight. He replied quickly, "Chicago."

"Chicago?" Owen shook his head at the very literal answer to his question. "My father is in Chicago?"

"I am uncertain," Walt replied.

"I don't remember anything before boarding school but my birth certificate on file with the school indicated I am from here. I guess that's why I gravitated back."

The pair sat in silence in their quiet escape at the back corner of the shop. Owen sloshed the remaining sips of his coffee in its mug.

"Walt, can you take me to my father?"

"No."

"Why is that?"

"You must find your own way."

"I can't go back to university and the way things were, not after all of this," Owen said. "I've waited my entire life for real answers. I've searched for the truth and come up with nothing. I don't know if it's my misplaced hope or if I actually believe you, but Walt, I have to see this through. I have to know where this goes."

Walt nodded. There was that nod again, Owen thought.

Owen turned to his cup and his mind settled on studying the last drops of liquid as he rotated the cup from side to side. And what of Walt? The man hadn't said a word the entire six block trip and when Owen mentioned he needed to stop and think—Walt had simply nodded. The man was odd, that was certain. Even so, the walls of the cup Owen clutched brought comfort and with it, resolve. He broke his stare in order to finish his drink. As Owen tipped the brim to his lips, he casually looked at Walt, who sat patiently, opting not to partake in a beverage himself.

"Walt, how do we solve the riddle?"

"You must find your own path."

Owen held up an open hand of annoyance. "Okay, I get it. Solve the riddle to find the answers and keep from getting pummeled by mister black car behemoth. This'll be no problem at all."

*****

A gentle breeze passed over the café patio as Clare sipped a freshly squeezed blend of fruit juice. The drink was always changing with whatever ingredients they could get as no single supply of anything remained steady. Clare didn't mind the differing concoctions and enjoyed the little break from monotony. The occasional drink was one of the only luxuries Clare afforded herself. In this case, it also gave her an excuse to be in her spot. She sat casually but kept her eyes vigilantly trained on the building across the street. The structure had charm, but its brick exterior was a reminder that time shows no mercy. The old canning factory stood silently as Clare debated what to do about Owen Bradley.

The whole thing tugged at her stomach. She watched as

people went casually about their day, entering and exiting the building. They carried books and walked in pairs, trios, or even the occasional quadlet. There was so much exposure with eyes and ears everywhere. Clare was the right age to fit in easily on a college campus. But if it came down to some physical altercation or intervention to protect this Owen fellow, there would certainly be witnesses. Which made her wonder, why was he in trouble at all? Who would take the risk?

The 100K thumped loudly in the back of Clare's mind. Those with money and power, she thought, they would take the risk. If Owen had really discovered something as huge as a new energy solution, Clare was sure people had been murdered for a lot less.

Clare pondered this and a thousand other questions as the café's quiet radio went to a news break. The name being mentioned caught Clare's attention.

"Amarth Corporation announced today a new contract to develop deep space transports. The hope being that one day humanity will be able to mine the materials needed to solve the energy crisis from far off planets. We think that the money would be best spent on finding the solution first. And in other news, a West Virginia sheriff of thirty years was found dead on the side of the road in his cruiser from an apparent heart attack. The man's death has rocked the community. Believed to be an exemplary officer and respected among members of State Congress and the Governor, the discovery of a sex-trafficking operation out of his home has brought everything into question. An investigation is underway into his contacts and the extent of the operation. We only hope that this brings some small semblance of closure to his victims."

Clare smiled with the news and gritted her teeth at the

name preceding. Amarth, the company founded by Vigo Amarth. A man certainly willing to stop at nothing to seize power and a constant ache in the back of Clare's mind. Are you tangled up with Vigo? Clare thought as she considered Owen Bradley. She knew it was probably her own desire to blame Vigo that forced unwarranted conclusions as she didn't have any other basis for Owen's case. The desire was enough to convince her though, she needed a closer look.

Clare threw back the rest of her juice and swiped her wrist across the table to pay. She needed to hurry so she could catch the 1:30 train to Pittsburgh. She had a job in Steel City that couldn't wait one more night.

The train ticket for the four-hundred-and-sixty-mile journey was not cheap, but it was cheaper than taking her electricycle and certainly way faster. It would come out of her operating expenses, something her client covered up front. Clare slipped on the custom bracelet that Malcom had made her. They were illegal but really hard to catch. The bracelet overrode Clare's implanted identity chip on her wrist. It allowed her to be Sue Grant, an accountant from Portland that was ironically in the vicinity of several suspicious deaths. This was Clare's vigilante profile, with accounts set up by Malcom to use her operational funds directly. So, when she swiped her wrist to board the train, Clare Furmore wasn't on the record and nothing tying her to a trip to Pittsburgh would be either.

Clare made her way across the street with a casual quickness. She appeared determined to get where she was going but not in such a hurry as to cause alarm.

Approaching the building, she studied it further. Clare took note of the exits, windows, and large trees near enough to the structure to provide quick cover if needed. She wasn't expecting trouble but the best plan was to be prepared for anything. Preparedness and considering multiple options were what made her good at her job.

Malcom's intel told her that Owen's apartment was 2B. Her plan was to walk to it as directly as she could and knock. She didn't have anything prepared to say. She decided to feel it out and be direct if she had to be. If Owen was entangled with people as powerful as Clare thought they might be then he should be made aware sooner rather than later.

She approached the double doors. They were glass and she could see as far inside the building as the light penetrated. Being able to see in was a good thing, as Clare saw two men stampeding out of the building. She pivoted back on her heel to avoid the swinging door and grabbed it as it shot open.

Some people are so rude, she thought to herself. The pair of men barreled past her without even a customary head nod. Clare watched in disbelief as the two men hurried off. One of them nipping on the heels of the other, trying to keep the pace.

At least they opened the door, Clare thought, and moved inside. The building was like any other in the city. The foyer walls were mostly blank and dimly lit, the lone standout was the bulletin board with various notices and listings of items for sale. Clare made short work of the stairs and found the entrance to apartment 2B.

She took a deep breath, then she knocked.

The door wasn't fully latched. She noticed the gap between the door and the frame was too much. Clare looked up the hall then back the way she came. She took a slow breath, focusing her senses. She didn't see anyone else. The only noises were of laughter somewhere on the floor below.

She lightly gripped her knife. Clare knocked.

The door began to open under the weight of her taps.

"Hello?" Clare said. "Hello, I just moved in down the hall and was wondering if you have a screwdriver?"

The statement sounded silly in the stagnant air but it justified why she was there. The door had stopped only partly open. She pressed against it with her hand flat, keeping her weight balanced on her feet.

The door fully opened. She could see the extent of the apartment from the threshold. There was an opening diagonally from her. Bathroom, she thought. She repeated her question.

Nobody answered.

Satisfied that Owen wasn't home or worse yet, prone on the floor, Clare closed the door behind her. Releasing her grip on the knife, she began to look around the apartment.

Owen's world was full of textbooks and notes brimming with mathematical equations. Papers were stacked in several different places in what appeared to be a chaotic mess to Clare. But they were in stacks, placed deliberately with no sheets on the floor. Clare didn't get any sense that there had been a struggle. The way it appeared had to be the way Owen lived in it.

Clare breathed a sigh of relief. She hoped there was still time to help Owen and he was simply bad at closing doors all the way. Clare crept along, fingering through some notes on Owen's desk. She didn't know what she was looking at. She could only guess that the solution to the world's energy crisis wasn't laying around on a loose paper. Or that Owen wouldn't have left a big note stating what was happening or why he was in danger.

Everything in the apartment screamed messy academic except for one thing. A single framed piece of art hung on the wall. Clare moved closer to see what it was.

Inside the spotlessly clean frame were familiar lines of a beloved character Clare recognized. The sight of the noble hero walking endlessly through a deep forest sent Clare's mind tumbling. The brick walls of the canning factory faded away, replaced by the dull grey of her high school's plaster.

Clare had been adopted by an older couple that were unable to have children of their own. They raised her on a farmstead in Southern Illinois. The farm was a great place to grow up, but Clare always carried the pain of childhood trauma.

As Clare grew older, the fragmented memories of her parent's car wreck defined her general distrust of everything. Entering high school, she was more likely to wear a scowl than a smile. This made it hard to make friends, even among the other athletic girls. She instead, focused on her martial arts training and schoolwork, the things she hoped would help her find answers. Or at least quell the burning passion for some sort of restitution.

Then, she met Malcom.

Sitting down in her spot near the undesirable's corner of the room, Clare noticed another solitary person sitting not far away. She hadn't seen him before but now noticed him from behind the edges of his book. The bookworm stood out because he did not have anything to eat and Clare knew it was absurd for a teenage boy to forgo food.

Clare was tough but she wasn't mean, so she unfolded the knife she wasn't supposed to have at school and cut her sandwich in half. Passing by him to throw away a banana peel, Clare slid him one half. She watched over her shoulder as his eyes lit up in surprise. Clare couldn't imagine having to face even a minute of history class on an empty stomach.

Malcom's reaction sparked something new in Clare. A fullness coated her heart, Clare's spirits lifted simply on the satisfaction of lending a helping hand.

The next day brought on the start of their friendship. Clare bought two lunches and sat down across from Malcom to share.

Malcom looked from the sandwich to Clare, then back again. "Thank you, but I…" He paused, shifting back and forth in his seat.

Clare wasn't sure what he meant to say, but he had said thank you and that was enough for her.

"Don't worry about it," she assured him. He didn't move. She grabbed her own food between both hands and took a bite. Even with her mouth full, she said, "So, I know that guy but can't quite place it, who is it?"

Clare motioned towards Malcom's chest. Appearing befuddled, Malcom glanced down to see what she was talking about. The realization hit him and the resulting enthusiasm helped him find his voice.

"You know *Samurai Jack?*"

"I used to," Clare said, grasping for memories she didn't fully have.

"That's so cool," Malcom replied, his eagerness bursting forth. "I didn't think anyone watched old cartoons anymore. The artwork is so good. And I just love the classic good vs evil aspect, plus the idea of a Samurai having to navigate a futuristic world—brilliant. I'm so glad they got to finish it." He trailed off. "Anyway, thanks for lunch."

Somehow unfazed by the awkwardness of her youth, she held out her right hand and said, "I'm Clare, by the way."

"Ummm, I'm Malcom," he responded, slowly returning her handshake.

"What's your favorite episode?" Clare asked, listening intently between bites.

"Oh, great question. I like the one episode where a city is being terrorized by this enormous robot that went rogue and could no longer be controlled. Jack has to operate a different super-sized robot in order to take it down."

Malcom continued to talk but the details were fuzzy to Clare after so many years. She did recall feeling something familiar and comforting about Malcom, him and that shirt. The Friday after they met, she happened to remember very well.

Clare had opened her locker to find a crudely wrapped gift. It appeared Malcom had been doing some sneaking around. His ability to get into her locker was impressive. The excitement welled up in Clare as she tore at the paper. Underneath it revealed a tattered paperback copy of *Jurassic Park*. Inside what remained of the front jacket was a note that read:

Dear Clare,

Thank you for sharing your sandwich with me that day. I struggled to come up with a worthy gift in return until I saw this on my shelf. It is my favorite book and this is the copy of it that I read for the first time. I want you to have it. You sure do remind me a lot of Muldoon… it's a good thing.

Sincerely,

MalcomTRex

P.S. I'm actually partial to turkey instead of ham, k thanks!

Clare smiled in a happiness she hadn't felt since her

family died. She had a friend and from then on, she bought him sandwiches as often as she could.

Now, standing in Owen Bradley's apartment, looking fondly at the same character she had come to know and love, Clare found herself confused. How was it that Malcom and Owen had an appreciation for the same cartoon? The show had a relatively short run and it had been decades since it aired. Something wasn't adding up in the back of Clare's mind. The heat in the small apartment seemed to increase as an odd familiarity swept over her.

She looked away from the artwork and was surrounded once again by the living arrangement of an academic. Clare smiled and thought: was it possible they were both just nerds?

Checking her watch sent a bit of panic into Clare's veins—she needed to hurry. Taking one last glance around, she didn't see anything that told her what sort of predicament Owen had gotten himself into. She hadn't decided to take the job yet, but she was more curious than before. She needed more info.

Entering the hall, she made sure the door was closed all the way before digging out her phone. She began to text Malcom what she had found.

Moving to the end of the hall, she focused on her phone. Clare couldn't wait to share in the sentiment with Malcom.

A shadow passed over her. She started to look up. Thud.

Clare ran straight into someone. She fumbled her phone but managed to grab it before it fell to the ground.

"Sorry," she said. "I really should pay more…"

Looking up, Clare saw the largest man she had ever laid eyes on. The top of her head barely reached his powerful looking chest. Her heart thumped. But it wasn't the man's size that struck Clare, it was the fact that he wore a full suit.

Clare stood slack jawed—she knew who this was.

The man grunted softly; his expression unchanged. The man's eyes were focused down the hall. Clare forced herself to move to the side. The large suit moved forward. Clare watched, trying to get control of her breath. She watched as the man lumbered forward, then stopped.

Red lights flashed, sirens blared, Clare could only look on. Vigo Amarth's bodyguard and suspected enforcer entered apartment 2B.

Chapter 7

Owen slid the empty coffee mug to the side. He was finally ready to ask. "So, who was that guy from the car?"

A curt shake of the head indicated Walt did not know.

"You knew he was coming or at least, that someone was coming. Do you know who he works for or why they are after me?"

Once again, a small no.

"And what about my father, is he alive?"

"Your father told me help guide you on your way however I could." Walt's expression remained unchanged.

"And when was this?" Owen asked.

"Two days ago," Walt replied.

"So, he is alive," Owen added, his hope pushing logic to the side. "And why can't you take me to him?"

"There is only one path forward. We must follow it."

Using his thumb, Owen spun the state championship

ring on his finger—he wasn't used to its feeling on his skin yet and the absent-minded activity calmed him. Walt was proving to be of little help. He didn't seem eager to give any information about the situation they were in. Owen believed it meant that Walt either didn't know or that the situation was much graver than he imagined. Owen shook his head, he had to approach this one variable at a time.

By one path forward, Walt must have meant the package. Owen's father must have sent it when the trouble first started. Maybe there was only one path to freeing his father and it wasn't direct. The black car screamed power and money, which meant influence. Was it possible his father had to conceal the way forward so that it would not be discovered by anyone but Owen? The image of the SOR guzzler remained in his thoughts; it exuded a carefree indifference to the world. Surely owned by a power that stretched far and wide, even possibly into the police and the security infrastructure across the city. Owen had to be careful. He wasn't sure about Walt yet, but he had to start somewhere. He pulled the slip of paper from his pocket and pressed it flat on the table.

Celestial bodies abound in close family heirlooms found.

Owen instantly stopped spinning the ring on his finger—the ring. *Close family heirlooms found.* There it was, plain as day. Owen glanced from Walt, to the paper, to his own hand. The earthly aroma of coffee grew stronger in the air. Owen believed everything had its purpose, such that coincidence was left to the unexpected sighting of an acquaintance on a street corner and everything else had an orderly, logical process. The ring was a family heirloom. It had been found. If he hadn't been right of the middle of it, Owen wouldn't have believed it himself. He now understood the last part of the riddle.

Walt said he was there to help in any way that he could, so Owen engaged.

"Tell me Walt, what does the phrase *celestial bodies,* mean to you?"

"Entities in space," Walt replied.

"The sun, the moon, planets; things like that?" Owen asked.

"Correct."

Owen shook his head. He'd been over that before. Walt had said there was a path forward. The ring corresponded to the riddle and so, Owen knew that the riddle held the key to where they should go. He took the ring off his hand and inspected it. A fragment of understanding held just on the edge of his thought. He couldn't quite take hold of it.

The hiss of the espresso machine pulled Owen from his thoughts. He hadn't gotten anywhere with staring so why should he expect it now? Then it came to him. The statement, from class, one of his students had said that the riddle felt like it was saying that the celestial bodies were contained in the heirloom: *celestial bodies abound in.* Someone had mentioned a snow globe, Owen smirked at the memory. How could huge objects from space be contained in the ring he held?

Did it have something to do with rings, like around a planet? Owen quickly scanned his mind for everything he knew about planets and their rings. It didn't make sense. Owen knew that was a dead end, his own logic telling him it had to do with the ring he was holding.

How was it possible to contain the stars and moon in the ring? Owen held it up, squinting one eye to study the inner edges of the ring. The stains of the ceiling came in and out of focus through the circular ring like twinkling stars against a sea of black.

Owen paused, holding his arm there, mid-air—that was it! The ring perfectly created a tunneling effect to the ceiling behind it and gave him the exact clue he needed.

"Tell me Walt, how does one view celestial bodies?"

"Look up at night," Walt said, still not betraying any emotion.

"Telescope," Owen said, slapping cash on the table next to his empty cup of coffee. "A big telescope. And that's precisely where we need to go, Chicago's largest telescope, and it's not far. But first, a supply stop."

Owen rose with a new energy that replaced the skittish one of struggling to keep up. Now, he had a goal, a purpose.

The deafening street noise greeted Owen as they exited the shop. There were people everywhere. The street was packed with pedicabs, e-cycles, and only a handful of SOR powered vehicles. Being able to afford to operate such an energy hungry machine had shrunk the number of them on the road tremendously. Everyone not fortunate enough to sit in one was red faced and those with a free hand used it to fan themselves in the break between stops. Owen's discovery gave him fresh perspective. The scene around him felt native and yet foreign to Owen, like every corner held something new but also hidden just for him—he only needed to find it.

Making quick work of the next two blocks, Owen stopped outside of a large glass-fronted building. "Stay here and give me five minutes," Owen said, holding up a five so that Walt understood even if he didn't hear him. As Walt nodded, Owen opened the large door and entered the bank.

Withdrawing a large sum of cash might indicate to

Owen's pursuers that he knew he was being followed, but he had no other choice. He figured if whomever was after him could trace a simple cell phone, then they could easily trace a debit card. It was worth the exposure to get what he needed now. After some quick mental calculation, he pulled out what he thought they would need for five days. He didn't have much. If they needed to stay multiple nights, then they would have to do it cheap. Owen figured it was probably better that way anyway.

Returning to the street, Owen found Walt almost right where he had left him. The man had only pivoted so that he now stood with his back to the building. Owen looked at him as Walt's gaze seemed fixed on the shop across the street. Owen brought his attention along the same path but found nothing out of the ordinary. He turned back to Walt and noticed the man was hardly moving. Add a uniform with a funny hat and the man would have been fit to stand guard outside Buckingham Palace.

Owen didn't know what to think about this guy yet. He didn't seem overly eager or overly suspect, or overly anything for that matter. The lack of information that Walt was willing to provide was strange, but Owen figured it had to be for a reason.

"Come with me." Owen said as he hailed a ride.

They both climbed into the backseat as Owen gave out the instruction. "Alder planetarium please."

The city began to slide past the window as a smile spread across Owen's face. He was on a journey to discover his past. It was a trip Owen had been making his entire life, but for once, he actually had a destination.

*****

A thin wall separated the two desks where the chief executive officer and chief technology officer worked. Each desk had a clear view of the freshly painted letters on the glass door leading into the space: AMARTH CORPORATION.

Vigo, as the newly founded company's CEO, had wanted a flashier office, but James had convinced him to keep overhead costs low for the time being. The topic was one of the first arguments between them and they were having another one now.

"Listen, we get some help, put a team together, and they can fulfill the contracts with the Department of Defense," James was saying to his anxious co-founder.

"Yeah, but you have to lead them," Vigo Amarth was saying. "As CTO, you need to oversee this and make sure we deliver so we can win further contracts and grow the business."

"Wal…" James started before catching himself and clearing his throat. "Vigo, I hear you but I'm telling you, we need to get ahead of the end of oil. We may already be too late."

The heat from Vigo's anger caused the wall unit to kick on, the thermostat set as high as they could without sweating to save on electricity. "Just give me a few months, six at the most. Let's get established and get a revenue stream so that we can fund your energy project," he said, surprisingly making sense despite the fury displaying around his neck.

James looked at their grubby coffee pot, leftover from his college days, and sighed. He felt that yet another weapons manufacturer in the industrial machine wouldn't do a drop of good for the world, but he was married and they planned on having a family someday. The dingy one-bedroom apartment with its 2 A.M. parties next door wasn't the ideal space for bringing home a baby. He could use a good salary and if they could get Amarth Corp. established, then he could use the money from the defense department's contracts to do the real work. A necessity the world needed that he saw coming but no one else cared to even acknowledge.

James stuck out his hand to strike a deal. "Six months. Then I want my own lab."

Vigo's mood instantly spun around as his face burst into his characteristic toothy grin. Shaking James' hand, Vigo replied, "In six months, we will be on our way and you can have a whole building. That way I don't have to look at your ugly face every day." Letting go of the shake, he playfully punched James in the shoulder.

"Hostile work environment!" James exclaimed jokingly in return as he bounced spryly on his toes, pretending to spar with his business partner and friend. They danced around each other in a fake boxing match like they had when they were kids. Vigo's temper could flare without warning but it was times like these that the stress melted away and they could just be friends. The occasions were getting farther and farther between. James wouldn't admit it, but he feared someday they would disappear and what was left of his friend would fade away for good.

*****

Owen and Walt stepped out of the electric-cab, or e-cab as everyone had taken to calling them. The small two-seater had become the preferred means of inner-city travel for anyone not on a bike or their own two feet. The occasional SOR converted car traveled the busy streets, but it was a luxury left to those with more money than they knew what to do with.

Owen purchased two entrance tickets then the pair hurried along the pavement. They made their way to the circular building nestled into the bank of Lake Michigan. The sun was setting to their backs as the chilling wind off the water stung their faces and worked against them as they opened the large metal doors to enter Doane Observatory.

Darkness flooded around them as they entered the cylindrical space. A quiet stillness replaced the howling wind of the shoreline and the pair stood motionless to adjust. Owen was as unsure as a gawky teenager entering the cafeteria on the first day of a new high school. His eyes scanned the room as its features came into focus. Was this the right place? And what would he find if it was? All he could do was press forward and hope.

Moving beyond the entrance, Owen realized they were the only ones there. The depth of the expansive space lending soft echoes to their cautious footsteps. The building was set up as one large ring around the telescope at its center.

What was he looking for? Owen had guessed the riddle led them here and now that he stood in the space, he was conflicted. The room was unfamiliar yet something about its orientation, its architecture, was known. Owen couldn't remember ever being in that space but his heart ached for there to be a connection. Every step felt right, but what had he expected—a middle aged man standing at the center of the room with arms outstretched? The thought bore into Owen's chest and his hope once again faltered. Would there be answers here?

Walt, a few paces ahead of Owen, broke the silence with a surprising question, as if a display on the wall about planetary orbits around our sun had triggered an idea. "What do you know about the ring?"

Instinctively, Owen touched the ring on his finger with his thumb, double-checking that it was there. "I'm not sure. Nothing, I guess. It fits perfectly, but that doesn't mean anything."

Continuing their methodical circumnavigation around the large telescope, Walt added. "And what of your father?"

Owen balked, his steps stuttering in their pace. Didn't Walt know? Hadn't he made it clear? He didn't know his father or have any recollection of him or his family. For all he knew, Walt could be his father, even though they looked nothing alike and Walt appeared to be ten years younger than what his father must have been. Owen grappled for a while with the question but didn't know what to say, so he let it fade into silence.

Walt stopped, having traveled halfway around the large telescope. The massive apparatus now loomed over their heads as they stood under the great cutout in the roof. Walt waited, clasping his hands behind his back, gazing at the structure in front of him—an impressed look on his face.

Owen continued to look around. He was sure something would stick out; something would strike an idea in his head. Why couldn't he think straight? This was all very new and Owen had no idea what this journey might hold. His intuition had told him to head to the observatory. He questioned it now as he looked over the various plaques and exhibits, unable to tell if it was misplaced hope or actual recognition that tickled the hairs on the back of his neck.

There was the customary graphic on the solar system, with characteristics and fun facts about each of the planets. Then was some detailed information on different types of stars: neutron, dwarf, giant—all great stuff but nothing that Owen didn't already know. He moved further around the ring. There were pictures of the building and its construction. A brief history of the place as well as famous visitors lined up next to it. There was an interactive display of facts on everything related to outer space. Owen guessed it was a hit with grade school field trips.

Owen circumnavigated the room and came to stand beside Walt, who had moved to read the display on the history of the observatory. Walt stood as calmly as a man without anything to lose. Owen wondered what it would be like to be content to take in the experience without the weight of your entire future in the balance. Owen let his eyes roam as he rested his hands on the railing. The smooth piping was the only thing that separated the observation area from the rotating platform housing the telescope. The tension of Owen's unanswered questions was deafening as the seconds ticked away in his mind. What were they doing here?

Walt's gaze came off the pictures and turned to Owen. "The walls are different; it appears they have remodeled."

Owen stepped down on to the platform and hesitated. The words danced in his ears. A hint of an image flashed before his eyes. He needed to unlock it. He grasped at a familiarity to the space, a faint memory that lived beyond the walls and domed ceiling, pouring out of the stars above and deep into the dormant strings of his heart. Owen squeezed his eyes shut, like a child hiding from a nightmare. The room swirled in his thoughts; he had been a child. Owen struggled to comprehend a time before boarding school, when he had last known his parents. His mind pumped energy into dormant recesses of thought and he saw the same sloping curve of walls. The same spacing of seams. The walls were green now but they had been… grey—he had been here before.

Owen stumbled back, reaching for the railing once more. He could see it, the telescope, not how it was now but how it had been almost twenty years ago. He had forgotten this place, somehow filed away with the shuffle of pain and loss.

Opening his eyes, Owen smiled. A veil had been lifted

and a new memory began to establish itself. Trying to concentrate on it, the memory faded. He quickly learned that he had to breath and let his mind make the connections for him. Slowly, the paint scheme from all those years prior revealed itself. Owen knew that buried beneath the fresh coats was what his mind now saw. There was a new banister and textured floor tiles had replaced the brown shag carpet. The smell of grease, the thick kind used for heavy gears, it was distinct and the same. His thoughts were clearer now, the room aglow with soft light as his father… his father… stood in the center, a big waving motion with his hands as he explained wonders of the universe to his young son. Owen could see the man, his details a blur, but there was brown hair and a corduroy blazer—as real as they had ever been. Owen's thoughts burrowed down, trying to wrap his consciousness around the sight of it—to relive the moment.

"I have been here before… I think, I think it was the last time I saw my father."

The words choked Owen's throat as he began to move towards the telescope, freely running his hands over its various parts. His chest swelled with an ache reserved for tears. It had come back to him, a moment with his father. Owen knew the memory was true. The fluttering beat of his heart told him that it was more than just hope.

"My father used to bring me here. We would come here just to hang out, I think he knew the lead astronomer. He would tell me stories and I would recount tales we had read from my mythology picture books. He would tell me about his favorite stories and music, shows he'd been to, places he wanted to visit—just sharing his life with me. For some reason, even that young, I didn't find it boring. I seem to remember that he was quite the story teller even though I didn't see him all that often. But this place, it was our special time together—father and son, just as it had been with his father."

The family ring warmed on his finger.

Taking a step back from the equipment, Owen's vision blurred from tears. "I can remember it now, clearly. You are right, the room is different. Even the telescope looks different. But this is the place, I can see it in its bones. Dad and I used to lay down right over there and look up at the stars through the slit in the roof. We rarely looked through the actual scope. I actually remember one time when it started to rain and we were in big trouble because we had left the roof open." A smile spread across his face, the kind that forms in happiness and swells in recounting fond memories.

Moving steadily with a sad lightness in his heart, Owen lowered himself onto the floor. He could faintly hear the sound of his father's voice filling the walls with splendor. The ground embraced him as his heart filled with the love and belonging that he had so desperately sought his entire life.

Staring out into the darkening sky above, Owen watched as the first star peaked out from behind the sun's drowning rays. Celestial bodies abound… the connection to his past had been buried over years of solitude. All he had wanted to know was that he was loved, that he belonged—and now he knew. He was part of a family, they still lived inside him and now he knew where to look. He didn't know what had happened to them, but now he knew that he wouldn't rest until he found out.

Another star popped up to his right, and that was when he saw it, just in the corner of his vision. Taped under a control arm for the telescope was a small manila envelope, impossible to see from any other angle. His eyes instantly focused as he scrambled awkwardly to retrieve the envelope.

Turning it over in his hand, there were no markings on it, but he knew—it was for him.

Sliding the carefully folded paper out of its credit card sized sheath, Owen's hands started to tremble. He could see words bent in the creases, and noticed how they were hand-written. These were his father's words, penned by his own hand. He cautiously unfolded it, careful to preserve the secrets kept in its folds.

The page was remarkable, the writing on it looked like his own. The traits of the lines and gaps were eerily similar. How? He actually could have written it, how was that possible? The biological connection strong despite the gap in proximity. His heart leapt with the realization of that small fact, stoking his hope. Silently, he began to read.

Owen,

You are standing in a very special place. A space where we spent many nights together just gazing at the stars and chatting the night away. The same for you and I was the same for myself and my father. There is a history here, and your holding of this letter proves you are part of that history as well.

This is where my father first told me about the family ring. You will be the fourth to wear it, but it comes with a price. You see, your great-grandfather Louis won this ring in 1941 at the Illinois state wrestling championship, completing an undefeated season his junior year of high school. He was all set with a full collegiate scholarship before even entering his senior year. His future was bright and every match made the local news—an uplifting story in a dark time for humanity.

Then the United States entered the war and everything changed. On his eighteenth birthday, February of 1942, in the middle of yet another undefeated season, Louis left all of his dreams behind and enlisted. The ring served as a stark reminder that even champions have to deal with the evils of the world and defend those that cannot defend themselves.

He wore the ring throughout his deployment to Africa and Southern Italy. He told my father that it brought him luck but mostly, it was a reminder of his promise to himself—fight for what is right.

I told you once, in that very observatory, that when you were ready, the ring and that promise would be yours. That is the price of wearing the ring, you must be the man that I know you can be. You must fight for those that cannot fight for themselves. Uphold decency, valor, and respect; that is his, yours, and our legacy. I have watched you from afar, I know that you are a kind, good hearted and respectful man. You must continue that in all that you do, no matter what happens.

There isn't much time. You must continue on this path to find your roots. I am sorry that I cannot be there with you and this all seems so convoluted. I promise the answers will come. Stick with Walt, I have entrusted my life to him and so should you.

Godspeed.

Owen sank down to his knees. A single tear slid quickly off his cheek, landing silently on the corner of the sheet. His father knew him, even after all these years. A conflict rose from deep inside of Owen. A burning desire to scream out the years of desperation. If his father had watched him from afar, where had he been? Why had he left him there at that school, questioning everything and if he would ever belong? The large black car once again flashed before Owen's eyes. This letter proves that his father would never have abandoned his son, so there must be a reason. Owen had to know the truth.

Whispering solemnly, Owen said, "I will give it everything I have." As the ring on his finger found a new weight, bringing meaning and purpose to the blood pumping through its enclosed circle.

Gathering himself, Owen wiped his face and smiled. Whatever lay before him, it was worth it. This note and the ring of his family was worth it. He didn't know what other mysteries would be revealed, but he was going to find out. For at the bottom of the letter lay the next clue.

Two Bohemians hang a right hook and find themselves in the cellar.

CHAPTER 8

"You know," Vigo started speaking while keeping his gaze out the window. "While you were off getting your doctorate, gallivanting around in lab coats and scribbling over white boards, I was in the trenches. I was working eighty-hour weeks. I was busting my ass off for this opportunity. Now… now you are complaining to me?"

He finally turned away from whatever distant object had held his attention so that he could face his co-founder, Dr. Stevenson.

"Listen I get it," Vigo kept on, walking towards James now. "You have things you want to do. You have to fix an energy crisis that doesn't exist and a world to save that doesn't need saving, but that's bad business. We have contracts in house right now that need your attention. We are growing faster than we could ever have imagined and this company needs you working on the things that are going to make us money."

James sighed, his attempts to get through to his colleague were instead, building his own despair. It had been a long, drawn out struggle in attempt to free himself from Vigo's micromanagement and get his own lab, but it appeared he still wasn't going to be successful.

"James, my old friend," Vigo said, leaning against the front of his large mahogany desk, any hint of their actual friendship lost months ago. "You have two kids now, right? Quite a handful you have there. A growing family needs a stable income, a nice house outside the city, good schools. We need to deliver on these contracts so you can do that. You are by far the best technical lead in the country and this company needs you staying on these projects."

James couldn't meet Vigo's eye line for fear of the anger and frustration that was welling up inside himself. He instead looked around the room, noticing the opulence of Vigo's office in such stark contrast from his own. Although they had changed buildings, James kept their original glass door. The painted title of the company they both had founded already starting to fade. It marked the entrance to his solitary office where his father's old desk sat, covered in technical specs and notes on new designs. The space was homey and welcoming to open and honest discussion. An unassuming space where the work could be done that would change the world. An office completely the opposite of the oppressive space Vigo liked to show off.

"Vigo, I don't know how many more times we can have this conversation. The energy crisis is coming," James said.

"Where's your proof?" Vigo responded, as he moved towards one of a handful of crystal decanters sitting on a side table. Each one filled with enough liquid to win lucrative contracts and have clients believing in Vigo's promises that were beyond the company's current capabilities.

"I've shown you before, multiple times. I don't know how else to explain it. Oil and gas sources are drying up. We keep using them at an ever-increasing rate and nobody has accounted for that."

"You don't think that the oil and gas companies would be prepared? They have to increase production to meet demand," Vigo barked, amused with his own reasoning.

"No, I don't," James responded. "They either are making so much money that they don't care, or are so ignorant that they don't know. I'm not sure what is worse. Those companies have made trillions over the years. They could give less of a shit what it does to the earth or to the hundreds of thousands of people relying on the jobs that made all that money. Let alone the billions on the planet and the wars that will break out plus the children who will have to clean up for our stupidity!"

"Always the pessimist." Vigo chuckled again.

"I am telling you, if we get out in front of this thing then we can do it our way. We can be set for life and our children's lives. We can save our planet and make millions in the process. Can't you see how lucrative a clean, reliable energy source would be?"

Vigo's smile turned stern again. "I don't need a lecture from you, Doctor. I built this business from the ground up. I am the one pressing the flesh and getting us paid. The country is scattered with the cold, dead remains of countless hopeful companies wanting to make clean energy. There is no evidence of an energy crisis and we just can't afford to lose any momentum right now. We are going to make our initial public offering in a few months and then we can discuss getting you setup to work on pet projects."

"You know why those carcasses exist? It is because oil and gas crushed them, but you wouldn't let that happen. Come on, we can take them on and win!" James said with all the belief he had in his body. He knew how to get Vigo on his side. Vigo needed to be told he couldn't do something. He needed a challenge that would bolster his ego.

Vigo nodded and strolled silently around his desk back to the window once again. "After the IPO, then you can have your own division to develop whatever you want."

James knew that any promise from Vigo was a complete lie, but still he had to accept it. He understood that the IPO would generate revenue to expand their capital and stabilize cash-flow. The offering would also make Vigo's stake in the company worth millions, while also setting up the Stevenson family for life. With two kids, James had to think of securing their future. His model indicated there were at least six to seven years left before fossil fuels ran dry. A few more months of delay wouldn't hurt he thought. James just hoped that those few months wouldn't mean the difference between an answer and collapse. A failure that would then lay the burden on the very children he was trying to protect.

James left Vigo's office and checked his watch. He really hoped he wasn't late, especially after yet another dismal result. Testing day was the first Saturday of every other month and provided each student the chance to earn their next belt. If Clare managed to pass the test, it would mark the third test in a row she moved up.

His chest swelled as James opened the glass doors to the dojo. The perimeter of the room was lined with people, each grouped in their families. The air of the room was a calm reverence. Each person was there to support someone in their martial arts journey, the skill and discipline of which was not lost on those closest to them. James found it as fascinating as it was powerful.

A small hand arcing back and forth caught his attention. It seemed that young Owen had been watching the door for his father's arrival.

James made his way slowly through the crowd, being sure to interrupt as little as possible. Testing went on for most of the morning, moving up the belts in order. Each student was encouraged to stay and watch those above them, every opportunity was a chance to learn.

"Hey Dad!" Came Owen's voice as James emerged next to him.

"Hey kiddo, your sister go yet?"

"Nope, they're still on yellow belts."

"Good," James said as he picked up Owen and sat him on his knee. He tousled the youngster's hair as he asked, "What have you been doing this morning?"

"Learning."

"Oh really," James said, amused. "Care to share?"

"I've been watching and I learned that martial arts are for everyone."

"True, but how did you figure that out?"

"Well," Owen replied. "In the last group, it was mostly kids, but there were adults too. So, it made me think that you can do it at any age."

"Very observant of you. That makes perfect sense." James said.

"Of course it does," young Owen added. To which, James laughed and turned to look at his wife. She sat with a smile as wide as the horizon.

"Glad you made it," Mairéad said.

"Didn't want to miss it."

"How was the meeting?" she asked.

"Unproductive," James replied.

"Still giving you the run around?"

"He just won't listen. And now I have to meet with him on a Saturday? I just don't know how to get through to him."

"At this point," Mairéad replied, "it doesn't sound like he's ever going to listen. The only thing that speaks to him is money."

"Well, selling half his crystal decanters and ridiculous artwork from his office would be enough to get started. But something has to be done soon."

"You've given him almost eight years," Mairéad said, bringing a hand up to rub James' back. "Vigo isn't going to let you do want you need to do. I see it eating at you every day. It's time to do what you think is right. You don't owe him anything. You know I support you in whatever you decide."

"Thanks," James said, letting her words calm his heart for the moment. She was his backbone, the steadfast rock in stormy seas. When the entire world doubted him, she was there to believe in him.

"How's our girl this morning?" he asked.

Mairéad nodded towards the line of matching white gis sitting at the edge of the mat. Each of them were focused on what was going on except one. James' eyes met hers. He raised a hand slightly to wave. A young Clare smiled at him. Her face beamed with joy that brightened the room with its radiance. James looked at her, his chest puffing up with pride. She was remarkable, full of life and the promise of filling a million rooms with her spirit.

James ran his hands over his knees. He could feel the course texture from each fiber of his pants along his fingertips. When Clare and Owen were born, he fell in love with them. When he rocked them in the early morning hours, he vowed to protect them. And now, seeing them with their own lives and personalities, he knew he had to ensure their future.

"I'm going to do it," James said. "I'm going to leave Amarth. I don't know what'll happen or how, but I have to find an answer to the end of oil."

Mairéad nodded. She didn't need to say a thing. James knew she agreed.

"Dad, its time," Owen said, attempting to climb back up on his father's lap. James scooped him up and they all turned their attention to Clare as she walked to the center of the mat.

James wasn't sure what she was supposed to be doing, but what he saw looked like the movements of a precise warrior. Clare demonstrated her skill and range, showing the results of her meticulous practice. She finished the test and bowed to the sensei. He returned the bow then waved her over. They talked to a minute or so, then Clare backed up and bowed again.

"Did she pass?" Owen asked, his head craning back and forth to try to discern anything.

"Not sure. She looks happy though," James replied.

The three of them waited as the rest of the testing at Clare's level completed. The group took a break and Clare bounded over to her family.

"I didn't pass," Clare said, a smile still on her face. The others exchanged confused glances, unsure how to process the information and corresponding mood.

"Sensei said that it isn't a lack of skill. He said that I know everything perfectly. He said that I didn't pass because now I must learn the hardest lesson of all."

"And what lesson is that?" James asked.

"Patience."

They all nodded their heads in silent consideration of the lesson at hand. James knew this wasn't about him, but the principle still applied. Marital arts were about discipline and knowing when to pick your battles. James believed at his core that he could solve the energy crisis that was coming. Now was the time to begin. But for the moment, he wanted to enjoy his family.

*****

The ultralight maglev train made quick work of the distance between major cities and Clare was soon exiting the passenger car before six o'clock. One thing was certain about the energy crisis, things had to be more efficient and the mass transit system was no exception.

As shipping and transportation costs soared, corporations were more and more enticed to join forces and upgrade the infrastructure. The result was the greatest overhaul of railroad transportation since the Industrial Revolution. The clunky workhorses powered by diesel, coal, and electricity were replaced with more efficient magnetic levitation locomotives.

The feeling Clare got when she rode the train was that she was floating, and it was true. The train levitated using the magnets and an alternating electrical current pushed and pulled the train along. As a result, the tracks were able to control the freight easily and could move at much greater speeds, cutting a previously nine-hour trip in half. Clare didn't much care how the train worked, she just loved the feeling and thought it was the closest thing she would ever get to flying.

Clare moved through the gathered crowd and waved her wrist at an electricycle rental rack. A bold yellow one came off the carousel, not ideal for staying incognito but she didn't plan to ride it within a quarter mile of the target.

The job was simple. She had been hired by the ex-girlfriend of a scumbag to rough him up and get him to leave her alone. Domestic disputes were something Clare normally wouldn't get involved in, but the man was becoming increasingly more and more violent. The latest video Clare's client had sent showed the ex-boyfriend grabbing her client by the back of the head and slamming her head into a wall. The collision left a hole in the drywall the size of a watermelon. Clare was happy the blow managed to be between the studs.

The client hadn't felt as lucky and begun to fear for her life. The woman moved and changed her phone number but he kept coming since there was one thing she couldn't easily change. She couldn't move the coffee shop that she managed and she couldn't leave entirely until she had another job. Unfortunately, the violence of her ex escalated quicker than the interview process.

So, Clare set up with a good view of the front door to the coffee shop and waited for closing.

Watching as patrons came and went happily, Clare's mind drifted with the endless flow of people. She thought about Owen Bradley. How had he gotten tangled up with Vigo Amarth? The guy must have discovered something and Vigo wanted it. Clare certainly didn't know the world of academia or corporate profits but she knew Owen should be careful.

Clare hadn't told Malcom yet what she found at the apartment. She was afraid of telling him that it felt like an opportunity. Clare felt a toss-up between unease and guilty pleasure with the situation. Normally her methods were clear cut: was the target a person who committed a heinous crime beyond a shadow of a doubt and somehow slipped out of the Swiss cheese inspired justice system? Then the choice was easy and Clare took them out. This situation was so much different however, and she wasn't sure what to do. Her thoughts seemed clear—stay away—but something in her gut kept nagging at her.

Her watch beeped at her, with ten minutes to closing time she needed to hit the restroom and get ready for a fight.

Returning to her vantage point, she immediately noticed the stocky man roaming close to the coffee shop building. He was trying to appear inconspicuous but Clare instantly recognized him from the client's description.

The lights began going out in the shop and Clare took several breaths to steady herself. Slipping out from her hiding spot, Clare set out in pursuit of her target. The client exited the shop out the front while her ex-boyfriend followed sluggishly fifteen feet behind her. The street was in a strange transition period as the shop owners and patrons of the day, gave way to the barkeeps and owls of the night.

The three of them walked the street in growing darkness. Shops were closing up with the loss of natural light, leaving their lightbulbs to collect dust. The distinct aroma of wax drifted in the air as tiny flickering began to appear in random windows.

Clare kept a short distance behind as she began to look ahead and time her move. She wanted to catch the man by surprise and knock him into a deserted alley in order to take care of business uninterrupted. She easily got to within five paces of the man as his steps varied in speed and direction. Clare was unsure of what was going on with him—something certainly seemed off.

Clare looked up to see a young couple approach, walking arm in arm, smitten with each other and utterly unaware of the vigilante woman stalking the despicable man, who in turn, was stalking an innocent woman. They passed by Clare without incident and she saw her chance. Her client was moving to cross the street with no one left around but the players involved. The man took a slight stumble and Clare barreled into him, throwing her entire body weight into shoving him down a small space between buildings.

The man was more solid than he looked and didn't move more than a few stutter steps, surprisingly keeping his feet against her advance. Clare quickly shoved him again, lowering her body this time, wanting to get him deeper into the solidarity of the alley.

She stepped back and caught a glimpse of the man's face, slightly slack and confused, but not afraid. Clare wasn't sure what she was dealing with, the look giving her a slight hesitation and allowing him to set his feet. She moved in to strike him. Her plan was to rough him up, make him forget every impulse he had to raise a hand to her client, or any woman, ever again.

As she closed the gap, the stench of fermented malt hit her nose—the man was drunk. The realization brought a smile to Clare's face. He was a built man, his sheer leverage able to resist the majority of her full weight being put into a shove. The man may have been big, but he was loose on the edges and his drinking certainly wasn't helping him keep his focus.

Clare struck, a jab right to the jaw. The blow only

seemed to awaken the man, a fierceness building behind glazed eyes. Clare struck again with her left, then went for a punch with her right, but the man ducked it, bringing his own arm up slowly to block at the same time.

Panic anchored Clare to the spot. Then, as the man moved, the inside of his bicep was exposed. What Clare saw terrified her, her flight instinct momentarily overpowering her fight. In the space of the man's arm lingered a tattoo, a faded emblem only given to a select few in the military. He was ex-special forces.

Clare wasn't punishing a drunk man; she was awakening a warrior. The hesitation it caused in her gave him the ability to seize control of the skirmish. He quickly grabbed at her, causing her to spin around. And before she could catch up, he landed a solid blow with his elbow—her vision flashed white as her chin was quickly full of the warm sticky feeling of her own blood. Clare brought her hands quickly to her nose in an instinctual reaction as her mind swam. Special forces? How could she have been so stupid? How could Malcom have missed that important detail? The questions came fast and went fast, as she needed to get control. This man was much stronger than her, well trained, and now she had lost the element of surprise.

Staggering back, Clare moved to gain distance between herself and the man as he squared up to face her.

"Who are you?" The man shouted; his speech slurred.

Clare's focus honed in just in time to see the faintest slide of his right shoulder backwards as he went for a weapon on his hip. Her training kicked in and she landed a powerful round-house kick to the side of his head in the same instant that he pulled the gun from its sheath. The blow caused him to lose balance and wince in pain, giving Clare enough time to take hold of his gun wielding wrist and spin rapidly underneath. Carefully she avoided the barrel as the first shot rang out, the bullet burying itself innocently in the nearby brick wall.

Now standing to his side, Clare had the man's arm twisted tight but he was skilled and he spun inward to make her lose the advantage. Standing shorter than the man, Clare had no choice. She brought another powerful kick to the back of his kneecap closest to her. The strike setting up her next move, as he bent slightly under the power of her years of training, she brought the heel of her hand blazingly fast into his elbow.

The man's arm shattered in two with a resounding crack to match the gunshot before it. A howl of pain rang out as the gun slipped from his grip and hit the pavement. Clare swept it away quickly with a flick of her foot and released the man's wrist. She then stood fully in front of him as he clutched his dangling appendage with the other. A wicked grin spread across his face, causing a rage to boil over inside Clare.

Her foot was fast, the kick landing cleanly across his face, erasing his upturned lips. She felt the man's jaw crumble under the strength of the dedication to her craft. The special forces warrior collapsed resoundingly onto the ground; teeth scattered like they'd exploded from his face. Standing over him, Clare grabbed his collar and hoisted him up enough so she could whisper in his ear.

"Raise your hand against another human again and I'll come back for your life."

She released him to slump into the pathetic human that he was. The groan that emanated from his slack body spoke the fact that he wished life had taught him this lesson the easy way. The adrenaline subsided as Clare touched her nose again. It wasn't broken, the bleeding now just a trickle. A faint sound of a siren reached her ears. Someone must have reported the gunshot. She turned quickly to head away from the alley and down the nearest side street.

Passing into the shadows of the buildings, she broke into a run, making up two blocks in less than a minute. She choose a path without any shops along it, so that no one would notice her. She passed into a park and headed straight across it to her parked e-cycle rental. The trees cutting her moonlit steps as she kept her eyes scanning in order to avoid running into someone. A petite blonde woman with blood all over her face would certainly rouse suspicion.

She slid silently behind a large tree twenty yards from the dimly lit parking lot her ride sat in. She pulled off her dark colored black shirt and rubbed methodically at her face. She had no idea if she was getting it clean, but she could take her time. The park was desolate at the late hour. Clare finally relaxed enough to take a deep breath, she made it out of there and didn't think the man would be able to remember her face. All she had to do now was clean up and make the midnight train.

Clare stuck her aching right leg out into the moonlight, a shiny streak of maroon due to her night's activities stared back. She had fresh clothes in her bag but not extra shoes, she would have to risk it and rinse them back at the apartment. Now confident that nobody was around and the parking lot was empty, she slid her shirt back on and speed walked to her waiting electricycle. She grabbed the pack out of the locked compartment and quickly made her way back to the tree. Nothing moved but the night air attempting to cool in the absence of the sun. She grabbed her water bottle and splashed her face, feet, and anywhere else she found blood, Clare laughed. Malcom owed her big time for this!

He was never going to hear the end of it. His research had turned up an ordinary male in his mid-thirties that was a dock worker; no mention of combat training whatsoever. Clare was going to hold this over his head for a while. The U.S. government had kept a secret from him.

Pulling her fresh clothes on, she felt confident that she wouldn't get noticed on the train. Just a young girl out on the town, looking disheveled as was the style these days. The irony of appearances made her smile once again as she turned from the tree to head to her ride and out of Steel City.

Clare froze, every hair on her body instantly rigid, the smile wiped rapidly from her face. A uniformed cop stood next to her bike and he was now staring at her. His headed tilted, assessing the situation. She could feel her cheeks warm against the start of a bruise.

She had to act natural. There was no reason for him to suspect anything of her. She was young and naïve; not an amazingly efficient secret vigilante that had just permanently messed up an ex-special forces asshole a few blocks away. She took a big breath and forced her legs to continue to walk towards him, but his expression said he had already seen the look of panic in her eyes.

Clare tried to think of everything that she would normally do, having to check off all the small movements that usually came naturally. She forced herself to take out the cycle's keys and continue walking in a steady pace. The cop just continued to stare.

Within a few feet of the cycle, the cop finally spoke.

"What were you doing in there?" His voice curious, but not overly accusatory.

"Evening officer," Clare mouthed with strained words coming out. Small flecks of blood on her shoes reflected bright and silvery in the street lights, a beacon of guilt waiting to be discovered. Clare tried to maintain composure. "I was a… cutting through the park back to my ride." She motioned slightly with the key in her hand.

The cop surveyed the yellow bike and then her again. "You know, the park closed at ten. You should be careful walking through there at night. A guy, big guy too—he got badly mugged only a few blocks from here tonight."

Relief surged through Clare's veins. He didn't think she could have done it, not in a million years. "Oh no, well I'm just coming from friends and saw this park to cut through. I agree, it was stupid." Clare said, suddenly able to hone her innocent girl voice.

"I understand, but try to stay on the street where there are lights and walk in groups." The cop said, acting like it was his duty to educate this naïve young woman.

"Yes sir officer," Clare said, slinging the bag over her shoulder and sliding onto the bike. "I have been thinking about one of those self-defense classes but haven't done it yet. Maybe I should, but even then, I should be more careful." She started up the electricycle and slid on her helmet. "Thanks!" She said with a fake smile. The cop nodding politely as he watched her speed off on the bike.

Weaving through the streets, Clare went directly to the train. Once boarded and comfortably in a seat, Clare let her guard down and relaxed. Pulling out her phone she powered it on and sent a text to Malcom.

Hey a-hole! Next time, I feed you to the raptors… Nedry was special forces!

She laughed at the thought of him getting the message in the middle of the night and it keeping him up. Clare's jaw ached, focusing her on what had gone wrong. Patience, she told herself; she needed to remember patience.

The train slid quietly into motion as the steady hum of electric magnets powered on. Clare powered her phone off and closed her eyes. A hint of Owen Bradley's case lingered in the back of her mind as the train rocked her to sleep.

Chapter 9

"You aren't listening to me!" Doctor Stevenson screamed at his former friend. "It is happening… it is happening NOW!"

"There is no evidence of that," Vigo said calmly, staying in his seated position behind his large mahogany desk. It had been only two months since their last discussion of this nature, but James couldn't wait any longer.

"Okay, fine. I'll explain it in terms you understand—money," The doctor stated in frustration as he turned from Vigo's indifferent stare to pace the large office. "Look at the transactions for the five highest employees in each of the top oil and gas companies of the world. They have all dumped their stock and most have moved on to executive positions elsewhere. Why would they do that? Gas prices set all-time highs every other week and nobody is reporting any sort of slowdown in the supply. But wells and refineries are getting shut down all over the place, quoting consolidation of the resources but the truth is that they have nothing to do so they are cutting costs. They are setting us up and any day now they are just going to shove us straight over a cliff! And who… who the hell is this and why is he just staring off into space?"

Vigo chuckled at James' mentioning of the large man standing to his right, void of any reaction to this meeting. Vigo replied, "This is Fitz, he's my new assistant. Don't worry about him, his job isn't concerned with the business side of things. He's more on the security side of things."

James took one more look at the man and through his rage, instantly assigned him a nickname. Mondo—Mondo Bot. The name came from a giant robot in one of his son's TV shows that was on a constant loop at his house. The episode featured scientists losing control of Mondo Bot so that it was left to lumber around in mindless destruction. The Samurai hero in the show had to work a new robot in order to take down the one that had lost control. James faced the same one-sided battle here, unless he could find his own way to even the odds. He turned his attention back to Vigo.

"The world is on the verge of an energy crisis that will shatter our way of life and lead to global war beyond belief, yet you concern yourself with hiring some massive robot to be your bodyguard? Why on earth do you need a bodyguard?" James asked, the fire still blazing in his eyes.

"Well, I am in and out of meetings with congressmen and prominent businessmen so I need to look professional. He drives the car, checks surroundings, those sorts of things, and it lends an air of importance to the process. It will help us win more contracts," Vigo said, resuming his normal stern gaze towards any question of his authority.

"Don't you think, and no offense to him," James replied. "Don't you think that maybe his salary could go to something important? I don't know... like maybe the clean energy project you promised me almost a decade ago when WE founded this company!"

The exotic plants lining the wall could be heard gasping as Vigo finally pushed back from his desk and stood. Straightening his custom Italian dress shirt and tie across his front, he slowly walked around to where James was rocking in place, awaiting a response.

"I told you. The new building has an entire floor dedicated to you and your project. Just hang in there until we move in next month and you will have a state-of-the-art lab to work on anything you can imagine. We have to seize the market share, establish ourselves with a steady revenue stream—we have to take the respect we deserve."

"What happened to you?" James barely whispered. "Where is the boy I knew... the one who wanted to change the world without the need of money and power? The end of oil... it isn't a battle that is going to be fought overseas on some desert battleground far from sight and far from mind. The bloodshed is going to be on our city streets, your money and power will be worthless against even the most basic of street thugs just trying not to starve to death."

"These last few years, you have become such an alarmist. Is it the stress of this job?" Vigo said. "You know it won't come to violence, there is plenty supply left, pump prices are still within reason. I think you need a vacation, some time to cool off; come back with a clear head."

"Really? You think pump prices indicate supply? You don't think they can be artificially held down so the big companies can build a stockpile on the cheap?"

"That's not happening, there are protections in place."

"By who? The government? Who the hell do you think

is stockpiling it? Developing their own personal little armies because the national one will be the first to fall. It is going to be an every man for himself free for all and you know it."

"Well, I've lived the streets and done the time. Now it is time to get mine," Vigo barked, his temper rising.

"Is that what this is? You feel like you deserve something? Why? Because you worked hard to get here? If anything, it should give you a sense of responsibility, an understanding of the basic needs of humanity."

"Let them struggle like I did," Vigo said. "They are weak and need to be taught the value of work. Plus, I didn't see anyone looking out for us."

"I don't recall you ever going hungry, ever sleeping in a cardboard box, or ever struggling to find clean water to drink.'

"We were poor," Vigo said, disdain in his voice.

"You may not have had everything but you weren't destitute. Hell, we had enough spare change to hit the arcade and comic book store once a week. We had it great."

"We were laughed at, looked down at; made a mockery of by even the middle class."

"That's why we vowed to change things, the right way. And it is precisely the opportunity we have earned. A chance to make a difference."

"It is bad business, a waste of money and time."

"Why does it always have to be about money?" James asked.

"Because cash is king! You want a pet project? You need equipment, space, technicians; consumables cost capital."

"No, you are talking profit, we have the money and can start small by just freeing up some of my time, but if we don't start now then we will be too late... we may already be too late."

"I'm not going to do it." Vigo said, definitively.

"Our fathers understood the value of honest work. The kind of work that had reward beyond the tangible."

"Don't bring my father into this, he knows nothing of success! The extent of his aspirations topped out at custodial manager."

"Maybe, but he had a good job with steady pay that kept your growing belly full," James said. "And a schedule that allowed him to volunteer, to become a strong influence in the community. I believe he introduced you to the congressman and got you the internship, the one that set the wheels in motion for this whole enterprise. It seems to me that we owe your old man everything and should take a page from his book, which was far from indifference! He would do anything he could to curtail even a fraction of suffering."

"Because we are old friends, I am going to let your comments slide. But if you ever compare me to my father again, you'll find yourself far from any lab and pushing a broom yourself. Do I make myself clear?" Vigo asked, jaw clenched.

"Do the right thing Vigo, approve the lab and research budget. Allow me to save the world from this crisis and make you a hero in the process."

"Get out of my office."

"Walter, time is running out," James said, slipping into old familiarity in search of sentiment swaying Vigo's decision.

"I said, get out of my OFFICE!" The large man bellowed through taut muscles. James could see the struggle welling in his old friend's eyes. There was conflict there, years of being ridiculed by peers not easily forgotten.

James studied the face of a man he had known his whole life but had never truly understood who he was underneath.

James had wanted to take on a look of betrayal but he had already known what Vigo would say, so the emotion didn't come. Instead, he felt only an intense sadness at the passing of an era, one that stretched farther back than he could put into a number. He had only one choice left. He couldn't put off his calling any longer.

"I hereby tender my resignation," James said clearly and succinctly, letting his words sink in as he stared deep into Vigo's eyes. "I will finish out the week to clean out my stuff and turn in all of my keys. I would tell you good luck, but it seems you make your own."

With that, James turned from what he had built and walked away. His mind spun with conflicting emotions and the ramifications of choosing to leave everything behind. His hopes, the passion and sense of responsibility seemed to pulse with every step further from Vigo's office. He needed to call his wife and tell her that he had finally done it—he had stood up to Vigo in the only way that he would understand. She knew the monster that Vigo had become and wanted him to leave years ago.

James tried to focus on his family. They were the reason he cared so much. He needed to protect their futures. The idea of Clare and Owen growing up gave him all the motivation he needed. They would go away for the weekend and enjoy some time together. The crushing responsibility of having a young family and knowing that a global energy crisis was coming could wait until Monday. He had finally stood up to Vigo and that was reason enough to celebrate.

*****

Owen traced the contour on the outside of his pocket provided by the one and only note he had from his father.

There was a peaceful reassurance in its presence. The simple fact of the note's existence meant Owen had fully let his hope of reconnecting with his family come alive again. He sighed and waited patiently alongside his counterpart, Walt. A man his father had told him to trust.

The pair stood in silence, having barely exchanged words after the revelation of his father's note. Owen had looked up upon gaining his composure on the observatory floor and met Walt's gaze. The man had simply nodded with only the smallest hint of understanding in his eyes. Owen still felt uneasy about Walt and his demeanor, but there wasn't much to feel easy about on this life shattering journey of discovery anyway.

The two of them agreed, shortly after they hurried out of the observatory, that they should get some food. Now void of any phone, they waited for the bus in the planetarium parking lot as a handful of solar powered lamps came to life. The sun finally finished tucking under the horizon and the change caused Owen to notice he was drained. The events of the day left his mind spinning with hope, fear, and always more questions. He was so caught up in his own thoughts that he actually came to enjoy the calm quiet that was becoming a characteristic of Walt. It seemed the man only spoke when it was necessary, choosing to let Owen lead the conversation, and it was helpful in those moments of reflection.

The street lights reached their full brightness as they boarded the bus and took the closest empty seats. A few people were riding already but they didn't seem to notice or care about the two new passengers.

The bus lurched forward as Owen continued to ponder. He couldn't be sure what else was locked away deep in his subconscious, lurking and waiting to be unlocked. After finding a connection with his father, his thoughts naturally drifted to his mother. What about his mother? Did he know anything about her? Owen strained with concentration in an attempt to drum up some sort of recollection. The thick fog of time remained and he longed for something to spark his memory like the observatory had provided with his father. A special spot, a letter, a picture, or her favorite phrase; anything that could clear the cobwebs of the past. The idea that the memories were locked inside his own head was infuriating as he only needed to find the key.

Sitting back, Owen let the thoughts pass on and instead turned his attention to the next clue. As the city rolled by, Owen decided that maybe Walt could provide some insight.

"What do you know about Bohemians?" Owen asked.

"They are people from the Bohemia region in the Czech Republic." Walt answered.

"Don't they have a major population in this area?"

"Correct. Chicago has one of the highest Czech populations outside of the country itself."

Owen wondered, his mind grasping faint hints that disappeared before he could connect them. He just had to find the connection between the culture and his history.

"Wasn't there some movement related to Bohemia several decades ago?" Owen asked.

"You may be recalling the Bohemianism movement of the 1960's and 70's. It was associated with free-flowing clothes made from long fabrics, nonconformity, and an easygoing lifestyle. The free spirit ideals were commonly linked to artists and writers." Walt said, almost like he was a living encyclopedia.

As the words sunk in, Owen noticed the next stop and made a snap judgement. Hoping for a long shot he jumped up out of his seat and said, "Come on Walt. Let's find something to eat in the art district."

After a few minutes of walking and milling around searching for something but not knowing exactly what it was, the pair found themselves seated by the window of a small café.

"So," Owen started in between bites of his toasted sandwich, "*two Bohemians hang a right hook and find themselves in the cellar.* Were they fighting and then they somehow fell into the cellar? Or maybe it is a metaphor for hitting rock bottom or possibly a jail cell?"

"A right hook is a punch in boxing." Walt added.

The comment seemed odd to Owen but he brushed it off and continued to think as his sandwich turned to mere crumbs. What was he missing? The clue sounded like some sort of old limerick but he had no idea what it meant or where it may have come from. His thoughts tumbled on and on until he noticed the desolate café. It was getting late.

"We should probably find somewhere to rest." Owen said. "It's half past eleven and I'm exhausted."

Walt simply nodded in agreement, showing no signs of weariness. Owen shrugged off the observation and figured this journey wasn't as emotionally draining for Walt as it was for himself. Using cash once again to pay, they asked the waitress if there was a place to stay nearby. She informed them that they were in luck. Only a few blocks down was a nice hostel that usually had vacancies.

Exiting the café, they entered a different world. The serene, comfortable atmosphere of the eatery was replaced with a bustling nightlife wandering the streets. There were boisterous people laughing and dancing as they walked along, headed to this party, or that show. Taken aback at first,

Owen soon realized this was the norm. They were in the art district and this area came alive in the dark hours of the night. Creative types stayed up, blowing off steam from a day of drifting through thankless jobs so that they could spend their evenings tapping into their inspiration. Their creativity kept burning alive and free despite the hardship of the post-Fuel Wars world.

Owen eased into the flow with Walt right on his heels. It may not have been Owen's scene but he wasn't unfamiliar with the mindset. As an academic, he often worked in the lab regardless of time of day. Here however, solitude and peaceful contemplation were replaced with rowdy human interaction. They would make their way to the hostel, as Owen still needed rest, but he was captivated with watching the people alongside him, letting the experience flow over him.

In the loss of major sports, big Hollywood, and cable television came the rise of the bard and the local theater. Small live performances with extremely low budgets became increasingly popular, sometimes only featuring a small two or three person cast and a stage—the art of the story propelling them forward.

They paused towards the edge of a gathered group. Everyone focused towards the center as two actors manipulated puppets in a brilliant display of skill. Owen didn't recognize the story, but he saw the look and awe in the crowd. The puppets were nothing but mere scraps from the garbage but the story held them in pure captivation. The actors were doing what they were meant to do—the performance was their purpose.

Owen thought about his purpose in life. The driving force behind all of his research, was all to control his fear of the horrors that would become true when the toll SOR was taking on the earth caught up with them. There was still a chance to not only survive, but to thrive. Owen knew it in his heart. They would have to stop stripping the earth and start rebuilding it or the earth would take care of itself and rid its surface of the parasite they had become.

But, so far, he had worked hard to no avail. He had increased efficiencies in the capture of solar energy and made breakthroughs in generator outputs, but he could never quite grasp the real answer, the idea that would bring them out of their dependence on finite resources. Sometimes he wondered if it was because he lacked something. He worried that he would never find the answer because he had some fundamental flaw within him, that somehow his lack of a family meant he wasn't good enough to be the hero. He tried to reason with himself that it was all just in his head, he was the man he was meant to be because of his experiences. He understood that everyone is unique, and it is what he did with his life that mattered, not idle words or promises, but actions, held meaning. Still, the doubt was there, no matter what his logical side argued; his emotions still remained, forever bolstered by the hormones beyond control.

He now could only hope that the Fuel Wars would truly become a thing of the past. He had searched for an answer for so long that he wondered if it had already become locked away in the recesses of his mind. He knew he was on a journey of discovery and somehow, maybe it would unlock the key to humanity's survival. He only had to see every twist and turn through to the very end.

The quiet man next to him was still very much part of that mystery. Perhaps it would be Walt himself that would jar the idea out of Owen's head. But in the meantime, Owen was unsure who to trust. The warmth of hope rose in his chest and yet, the ice of self-preservation flowed through his veins, keeping his senses always on alert, always protecting, always holding back.

The pair moved along, ever vigilant to keep an eye out for their destination. Coming to a corner, Owen noticed the small sign for the hostel a half block down a side road, away from the main thoroughfare.

Sighing with relief as the noise faded with each step closer to their lodging, Owen suddenly hesitated. A soft tune ahead replaced the sounds of the chaotic night behind him, and the melody felt oddly familiar. Owen tried to clear his head, reasoning that it was his tired mind, and moved closer to the hostel entrance.

A few paces ahead and they passed an old building, the thick wooden door propped open. Owen stopped and just stared into what appeared to be a bar, all sounds from the street behind him fading away. Through several tables of patrons clutching drinks in various shaped glasses, Owen saw the young musician. Several candles and an oil lantern illuminated her on a stage across the room from where he stood mesmerized outside the open door.

She sat embracing her polished cello, long hair flowing down over her opposite shoulder. Her hands flowed freely over the strings as her lips formed the words of her song.

Owen was compelled, despite the aching of his feet and dull throbbing of his head, to continue forward and he did, each step measured, intentional. His eyes focused on the muse before him. He couldn't take his gaze off her but it didn't matter that he was staring because he wasn't looking at her—he was listening to her.

The notes of her song floated to him. The vibration of the strings were soft and soothing, developed by years of tradition. The lyrics were Gaelic, a Gaelic lullaby that was as majestic as the rolling green fields it started on. Owen didn't know what was happening but the passion behind every plucked string, every word of the chorus, drove a fresh note of connection to his dormant memory. He couldn't help but listen and let himself wade in that space. Swaying gently on his toes, his eyes slowly shut. The world around him replaced with nothingness as there was only the rhythm of the chords and the stirring of her words.

His sight shrouded in darkness; a small light began to rise in the distance. The dim beacon was far off, yet warm and welcoming. Owen didn't chase it. He instead just rocked and enjoyed the gift of the musician's performance. Owen didn't want it to end, but alas, she slowly faded the chorus and brought the song to its conclusion.

The appreciative response from the small crowd brought Owen's presence back into the four brick lined walls. The small light he had seen remained with him. Opening his eyes, he noticed his face was streaked with tears. Turning quickly with the shock of such a deep emotional experience, he returned rapidly to brush past Walt still waiting outside the bar. They didn't exchange any words and hurriedly continued on their way.

Lying on the top bunk of the hostel bed only minutes later, Owen couldn't shut his mind off. He had a profound moment in that old bar and was left with something, a faint hint of a melody dormant in his memory. He knew it now as he lay there; it was his mother's favorite song. Memories came back to him—she had loved to sing. She brought joy to daily chores with her ballads, would make short the passing time with her soft voice, and she would ease him into sleep with her lullabies. The song Owen had just heard was one she sang especially for him. A song that her mother had taught her, a song from her country. He had heard it count-less times from his loving mother but not ever in the years since. Its timeless beauty left to forgotten tradition, until once again it emerged at this random bar.

Owen could hear it now clearly in the quiet of the night. It comforted him even from years removed. He wondered what had happened to her and why he couldn't see her face or recall her touch. He didn't know, but the reassurance of her steadfast song would stay with him. The soft words of her lullaby bringing him strength in the darkest of nights.

CHAPTER 10

James worked quietly to pack the remainder of his things. He couldn't believe that all of the promise, hope, and pure inspiration from that first day was now gone. They had formed a successful company and he had worked as hard as he could, but Vigo just couldn't be swayed. James had to pursue his calling. The writing was on the wall and the data proved his theory—the world was about to run out of fossil fuel. If James didn't stand up to his old friend, then no one else would. He had only hoped that Vigo would have been able to come to some sort of compromise.

James put away a few remaining files neatly in a folder. Silently, he hoped that he hadn't lost too much research time as it was. He had contemplated solutions when he could, but without dedicated time and equipment, he hadn't made progress. The day was getting late, about time for James to leave. He sighed and understood that Vigo wouldn't be coming around. He made a mental note to send a moving company for his father's desk since he couldn't move it himself.

"James." Came a familiar voice in a dark tone as the shadow of its owner filled the doorway.

James froze, three files clutched in his hands. Vigo had never bothered to visit his co-founder's office, and the sight was a shock.

"Come to see me off on my last day? I never took you as one for sentiment," James said with a smirk. He wasn't going to pull punches, not mere moments before he left Amarth Corporation for good.

"James," Vigo said again, stepping into the room. The look of concern on Vigo's face was a sight James had never seen before.

"It's your wife… and the kids… there was an accident," Vigo choked out.

"What? What do you mean? I haven't heard anything," James replied, suddenly very concerned where his phone was located. "I just talked to them a few hours ago… they were headed out of town."

"There was a car accident on the way… they couldn't get ahold of you," Vigo explained, the palms of his hands opening by his side.

"How bad is it? Are they hurt?" James asked, the search for his phone turning to panic.

"I don't know anything," Vigo said. "They said for me to find you and bring you to the hospital right away."

The files crumpled in James' hand before he released them, not caring where they fell. The man's stomach turned in on itself, causing James to double over. The organ felt like it was trying to solidify in defense of the unknown of what would happen next.

"Come on James, I'll drive you," Vigo said, waving for James to follow.

His legs knew what to do after so many years on earth but it was difficult. He followed, as his mind swam through a thousand possibilities and the safety measures of modern-day cars. Every iteration of the scenario bit at him like an exposed nerve.

*****

Clare's eyes opened mid-morning Sunday to the dim interior of her apartment. The side of her face quickly reminding her of the previous evening's activities. Popping on a small lamp, Clare got up from her bed in the dark space. As most people had grown accustomed to, Clare blacked out all of her windows to keep as much heat at bay as possible.

Moving to the small kitchenette, Clare searched for something cold to put on her nagging jaw. Unfortunately, a freezer wasn't a luxury she had, so she settled for a wet cloth.

Standing with her face in her hands, Clare felt the constant nag in the back of her mind. What was it about Owen Bradley? Why did she care so much? He was just a seemingly innocent scholarly man and yet Clare couldn't shake this weird connection. He certainly wasn't attractive, or his university photo wasn't doing him justice, but Clare knew the feeling wasn't physical, so what could it have been? Had she been in the business of hurting people for so long she lost touch with her compassion? She had plenty of clients that she helped out, but had it grown from a desire for justice to something different? Was she taking too much enjoyment out of her vigilante endeavors? Had she lost sight of humanity?

Answers to her questions failed to come in the same way that the cloth failed to soothe her face. The sting of it screamed at her that she had grown complacent. She had success because she was prepared beyond a doubt and that success had then made her sloppy. She could no longer just rely on Malcom's research. It wasn't his fault, but she was the one out there, it was her body on the line. She needed Malcom, that was for certain, but when it came to the questions deep inside her, she had to get the answers wherever she could find them. And there was only one question that she needed answering at that moment: who is Owen Bradley?

She slung the cloth around her neck to help stay cool in the growing heat of day. Powering up her phone she laughed, it instantly flooded with worried messages from Malcom.

> MTRex: Really? Are you ok? What happened?
> MTRex: I'm so sorry.
> MTRex: Let me know you're ok, I'm worried.
> MTRex: Saw the news report, no mention of you. Where are you?
> MTRex: Swipe has Sue on the train back to Chicago, I assume you made it home?
> MTRex: I don't know how this happened. I feel terrible.
> MTRex: Please let me know you're ok.

The concerned messages put a painful smile on Clare's face. Making him worry for a few hours was a slight recompense for his missed research. She would still hold it over him though, even if she needed his help now. She replied.

I'm fine, just a little lesson to my cheekbone. You owe me one...

> MTRex: Thank the great Crichton himself, Muldoon still breathes among us. And yeah, I feel pretty shitty.

Well we've got years for you to make up for it. Anything new?

MTRex: The protection gig is all we have and FYI, the money cleared the operations account. It looks like they aren't waiting for you to accept the job.

We can always send it back. I have a weird feeling on that one and last night reminded me to address those feelings before leaping into something. Find out more, there has to be something going on with the guy.

MTRex: I'm on it… glad you are ok friend.

Setting the phone down Clare felt her heart swell. She had her dojo and she had her revenge, but all of it wouldn't have been possible without Malcom. She owed him a lot more than an elbow to the jaw could erase. Either way though, she wasn't ready to tell him who she had run into at Owen's apartment. She wanted him to find any connection to Vigo Amarth through his own research.

Fixing something to eat, Clare let her mind wander over what it was she was really doing. The tattered remains of Vigo Amarth's picture still clung desperately to the mounted board. The path of retribution seemed to end with him. Yet, she still wasn't completely sure why he was her main target. There were still questions in her mind that needed to be answered, gaps in the story where she had just enough shattered memories to cause doubt.

She was six years old when the car wreck happened, old enough to remember. Her memory was as fragmented as time and tragedy will do, but it was still there, buried deep between the story she had been told.

Her adoptive parents, the Furmore farmers, as she liked to think of them, had been very upfront about how she came to live with them but never had any real details. They cited not wanting to bring up bad memories, but told her there was a car accident and that she was the only survivor.

But Clare could recall certain details, even now. She seemed to believe that her father wasn't even with them. A detail the Furmores just shrugged at, saying the mind plays tricks. She had the faintest image of no one sitting in the passenger seat, but it had been analyzed over and over again in her mind for so long that the details couldn't be trusted. Clare also seemed to recall being pulled from the car by a police officer. Then she was taken to a hotel for a few days before she came to live at Furmore Farms. She never really understood the transition, why didn't she go to the hospital? Or if there was a cop, then why not the police station? She didn't remember anyone else from the time. Her recollection played games with what she thought should have happened.

Clare also didn't have any memory of attending a funeral for her parents. Why was that? The Furmores assured her that they had gone to one and that she must have blocked out the event, but Clare felt they were lying as they were always quick to change the subject. She had struggled to understand any of the details she felt she deserved. All the while screams from that day plagued the recesses of her mind.

The battle between what was in her head and what had been said to her ears raged on. Over the years she began her own research, using old pictures from the farm to determine when she came to live with the Furmores. Once she had that detail, she looked for news about her car wreck. If people died, then it would have made the news. She checked every Chicago based news outlet and all of them in surrounding Illinois. She was certain she was from Chicago because she was old enough to know that information when the wreck happened. So why couldn't she find a single mention of her family? She had to admit that she was hunting half-blind though. She somehow couldn't recall her biological last name and had thought that some news article would have sparked the dormant recesses of her brain where that very useful tidbit of information lurked. But everywhere she looked, she seemed to stumble upon news about Amarth Corporation growing at rapid speed and building a massive building downtown. It had infuriated her and the lack of news coverage related to her family had struck a chord. The result left her believing that Amarth was somehow involved.

While she didn't take much interest when she was young, Clare knew that her father had worked at Amarth. He had told her a few times about his work and she overheard him talking with her mother in boisterous debates about it as well. He had seemed unhappy, or at least that was what she seemed to remember, it was so long ago. But Clare had the strong suspicion that her car wreck wasn't an accident and that her father had been the target. It was the only explanation she could find for the secrecy and the questions that no one seemed to be able to answer. Clare came to live on the farm, her family taken away and covered up, while Amarth Corporation hit it big.

Clare had placed all her anger and pain on Vigo after she saw a profile on him as the face of the company. Her father must have had something on Amarth and Vigo took him out to keep it quiet. He certainly had the power and based on whispers around town, he certainly had the nerve. Clare didn't have any truth to back her accusation, but it didn't stop her from developing a deeply intense hatred of the man. And if the night in Pittsburgh showed her anything, it was that she better be prepared, because Vigo was much more powerful than a bottle-abusing vet.

*****

Vigo didn't have much information other than there was a wreck and where they needed to go. After they had rushed to the car, the nervous silence settled in. The clouds overhead darkened the sky ahead of the setting sun as they drove along. James was unable to process anything about the situation and he certainly wasn't thinking about fossil fuels or the history he had with Vigo. Ever since that day at the library, his family had been his heartbeat. Without them, he wouldn't know what to do. So, the awkwardness and corporate disagreement between the two men were set aside for the time being; for the first time in a very long time, they appeared to be as friends.

The car was still moving, but once they were within feet of the emergency room entrance, James shoved the large door open and jumped out. Vigo could hardly even apply the brakes.

The doors split open to let James in as he rushed into the bright white of the hospital. His head turned this way and that, searching for the nurse's station. Every input to his mind was amplified as he struggled past rows and rows of waiting room chairs to arrive at the counter separating him from answers.

"The car accident… family of three… where are they?"

"I just got on shift, let me check for you," The nurse replied.

James drummed his fingers on the cold, lifeless countertop. The smell of stale coffee and three different cleaners wafted around his nose. He hated the smell of each of them.

The head nurse looked up from her paperwork with concern. "The only car wreck today on the intake sheet was taken in down at the medical examiner's office. Are you related to the…"

The nurse's voice trailed off in James' ears. He had a singular purpose and any deviation from finding his family was an unnecessary expenditure. He took a step back as the nurse continued to try and get his attention. Looking to the ceiling and the directional signs hanging over each corridor, he scanned desperately for the words he needed to find. His brain was in primal auto-pilot, everything functioned, but he lacked control. He found the direction he needed to go and his feet did the rest.

Running down the corridor, he was oblivious to the nurse yelling at him. He could only focus on the next turn in the hospital's never-ending catacomb of nightmares. Endless hallway after endless hallway of moaning doors unveiling pain at every turn. Finally, James found the words he had been following printed on a door at chest height.

Rushing up to the door, James threw a shoulder into it, letting the fire of the unknown drive it open. The door slammed into the filing cabinet behind it and the medical examiner standing next to it was taken aback by the sudden appearance of a distraught man in his office. Papers fell from his hands as James addressed him.

"The car accident this afternoon, what's their status?" His eyes swelled in stinging pain in the realization that he was talking to the medical examiner and not an E.R. doctor.

The hospital employee answered the question quickly, as if he was dictating notes. "Three deceased victims identified by the car and personal effects. A female, mid-thirties and two children, boy age four and girl age six." As soon as he said it and saw the look on the James' face, the medical examiner realized what his own shock had led him to do.

A sword of immense size buried into James' chest multiple times couldn't have done as much damage as the man's words. The examiner's face grew blurry as the little tiles lining the walls spread into a web closing in on James. Each segment, every intersection, a roadmap of decisions that had led to this point. James swayed to the side, reaching out to steady himself on the filing cabinet by pure instinct. A lifetime of memories past and future slipping rapidly through his every thought.

The medical examiner's look betrayed his confusion. He said, "I apologize. They should have contacted you. They passed at the scene… I'm sorry." His eyes cast down; he wasn't used to facing raw emotion.

James' breakdown hesitated long enough for the denial to take over. "I want to see them," he said as his feet took up a small pattern of pacing.

"Sir," the young medical examiner said, raising his hands and thinking this was all more trouble than his meager salary paid him for. "I don't recommend it. The bodies are badly burnt. It won't be an image you want to remember them by."

James moved swiftly. The movement caught the medical examiner off guard as James soon held the man up, dangling him against the wall. James pressed a forearm heavily into the examiner's throat, the man's toes pointing desperately for a chance at touching the floor. James looked up at him, surprisingly strong for a skinny intellectual, powered by the reserve of adrenaline now pumping through his weary veins.

"I said I want to see them!" His mouth barked as his eyes screamed violence. The examiner nodded as best he could just as a hand lightly touched James' shoulder. Glancing over, James saw that Vigo had caught up with him. The familiar face of Vigo allowed James to relax, letting the examiner slump into a heap on the cold tile floor.

James stepped over the examiner and moved to push open the double doors at the back of the office. They swung silently on their hinges as James was enveloped by the chill of the postmortem examination room. The room was only lit enough to see three silhouettes. Each member of his family lying prone under their white sheets.

The hands of the renowned physicist balled into fists so tight that no air existed in the folds of his burning skin. His heart laid ripped from his body, spread on those tables, causing a powerful agony to erupt from his mouth. A visceral scream bellowed out in denial of the tragedy he could not control. Its intensity bounced off the tiled walls, causing the metal instruments to vibrate in their neat little rows.

Finally, out of breath and with vocal cords cracking under the strain, James' face quickly turned into a sobbing wet mess. He would no longer be able to hold his little girl's hand or pat his son reassuringly on the head. He would no longer get to kiss his beloved wife simply before and after work. Portions of his heart were left to go dark. The brightness and life that once thrived there, forever sent to the shadows of memory.

James dared to lift the corner of a sheet. It isn't them, he thought. The bodies were unrecognizable as he struggled to accept that they were real. Something deep rooted told him that these people weren't his family, that these bodies couldn't belong to the young vibrant extensions of his own flesh and blood. But... he knew it was clinging to a false hope, denial the first step on the ladder of grief.

James turned to see Vigo and the medical examiner shake hands through the tiny square windows of the hospital room doors. Vigo stopped and pat the examiner on the shoulder, the odd exchange instantly etched in James' memory. But, the magnitude of the moment, the shattering events of just one day, easily cast aside the observation in the moment.

Chapter 11

The sun was up on Sunday morning and the calm of casual weekend business returned to the streets of the city. Owen yawned eagerly and was amazed at how well he had finally slept. Walt and he had a corner of the room in the hostel to themselves and it lent itself to a peaceful rest after a day of emotional turmoil.

Soon, the pair were up and once again out on the street, unsure of where to go to next. Owen's mind quickly warmed up and focused on the next clue once again. The next step in his journey was the only item occupying his thoughts despite the strong signal from his stomach that it was time to eat. They didn't make it far before discovering that the insightful bar from the night before had transformed into a small coffee shop. Owen was sure the proprietor had to cater to every hour of the day in order to squeeze out a living wage. The same was true for the few employee's and Owen's eyes easily recognized the young musician, now bustling between three occupied tables.

"Let's eat here," Owen said, entering without waiting for an answer from Walt.

The two sat at an open table on the edge of the room and looked over the mismatched decor. Owen tried not to linger with his eyes as he followed the movements of the inspiring singer he had seen the night before. But her every step entranced him once again as she moved smoothly through service of the tables already into their breakfast. Finally, putting the agony to an end, she approached them.

"Morning gentlemen, what can I get you?"

"Coffee, for now," came Owen's response.

"Same," from Walt.

She turned to get the drinks when Owen stopped her.

"Actually, I am curious. I caught your performance last night and I have to admit—I was moved. Where did you learn that song, I think it was Gaelic?"

The corners of her lips curled upward. "I… I first heard it at a show long ago. My father, mother, and I went to see an Irish band when I was young. My mother adored them and I begged to come along. They closed the set with that folk song and I have wanted to be a musician ever since."

"You are very talented." Owen found himself smiling sheepishly at the attractive young woman. "That song, do you know what it's about?"

Returning the twinkle in his eyes with one of her own, she said. "It's a Gaelic love song—about strength of family and the bond of lineage. The band that I heard it from were all siblings. It was really moving."

"That must have been really something, no wonder you remember it. Did you see them around here?" Owen asked, unsure why, just grasping for anything to keep her talking to him.

"Yeah, it's been years ago but it was at Thalia Hall, not far from here actually. It's a great place to see a show. I would love to play there someday. They say it is modeled after the opera house in Prague…"

She continued, her voice light and giddy. Her tone hinting at flirtation, but suddenly Owen wasn't listening, her phrasing snapping him back to his father's next clue. Prague? His mind worked quickly to connect dots. Prague, the capital of the Czech Republic. The Czech Republic, a country formed in the same area that was once known as Bohemia. There was that description again. They didn't have any other leads so he excitedly cut her off. "You said it's close to here? The hall?"

"Yeah, just a few blocks away on West 18th Street."

Owen shot a look at Walt, who hadn't reacted at all to the conversation. Owen said, "We have to go there, it's the only lead we have." Then turning back to the confused waitress, he said, "We're going to need those coffees to go. And a couple breakfast sandwiches. Please."

The waitress simply smiled at the situation and the abrupt turn of events. Nodding, she turned on her heel and went to get their request.

*****

Two hours passed with James sobbing in the tiled room, rocking unsteadily back and forth. He was unsure of what to do, chasing thoughts like a half-starved dog in a field full of energetic rabbits. The door cracked, letting in a wave of warm air and a hint of bourbon. Vigo approached slowly.

"I'm sorry," Vigo whispered. "I can't imagine what you are going through." James heard the words. Yet he could only think of how cliché they were, but what else was there to say?

"I can't go home," James replied, his attention remaining on the tables extending before him.

"I've got a key to your new lab. There are living quarters there and I've got permission to start using them while they put the final touches on the rest of the building," Vigo said, almost eagerly.

James nodded.

"Come on, let's get out of here. We can make arrangements in the morning," Vigo suggested.

"I need a bit more time," James replied, unable to look at his old friend. "I'll get a cab later."

Vigo nodded quietly and dug into his pockets producing a small keychain. He set the shiny silver on the table directly in front of James. The doctor shivered as the metal clanged against metal, but he didn't change his gaze, always burning a hole deep into the opposite wall.

"Take as much time as you need. I'll call security to let them know you're coming. They'll let you in at the front desk," Vigo offered, before taking slow steps backward until he was far enough to turn and leave. Reaching the door, he stopped as the distraught doctor spoke.

"Vigo... thanks. You have been a good friend."

A tiny shudder passed through Vigo Amarth's impenetrable armor before he straightened up and left the room. James watched as the gruesome grin of his foul character returned to Vigo's face.

James felt the weight of the key in his hand. Why did Vigo have it with him? Maybe it was just a copy of the master key that he kept on him so he could go and inspect the new shining tower of his own greatness. Still, James was a problem solver and his thoughts turned dark when faced with tragedy. Was Vigo hiding something? Why was he first to know of the wreck? Why hadn't the hospital called? Why did the exchange he witnessed with the medical examiner seem so odd?

The questions welled up inside James as he tried to focus on anything other than the burnt bodies lying before him. His senses finally sounded an alarm with the sudden urge to use the restroom. Whispering goodbye, he let his hand slide softly on the tables as he walked out of the room. He wasn't sure what the world had to offer for him beyond the double doors.

Washing his hands felt odd, like an unnecessary exercise in a cruel, abrupt world. He let the stream run over them regardless and occasionally splashed his face, raising his head to watch the streaks of clean water carry his tears away.

A pair of nurses entered the bathroom. They were distant shapes, moving in and out of James periphery. He didn't pay any attention to them until he overheard what they were saying…

"Man, sometimes I hate this job."

"Only sometimes?"

"We had to sedate a guy upstairs, totally strung out. He kept trying to hit anyone that got near him, mumbling something about kids, or no kids. I don't know, it was all gibberish. The dude was a total mess and wicked strong for a druggie."

"They always are, like some string bean comic book character with super powers or something."

"Yup, the guy couldn't have weighed 120 pounds."

"Treating for drug overdose?"

"No, car wreck."

Alarms blared in James' ears. He paused, his hands midway to his face, cupped with water. The nurses continued.

"Yeah, we're going to stabilize him, then he's the cops' problem."

"Well, maybe there is some justice in the world."

The nurses continued as the door squeaked on its hinge, then shut again. James let the water fall back into the sink.

Justice? He thought to himself, finally reaching for a towel. Could there ever really be justice? Was it possible to justify the ending of three beautiful young lives and the countless actions they would make to brighten the world? Was it possible to replace the hole they left in his life? Could there ever be justice?

James' heart turned cold, icy with a singular focus. A focus on confrontation. The man that took his wife and kids was in the building. He burst from the bathroom headed for the first supply closet he could find. If there was justice, James was going to find it.

*****

Clare accelerated her electricycle as she left the city limits. The wind passed through the air vents of her jacket in a poor attempt to cool her skin as she effortlessly wove through the minimal traffic on that Sunday afternoon.

She was headed to the farm where she grew up. Between Owen Bradley and the mysterious connection to Vigo Amarth, Clare had spent hours the night before searching for answers. Her mind constantly bounced back and forth between her past and Owen Bradley. She found only more questions, never answers. In her desperation, she decided she would press her adoptive parents for details of the truth. That was why she sped rapidly away from Chicago towards the farm with her mind in a fog.

Clare had only fond memories of the farm. The Furmores were loving and cared for her as their own. The nurturing environment was complimented by growing up working a dairy farm. Clare learned early on the value of hard work and using her hands. Caring for and tending the property taught her many skills and the discipline to be free from distractions. The chores provided the structure for her to build strength in her muscles, grit in her teeth, and determination in her heart. The long hours and repetitive tasks of caring for a herd of milk producing cattle built the foundation for the countless hours spent training on her craft. The image of sixteen stacked wooden boards were always in the back of her mind. The farm was a place of purpose when the outside world felt awkward and foreboding.

Off the farm, Clare never really fit in, always closed off with an untrusting chip on her shoulder. She had casual friends from her martial arts groups but mostly they were intimidated by her superior talent and unwavering focus to the craft. She also had Malcom but she never shared with him her deepest motivator. He believed they took on the evils of the world because of the pain and suffering they saw; that they had the skills and means so they had a duty to do what they did. The real reason Clare kept to herself, never speaking the intense longing for justice she desired for her family and... herself.

That intense longing drove her forward even now, seeking answers from a place she never fully accepted as home.

Passing the split rail fence she had repaired numerous times, Clare turned quickly at the faded red mailbox, a small cow silhouette sitting on its top. Riding down the tree lined dirt driveway leading to the Furmore home, Clare quieted down her thoughts. She wasn't leaving without details, but an uncontrolled rambling of questions and accusations would never get her anywhere. She needed to know what had happened and she needed to get there without betraying her emotion.

The front screen door swung open as Clare parked her electricycle and hoped off. Her adoptive father, Thomas Furmore or Big Tom in agricultural circles, was eager to greet their visitor and a smile spread across his face at seeing Clare.

"Hey sweetie, we weren't expecting you so early. You must have made good time," Big Tom said, taking a drink from the chilled lemonade sweating in his hand, surveying the scene from the cover of the porch. "Is that the new EC 2600?" He asked, intrigued by her bike.

Clare slid her helmet off and set it on the bike in question. She ignored his question, approaching the porch instead. As she climbed the steps, her adoptive father, owner and sole operator of Furmore Farms, moved to meet her. They embraced on the top step without a word. The lightweight short sleeved farmer motioned to the rocking chairs, before taking his usual seat.

"Looks like someone finally caught up with the judo queen of the Midwest," he said, an eyebrow raised towards the swollen purple along her jaw.

Clare nodded and let the comment slide past her—she had only one thing she wanted to discuss, and her impatience had grown past her civility.

"I need to talk about my family, my biological family," Clare said, her back stiff as her body leaned forward, keeping the chair from rocking. "I have so many unanswered questions and I really need to know what you know."

Big Tom's gaze rose from the porch and trailed off into the distance, his eyes revealing the search into the past that his thoughts performed.

"You have always been a curious one. I guess you get that from me," he said, the pace of his words as long as his breath was steady. "We have always told you there was a car accident and that was how you came to be with us. I always knew you were old enough to remember something from that time and had a need to question our explanation. We kept it from you because we were afraid. Afraid of the details that we didn't know or understand, and afraid of causing you pain. And now, I guess the facts will never quite add up in your mind and you are right to question them."

Big Tom sighed, content to have the faintest of breezes crawl through the porch beams as he searched for the right words.

"Clare, it wasn't an accident… it was an attempt to kill you and your family."

Clare's knuckles turned stark white as her grip tightened on the edge of the chair. Pain rose in her chest even though there was nothing at which to direct it. The screams returned, seeming to come from all around. They plagued her ears, tugging at her memory and filling her with hatred.

"Your mother's brother," he said, as Clare understood that he referred to his own brother-in-law and not her biological mother's kin. "An uncle you met once but never again. Well, he was a cop and father himself but still managed to get in some trouble with some rough people. So, when an opportunity came to cover up a car wreck by making it look like well… an accident, in exchange for making his debts go away, well, he had to take it.

"He hadn't realized however, that it involved kids. He may have had his demons, but harming children was not one of them. He saved you from the wreckage that claimed your mother and he brought you to us, to keep you safe.

"It took me a long time to piece together the clues since he had tried to keep me in the dark as much as possible to cover his tracks and give me deniability. Plus, it was just before the Fuel Wars and after that, information became harder and harder to come by, though I managed to complete most of the details."

Big Tom Furmore turned his head slowly to meet Clare's stare. His dark brown eyes full of kindness and sorrow all at the same time.

"Clare, it has been my greatest privilege to be a father to you. To watch you grow into the strong, confident young woman you have become brings such pride to my heart that I can't even describe it. You deserve to know that truth— your real name is Stevenson, Clare Stevenson. Your mother was murdered in a car accident by a very powerful force and it destroyed your family. I'm sorry that I kept this from you all these years; I was only trying to save you from the pain and the evil forces at work."

Clare's thoughts flew faster than she could keep up.

"I think…" she began. "I think maybe I have always known. I have fragments, images of that day. I hear things in the quiet, screams that must be from the wreck because they are so painful. But I was unwilling to believe it, always trying to deny it, to fight it—always holding on to my anger at something I have never fully understood."

"Clare, there's more."

Clare edged even further out of the chair, her every ounce of attention focused on his words.

"As far as I know, your father is alive. I could never find any details on the man, but I believe he is being held against his will or trapped or something—not really a prisoner, but not really free as well. Your uncle told me once that your father knew you were alive, and until he could figure out a way to bring justice to the one who tried to kill you, then you wouldn't be safe. But I know he is out there, watching over you. Every time I thought we would lose the farm, and especially in the aftermath of the Fuel Wars, something would come along and save us. A payment of a debt, a delivery of new equipment, a new contract to supply stores with our goods; all coming out of nowhere but feeling exactly like we had some sort of guardian angel watching over us. I can't explain it, but over the years I understood what it meant to be a father and I knew those actions had to be from him."

Clare couldn't believe what she was hearing. Her anger, her memory of the past, it had driven her to a life of retaliation, a life of a vigilante. The mother and father she lost were now more than just pain, more than a life she thought she lost… it was now a life that was stolen from her. Her mother's songs gone forever, and her father somehow trapped in his own self-sacrifice for her protection. She had always believed they were both dead and she had her accusations of murder, but now she had proof enough to settle her thoughts.

Yet, something still nagged at the pit of her stomach. A phrase he had said stuck with her, mulling around behind her focus. She was missing the real link, the real future she could have with her biological family. The half-formed memory of her past was the reason she came to the farm; the real hunch she had been trying to confirm. The phrase rose to the front.

"You said children…" Clare said, her voice barely above a whisper as her thoughts focused in on their conversation. "Earlier, you said he had his demons, but he wouldn't harm children."

The old man smiled. Big Tom's face beamed with the pride he had for her.

"You have always been very clever Clare… you have a younger brother and he is still alive."

*****

The hospital hall was like any other except for two uniformed officers standing outside one of its doors. They were the only police on the floor, so James didn't have to search for the room he was looking for. Clad in a white coat and clutching a random hospital chart, James approached the officers. The pair nodded to James as he walked past them and into the room they were guarding. It seemed the boys in blue were only concerned with the occupant leaving the room and didn't care who came in.

James entered slowly. He was afraid the attending nurse would question who he was. She instead paid no attention to him. She seemed to finish her duties as he entered and then rushed off in disgust, passing him by without so much as a nod.

He could hear the man mumbling, half hidden behind his bedside curtain.

James gathered himself, breathing out slowly and deliberately from his nose. He had to keep his calm. There was nothing that could have prepared him however for the chemical reaction that occurred upon setting his eyes on the man that took his family. His blood instantly boiled as his grip tightened on the clipboard he carried at his side. Visibly starting to shake as memories of his wife, daughter, and son flooded his thoughts, James' mind turned to intense violence.

James glared at the man, just lying there, restrained to the bed at his wrists and ankles. James was suddenly aware of all the ways he could kill the man with only the objects in the room. The only decision left was which one was the most brutal.

Then the man cocked his head to the side and broke the silence, "No kids doc, there weren't supposed to be kids."

James froze. Images of revenge were replaced with conflicting empathy. Something tugged hard at the logical center of James' mind but he couldn't focus on it. The room grew cloudy with the raw despair of the day.

"No kids doc, no kids," the man repeated himself, mumbling as his gaze turned towards the window.

James took a long breath and pretended to look at the chart he brought with him. Why couldn't he think straight? He saw the paper with lines, numbers, and words but they that appeared to be a foreign language.

"It says here," James began, his nerves shaking the syllables, unsure where this would go. "It says here that you were involved in a car accident. Can you tell me what you remember?" He asked his question and flipped up the front page of the chart, feigning reading in the same manner he had seen countless TV doctors do before.

"Only a guy," the man slurred. "Owed some money, needed to be reminded."

James shook his head; the man was incoherent. He wondered if the sedative they gave him hadn't fully worn off.

"You were in a car accident," James said. "Tell me about that."

The man's head wobbled back and forth as his gaze held steady out the window. James didn't know what he was expecting, but any comprehension of the events that had taken his family would have been a good start.

"Were you high?" James asked.

The man kept on without acknowledgement.

"Are you aware that you killed three people today?" James said, his teeth grinding together.

"I AM VERY AWARE!" The man barked, snapping his head to meet James' stare as the restraints on the bed snapped taut. The sudden outburst startled James, causing every muscle he had to pull away from the outburst.

"No amount of money will make me forget," the man said before slouching back down into his bed again. A fresh stench of sweat and body odor swept over the room as he did.

Money? James thought. What was this man talking about? He started to speak again but stopped, the commotion had summoned one of the police officers to step into the room. James turned to look at him, unsure what to say.

"You okay doc?" The uniform asked. "We had to restrain him earlier. Guy was muttering nonsense about kids. No kids, no kids; he said. Just keep your distance, he's actually wicked strong despite his looks."

"Umm, all good here," James replied. He didn't know what else to say, or do. His mind took off, racing to piece together an idea that wasn't fully formed. The lights grew brighter. James' palms started to sweat. A growing fear of everything took over James' body. He couldn't face the murderer anymore.

He brushed shoulders with the cop, who watched James leave with innocent curiosity. James didn't even apologize. He couldn't focus. The man had said. The cop had said. What was it?

No kids.

Why did that stick out? James searched his mind for the red flags. He kept coming back to the phrase. But what did it mean? Was the thought of his children clouding his logic?

James was three doors down when his mind coughed up a coherent thought. He stopped. A cleaning cart was rolling down the hall behind him, two of its wheels squeaked. The piercing sound of metal on metal penetrated the general roar of the hospital floor in the same way James had a singular thought.

The accident, it wasn't an accident.

James replayed the conversations over and over in his head. The idea of it was absurd, but he continued to arrive at the same conclusion. The man kept saying no kids and mentioned that a man owed someone money and needed to be reminded. Had he been paid to get in the car wreck? Had the car wreck been intended for someone else? Had he simply hit the wrong car? He'd said no amount of money would make him forget.

James needed to tell the cops what he thought. They would take care of it; that was their job. His family had been the innocent bystanders, the collateral damage to some hit on a man with a bad debt. He turned to go back and froze.

Past the cleaning cart, he saw a large figure approaching. James couldn't move. He could only watch in dismay as his heart pounded louder and louder in his chest. It was Mondo Bot, Vigo's bodyguard. What was he doing there? James searched his mind quickly and recalled that Vigo had driven them to the hospital, not Mondo.

James held his breath as Mondo approached the police officers. They nodded their heads with indifference as Mondo walked right past them and into the man's room.

James spun around again, his arm shooting out to stabilize himself against the closet wall.

A staggering sense of dread fused his muscles to the spot—Vigo.

It couldn't be possible. He wouldn't do such a thing. They had their problems over the lab and the direction of the company, but this? It didn't make sense? Vigo wouldn't have done this, unless he was cornered with no way out? Had James pushed Vigo to extremes by leaving the company? Vigo was power hungry and had lost touch with any humility he might have had, but this?

"Are you okay Doctor?" someone said towards James. He waved them off like a man that couldn't be bothered.

"Air," James said. "I need air." His legs kicked in and carried the increasing weight in his chest toward the stairwell.

Chapter 12

The screams that echoed forever in her ears, the ones that made her senses tunnel away into the faint slivers of a dark past… those screams hadn't been her own. Their true ownership was why they were so painful. The screams were her brother's—her innocent and defenseless little brother's.

"Clare," Big Tom finally said. "I'm sorry. I should have told you sooner, but it was dangerous. My brother-in-law had to move his entire family across the country. I haven't seen him in years just so that we could protect you and your brother. The people that came after your family think you are dead and I was afraid if you knew enough then you would go looking and wind up right in their crosshairs again."

Clare nodded as the new information sunk into the fiber of her being. She had been right all along, the instinct in her gut more than just a hopeful thought. But, was that everything? Did she have any kind of relief from the rage she felt?

"So that was why I don't remember a funeral? There aren't any pictures? Long lost relatives? Was it all because we couldn't risk anyone knowing I'm alive?"

Big Tom settled back into the rocking chair. The weathered wood of the porch groaning under the weight of his movement. He nodded his head.

"Stevenson," she recited. "The name given to me at birth is Clare Stevenson."

Stevenson? Something about that rang a bell deep in her memory. Was it just a faint recognition from before she came to live on the farm or was it something else? Something more recent, from her hours of research?

"I know that name, why do I know that name?" she said, her eyes darting back and forth, searching. Clare reviewed everything she could think of from before the accident, but something tugged her forward, closer in time to the present. The recollection was from her notes but she couldn't place it.

"I don't know your parents' names or anything; all I know is that your mother was the only one who passed in the wreck. Your father wasn't even there and your brother survived. My brother-in-law saved him as well, but we felt it was best you two were separated to help protect you both."

Clare's mind flashed to the crumbled mess of a family sedan, the stench of burnt mangled metal suddenly fresh in her nostrils. Her ears rang as someone pulled her painfully from the car. Her chest was bruised from the belt. She recalled the image, her brother next to her and her mother slumped over the wheel, half hidden by a deflating airbag. The passenger seat was empty—he was right, her father hadn't been there.

"So why? Why did I think my father had died that day? Why did you let me believe that? Where has he been?" Clare stammered rapidly, her mouth failing to keep up with the years of longing pouring from her heart.

The rocking chair just kept on creaking in its steady back and forth as Big Tom shook his head. "I don't know. I just know that your Uncle Ethan said he was in trouble. That whoever arranged the wreck was trying to get him and they weren't to be messed with."

Clare wanted to scream in agony, a tragic mix of chemicals racing through her veins. Why didn't he come find me? Why didn't he come save me? Protect me? I am his little girl—where was he?

Clare's hands shook as the turmoil welled up inside. She would never have those years back, all that time lost, and for what? What were they dealing with? Could she even make a difference and get retribution? Was there even retribution for seventeen years of separation and loss?

Then it hit her… she knew why the name Stevenson stirred her memory so vividly. The name was from her own past and the recent research she had done. The back-channel conspiracy articles she had read about… Vigo Amarth. Her stomach had always churned when she saw his face, now she knew it was more than intuition.

A man that had risen to immense power in the wake of human tragedy and suffering during the Fuel Wars. He was keeping her father, and his co-founder, James Stevenson, hostage. The attack on their car must have been a power-play, a move to solidify control over a man by taking away everything he loved. It was the reason her father had remained in hiding and why he had never reached out to her. Vigo was untouchable, in some ways more powerful than the President of the United States. The secrecy was really for her own protection. She couldn't believe it… but all of it was true.

Clare tried to control herself, taking a few cleansing breaths to steady her thoughts. She was okay, the farm was still here, the sun was still passing overhead; this was just uncovering a fresh wound already over a decade old. She gathered composure and realized there was someone just like her out there, a brother she had forgotten was alive and now she knew.

"And my brother?" Clare asked. "What happened to him?"

"I'm not entirely sure," Big Tom said with compassion in his face. "All I know is that he was going to be setup at a boarding school on the East Coast and that his name was changed to Owen Bradley."

"Owen Bradley!" Clare shot up to her feet shouting. "Are you sure?"

*****

Escaping from the hospital's bright lights, James wandered slowly into the night. His feet replaced each other without his consent, driving him down the city streets to a destination that he didn't know.

Betrayed.

Betrayed by his oldest friend.

How could it be true? He didn't want to believe it and searched every corner of his mind to come up with an alternate explanation. But each time he returned to the same conclusion… Vigo.

He had never known such a lack of basic understanding. The world was cold, but how could the winds of frost come from a friend? Guilt, sorrow, hatred, desolation; they all tugged at the cavity left in his chest. The rhythmic thump, thump of its beat was the only indication that his heart still pumped on.

A dim light bled onto the street ahead, the growl of his stomach urged him to stop at it. He had to think, process the meaning from only a few hour's details.

Entering the 50's reminiscent diner, James walked casually to take up a barstool along the unpolished chrome bar top. A couple sat hand in hand enjoying a pie in one of the booths to his right and a young college student sat in the back corner, walled behind a pile of books and a plate of chocolate chip cookies.

The waitress observed the state of her late customer and didn't even ask if he needed a cup of coffee; she just poured it and set it in front of him. James stared into the dark depths of its caffeinated warmth. A fresh image of his wife flooded his mind. They were in the mountains, a small cabin, single room, earthy breeze through the open expanse of windows. Mairéad was there, staring out at nature's majesty wearing one of his collared shirts with her long slender legs protruding out from underneath. She stood with a fresh cup of coffee wrapped in the gentle caress of her hands. The wisps of steam dancing in a seemingly random pattern, but James could still see their every movement. That moment was the moment that she told him about Clare. He was going to be a father; nervous, scared, excited, and everything in-between. He cherished that moment in the quiet calm of the mountains. It always brought him peace.

James smiled. The day's chaos faded into that serenity, washed away by the overwhelming love he felt for his family and the impact they had on his life. He let his remorse for the outcome and the fear of what lay next take a back seat as he addressed the waitress. He wanted to enjoy this feeling, no matter how fleeting it might be.

"Could I get some French toast with strawberries and whip cream? Also, six pieces of bacon."

"You got it." Came a cheerful reply from his gracious host who understood never to ask questions about a weird order from a customer that looked like a train wreck.

Sitting quietly, James rolled his memories through his mind, laughing at the images and feeling the sting of pain with the closing of each.

His daughter Clare wasn't a fan of meat at even an early age. James could see her now, early in life with just a few strands of blonde hair donning her smiley head. She sat in her high chair with her head held high, mashing up another failed attempt to eat a pancake when he decided it was time. He handed her the first strip of bacon she had ever encountered. She rolled it over in her hand inquisitively, puzzled by its crunchy texture. Convinced it wasn't poison, she buried it halfway in her mouth, attacking it with the same gusto she did everything else in her life. From then on, Saturday morning breakfast was where she would devour an entire plate of bacon without hesitation.

The smile that spread across James' face lit the chrome countertop of the diner. He could see her eyes; he could feel the pure joy she felt with the new experience of a food she would love for the rest of her life. A memory, a connection, James let out a sigh—thankful that he would always have it.

His food arrived, plates of comfort masquerading as sustenance. James took in a fulfilling breath before cutting into the perfectly cooked French toast.

His son Owen had been a brilliant kid even from a young age. Always asking questions and never afraid to get his hands dirty, the lanky boy never missed helping with Saturday breakfast. He would mix the batter for pancakes, or lay out the bacon in the skillet, but by far his favorite was the egg-soaked bread cooked to a golden hue, served with homemade whipped cream. James chuckled at the vision of his young doppelganger with a dollop of fluffy white heart attack on the end of his nose, smiling cheerfully as he listed every type of bread he knew of, which ones were best for French toast, and which ones he wanted to try next.

With every bite the memories grew more vivid in James' mind. With every detail that came back to him, a bit of the fear he felt faded away. He had to hold on to those moments. The little pieces of time strung together to make a life. They were extensions of himself and the building blocks of what his heart must become—something closed, warmth on the inside, long sharp barbs on the outside.

The diner lights seemed to suddenly dim all around him, sweeping his joy away with it. His perception darkened, James took a few more bites of each item in desperate attempt to savor any clairvoyance he found there. But, the sweetness of the food only brought the taste of bitterness to his thoughts. Finally, pushing his food around indiscriminately, the despondent doctor sensed a presence and he gulped in preparation to face it.

The sudden clatter of the bell hanging from the diner's door caused James to freeze; all of his senses heightened with gushing fear pumping through his veins. He could feel the two large bodies entering the space, and James instantly knew who they belonged to. Vigo was there. They had tracked him somehow, followed him here, but how? No one had seen him yet he felt a heavy weight in his pocket... the keys.

A cold shiver crept up his spine as James felt the presence of two hearts beating steady just behind him. Their slow pace despite the day's events, were an indication of the dark lengths they were willing to go. A stack of twenties appeared and were casually laid next to his plate as James looked up to catch a glance at the reflection of the last two people he wanted to see.

The looming presence of Vigo's henchman Mondo stood with his arms crossed between James and the door. James wasn't exactly sure why they were there. Had Mondo spotted him in the hospital? Had Vigo grown impatient as the night grew long? Or did Vigo figure out that the smart man who had propped him up all these years was able to surmise the true nature of the day? Either way, their presence there confirmed James' suspicion.

While Vigo came to stand at the physicist's side, he leaned down slightly so he could whisper.

"Let's not make a scene James…" He paused, his breath hot with bourbon and his eyes on fire with power. "It's time you come home, where you belong."

Chapter 13

Owen smiled as the pavement gave way to their destination. The outside of the building was amazing, with a stone architecture in a profound style that was convincingly European. Standing at the corner just outside the doors, Owen felt the tiniest touch of reassurance—they were on the right track.

The hall itself was closed during the day but the restaurant inside was open. Owen and Walt took a seat and looked around, unsure what they were searching for. They ordered some drinks from the lone worker and studied their surroundings carefully.

The stroll had been mostly quiet, unsure this was the right path but committed all the same. Now that they were sitting however, Owen wanted to talk. He needed to verbalize the thoughts in his head. There wasn't anyone else in the place except the waiter, who wasn't concerned with them now that he had delivered their drinks, preferring instead to lean against the bar with a tattered copy of *Jurassic Park*. Older copies of physical books had become more commonplace in the post-Fuel Wars world. The prints that existed were in endless circulation, tattered spines and all; while publishing houses sat collecting dust. The cost was just too high to produce new works and people had very little extra income.

"This isn't adding up," Owen began. "Why the charade, why the cryptic riddles? What is the end goal? Is my father standing at the finish line? What about my mother? Where have they been all these years?"

Walt only shrugged, offering nothing of comfort to the young man.

"So, what about that gargantuan man and his expensive ride? You knew he was coming, why can't you give me the details?"

"I am only here as a helping hand when the time is right. You must make the discovery for yourself."

Owen's fists balled up in frustration. "Is my father involved in something illegal? Is it dangerous? Is his life in jeopardy?"

"Your father is in control of his own path and has chosen it. He has given you this path and the option to choose as well."

Walt's words took Owen a moment to process. Was it really about a choice? Was this path about discovering his past so that he could choose his future? It seemed all so convoluted and the pain from years of boarding school didn't subside due to the thrill of a scavenger hunt. Owen had been abandoned, left alone with no memories, no tokens, no pictures, no stories to get him through the holidays and long solitary summers. Owen hadn't known where he belonged or where he came from. He didn't have roots built into his foundation. The early memories were coming back now, with prompting, but was it enough to make him whole? Was it enough for him to feel like he had a solid base so that he might look to his future? He had always struggled with the vision of his life. He preferred to keep his head down in academics and conquering the world's problems so that he wouldn't have to face his own. Even if he did solve the energy crisis, what then? Would this journey of discovery be enough for him to forgive, so that he could finally embrace happiness?

Owen opened his mouth to speak, to spill his heart out on to the table but he stopped. A TV mounted high in the corner of his vision caught his attention. The sight was odd because TV had become mostly a relic of the past. Most people couldn't afford the extra energy needed to run even the most efficient sets and because of that, new content production had ground to a halt. Owen had read about the years when there were too many channels to ever watch in one lifetime, but now he knew there were simply five channels. The news, famous sitcom reruns, kids and family, old sports mixed in with limited coverage of the new Capstone events, and westerns. For some reason Owen didn't quite understand, westerns had remained relevant and extremely popular. Maybe it was the analogous nature of the story and hard times to what they were currently living in, or maybe it was the simple plotline of good vs evil; either way they played on. But the TV Owen noticed wasn't on westerns, it was on local news coverage. The broadcast was muted but the unmistakable image of himself was splashed on the screen. The sight of it slammed his heart into his throat, as the rush of adrenaline flooded heavily into his veins.

They had his university faculty photo positioned just above the title: *Suspected Terrorist Loose in Chicago.* Owen could hardly breathe, what was this? All of his focus bore into the screen. The newscast closed captioning ran quickly and he read as fast as he could.

University of Chicago physics teacher Owen Bradley is wanted by authorities for possible terrorist intent. He has been seen snooping around several prominent buildings near downtown Chicago and has been escorted out of them by security personnel on multiple occasions. Anyone who has seen the suspect should report it immediately to police at...

Owen's focus on the TV waned as real worry sunk in. This was bad, really bad. The man in the black car and now all of law enforcement were out looking for him. It would be hard for Walt and him to move through the city with all eyes searching for his face.

Instinctively, Owen brought his hand up to cover a portion of his cheek. He was suddenly very aware of the man still reading at the bar. Had he seen the report? Did he recognize Owen? An agonizing minute passed as Owen's paranoia rose, then began to cool off to a low simmer. His senses returned, along with his logic; Owen began to search for meaning.

"Why aren't you mentioned in the report?" Owen asked of Walt, his voice barely over a whisper.

Walt, unsure of the meaning of the question, simply shrugged.

"The TV just listed me as a terror suspect, the whole city will be looking for me." His voice rose to normal volume, "But why weren't you in the report?"

Walt nodded in understanding, taking his time in response. "We are dealing with very powerful people, and it appears they are catching on."

"Who is catching on—WHO?"

"Your father felt it was best for you to find out for your-self so that you could form your own opinions and wouldn't be swayed by his choices."

Swayed by his choices? The response was infuriating for Owen; the man was his father only in his biological donation. Owen knew nothing of him and any decisions he may or may not have made. Why would that sway his own choices? This man that his father trusted kept deflecting and wouldn't give him a straight answer.

Owen let the air calm down, trying to take stock of what he knew. He had no idea what he was involved in and yeah, he could admit that his emotions of a possible reconnection with his family might cloud his judgement. He would have to process that in time. But, putting that aside, there had to be a reason why Walt wasn't mentioned in the report. If whomever was after him had connected the dots that he was on the run, surely they knew that Walt was with him. Unless, there was something else, something other than him being on the run, something he had that only they wanted to find… the package.

Since the package presumably had come from his father, was it possible the people after his father tracked it and were now after him? If they had the power to get the entirety of law enforcement chasing him then they could easily find out who sent the courier. It could explain why Walt wasn't in-cluded in the report, he was sent directly by Owen's father. The only people that knew about it were Walt, Owen, and Owen's father, nothing to track, bribe, extort, or steal. It made logical sense to Owen and he relaxed as much as one could, given the situation.

Now, adding fugitive to his list of problems, Owen de-cided there was only one way to proceed. He had to trust in a man he did not know. Through the years of loneliness and abandonment, Owen had grown up knowing only questions. The only path to answers was through the clues that his father laid forth. Owen only hoped that they would lead him to answers—real, concrete answers.

Owen felt suddenly free with the acceptance and with the revelation, his gut told him they were close. But the question remained of how to proceed with all of Chicago out to find him. Then it hit him fully, the clues, the cryptic chase across the city, it was to keep him on the move, out of sight and away from the usual locations that he frequented. His father had known this would happen. He had set all of this up.

"This isn't just about discovery; this is about staying on the move and away from the influence of my father's enemies." Owen said.

The smile spread wide across Walt's face. "Now they aren't the only ones that are catching on."

Owen chuckled at the first sign of levity from his companion. The trust between them was building with each revelation, but Owen still had plenty to worry about.

"I'm going to need to disguise myself, hide my face," Owen said as his eyes began to search the room. He already had three days' worth of stubble helping to cover his baby face from his university photo, but he needed more.

The restaurant they were in was associated with Thalia Hall as it was on the first floor of the same building. And that was when Owen's eyes found it—a small merchandise section near the front. There were stickers, patches, posters, t-shirts, and hats—that would do. A hat would help hide him from crowds and allow him to blend in. He needed to get one.

Standing, he approached the items, trying to determine which one would look best. His eyes scanned quickly when they latched onto something and lingered. There was a shirt that grabbed his focus but he couldn't quite place the reason why. There was an oddness in lettering across the front that stood out to Owen. It didn't really look like words, but soon his mind managed to read it:

Punch House: Where the hits keep coming, round after round, via glass, carafe, or bowl.

Something was there, a hint of an idea formed in the back of Owen's mind. His thoughts scurried to catch it before it slipped away.

"Excuse me," he blurted out towards the sole worker in the establishment without a care that he might be recognized. "What does this shirt mean? What is the Punch House?"

Not bothering to look up from his reading, the man simply replied, "It's the bar. Downstairs. They serve rum punch in these huge bowls."

Everything in Owen's vision shifted forward, giving him a sense of falling backward as the pieces lined up in his mind.

Two Bohemians hang a right hook and find themselves in the cellar.

In the cellar…

The bar is downstairs.

A right hook…

The Punch House.

He was on the right track. Hell, he was in the right building. Owen's thoughts immediately jumped to the day before and the observatory. His father had been here and hidden a note somewhere that only he could find. But where to look?

Owen quickly grabbed a hat from the stack and went up to the bar.

"I'm going to get this hat." He said. "But first, is there any way I can get a tour of the hall?"

The disgruntled service industry worker took his time looking up from his book. Giving Owen a simple look over, the man replied, "I'll tell you what. You buy this hat and a shirt for your friend, then I'll let you in there to check it out on your own."

Owen eagerly shook his head in approval of the deal and silently thanked Michael Crichton for being such a captivating author.

*****

James sat on a stool, slumped over a pristine lab table. He finally got the lab he wanted, but all he cared to do was roll a No. 2 pencil back and forth endlessly.

The entrance to the lab was on the opposite side of the building from the elevators, accessible only by a long hallway. James hadn't understood the architectural need for it in the planning stages but now he did—Vigo had been planning to keep an eye on the comings and goings from the lab all along.

James wondered when the mistrust had crept in. He didn't have a track record of keeping things from Vigo. In fact, he may have been too open. James had kept treating it like a partnership when in reality, it never had been. Vigo believed he had full control and was the better businessman when he rebranded himself and changed his name. Not that it mattered now, Vigo was willing to go to a level that James was not, and James lost anything that would push him to go there. All that he had left to do was wait out his days in the lab that Vigo had so graciously bestowed upon the man who had built the empire. A used tool left in the shed to turn out products and feed the machine.

Looking around the room, James took in the irony of the decisions he had made when designing the lab space. He often worked late or arrived early and needed to freshen up before a dinner or big meeting; the full bathroom suite included in the plans was now more than a convenience, it was a necessity, as was the attached kitchen, complete with cookware, refrigerator, and table space. He could easily prepare meals or have them brought up from the full cafeteria on the 1st floor. The design was meant to be an efficiency, but now, it just seemed practical. James controlled everything precisely, ate for the sake of fuel, and kept familiar aromas at bay, lest they trigger a painful memory.

James wandered over to the only side of the room with windows. Staring out into the heights above a bustling Chicago night, he should have been overjoyed. The room was filled with enough work area and tech to solve the impending energy crisis, it was exactly as he had pitched it. The lab was everything it needed to be and more. The area should have been where historical discoveries would be made, but the room no longer invited creativity—it invited only imprisonment.

The four lab tables, benches, and stools centered in the room were brand new and pristine, but all James saw was a new phase of his life. A phase void of the wholeness his family provided. Sure, there was purpose in his work, but what was purpose without those he held most dear to share in it?

James let the drive he had known his whole life slide into the recesses of himself. He didn't see the point anymore. Why did he feel the need to be the savior, the one who worked tirelessly to no avail? He couldn't prevent the end of fossil fuels and an energy crisis any more than he could stop his best friend from murdering his family. He would stay here and watch what he predicted come true, even if it was only to know that he would have some companionship in his suffering.

Days turned into weeks, the world spinning around as light came in the window and then went out again.

The rest of the building had been completed and business got back to work as usual. Dr. Stevenson became just a response at the end of an email. The understanding was that he had lost his family and that he needed time, or at least that was the narrative that Vigo wove. The work gradually came back his way as engineers and project managers needed his advice. The tasks were tedious, easy, and barely took up any of the hours that he spent stricken with sorrow.

The energy crisis that James predicted struck only four months after moving into his new living arrangement. An infrastructure completely dependent on electricity had no hint of a backup. The country, and world, quickly slipped into a blackout caused by the energy gap that oil and gas left behind.

Society fell into chaotic ruin almost overnight. Human decency was cast aside and suddenly, if you weren't related by blood, then you were the enemy. Much later people took to calling it Gaia's Reckoning, but in the end, it was humanity, always humanity, that would be its own downfall.

James watched for weeks with indifference. There was no way to tell of the full nature or the countless lives that were lost in that time. Civilization had returned to a time worse than the Dark Ages. James' shame weighed like lead in his heart, his only solace was that he had nothing left to lose.

Then out of the chaos arose a new company to save them all from total destruction. The company called itself Phoenix, revealing that they had developed a synthetic alternative to gasoline. Led by a handful of ex-oil and gas executives who knew what was coming, the company quickly became the most valuable in the world. The limitations to their new technology having very little impact on their meteoric rise.

The historic chemical breakthrough was called Synthetic Oil Replacement, or SOR, and worked in all gasoline applications except for one catch. SOR was unstable based on quantity and time, so its chemical components had to be mixed just before use. A massive market for convertors blossomed overnight. Everything from cars, to lawn mowers, to water heaters, to power plants, and M1 Abrams tanks; they all needed convertors that could take the chemical supply and mix it before injection into a normal gasoline engine. And the converter business was where Vigo took them, sticking with the military machine and his friends on Capitol Hill. Vigo led Amarth Corporation to get the contracts for developing convertors for a majority of the nation's military vehicles. All normal means of procurement were thrown out the window as laws were bypassed all in the name of establishing some semblance of a civilization.

James was skeptical of SOR and began to study its properties. He knew from his own research that countless attempts had been made previously to create a synthetic gasoline. They all had failed and he had to know how SOR managed to succeed.

The key, it turned out, was genetically modified algae. SOR was a mix of water and the waste of this new algae. The algae had to be grown in massive vats and fed pure sucrose in order to produce even a gallon of SOR. Almost overnight, SOR turned the reliance on fossil fuels into a reliance on sugar.

Even though its properties were not entirely understood, every government on the planet rushed out its approval and praised it as the replacement for gasoline. With the death toll from the city street war lords battling with each other over food, water, and the basic necessities now in the hundreds of thousands, there really was no other choice—the Age of SOR was ushered in with open arms.

*****

The wind fought hard against Clare's hearing as she dialed up Malcom via the helmet connection to her phone. Her mind was still reeling with the new information that her visit to the farm had revealed. She hadn't stopped to process it at all, foregoing dinner and any pleasantries that were planned with the Furmores. She just bolted and fired up her bike. When she paused before putting her helmet on her head, she looked up to catch the gaze of Big Tom on the porch. He gave her a nod of understanding and a look that said: just be careful. If Owen Bradley really was her brother, then she had to do everything she could to protect him.

"Hello?" The phone answered as Clare merged onto the interstate. Clare had forgotten the sound of Malcom's voice.

"Malcom! I need your help," Clare shouted, trying to hear herself as she weaved past another electricycle going slower than everyone else despite being in the left lane.

"Okay? Are you riding? It's rather noisy."

"I am. I have new information and we are taking the protection gig." Clare said between controlled breaths.

"We are? What changed?" Malcom asked, curious. "And why didn't you just text me? After the special forces thing, I was afraid this…"

"He's my brother," Clare said, cutting to the chase. "That's the new info I found out."

"He's your what? Your brother?" Malcom's voice trailed off as he worked quickly to try to connect the dots. "Wait, like from before you were adopted?"

Clare smiled, they had only talked about it a couple times but like a true friend, Malcom remembered when important things were shared.

"Yeah, I think he is my biological brother and I suspect that whoever hired us to protect him knows that."

"You serious? Hold on to your butts!" Malcom almost shouted before his voice dropped to a whisper. "Like some sort of genuine conspiracy theory?"

"Malcom," Clare said calmly. "You don't have to lower your voice, if they are listening than they can hear you either way."

His characteristically nerdy chuckle came over the line. "Yeah, yeah you're right. So… you find out anything else?"

"I'm not sure I ever told you, but it was a car wreck that killed my family. Or at least that was what I was led to believe. It looks like possibly it was only my mother that died in it, my brother and I survived while my father wasn't even there. Besides that, the only other thing is that my real name is Clare Stevenson."

"Wait, really? Stevenson? Like the famous silent co-founder of Amarth Corporation who hasn't been seen in public in years?"

Clare almost lost control of the electricycle with his quick account of her father. The memories were coming back clearer now. The fond details she had of him holding her hand in the park and taking her to her first dojo. Why had she blocked the name out and those moments out? Had her time on the farm caused her to forget?

"Clare?" Malcom came back after the long silence.

"Yeah, yeah, still here man. Just trying to process it all," Clare said, slowing her bike to a less concentration intensive speed. "What do you know about him?"

"Well, he co-founded Amarth but hasn't been seen in years. He is some kind of crazy genius, has a whole floor dedicated to his secret lab. Nobody really goes in or out of there and there are a lot of speculations about what goes on in there. But as far as the rumors go, he is still in there, tinkering away—a living ghost story."

Clare's heart pounded once again in her chest. Her brother was alive and now her father? What the hell had happened that caused them to be separated? What kind of evil were they dealing with? For the briefest of seconds, she was six years old once again, sitting on the dairy farm steps, crying with longing for the family she so desperately missed. The pain was fresh in her mind once again. Now uncovered after being hardened by seventeen years of training and taking charge to right the wrongs she saw in the world. The experience stoked the smallest ember of hope deep inside her. Could they become a family again?

"Malcom," Clare said, her voice steady, focused. "I am not sure why what happened to my family happened. I know Vigo Amarth is involved. The connection to my past and Owen being my brother, then I saw Vigo's bodyguard at Owen's apartment. It can't all be a coincidence."

"Wait, what do you mean you saw his bodyguard?"

"I went to check out Owen's apartment, trying to figure out what he had gotten into. I didn't find anything out of the ordinary, except then I ran into Vigo Amarth's bodyguard on my way out. He went into Owen's apartment. I didn't tell you because I wanted to see if there was a connection beyond my disdain for Vigo. Sorry."

"No problem, that's smart. I haven't found anything by the way."

"Listen, I am not sure what we are up against, but if there is a chance I can help, even in the slightest, then I have to try to help Owen."

"Clare, I am with you all the way," came the voice of her oldest friend without pause, without hesitation, and that was why she considered him a brother as well.

"Well then, let's find my brother."

Chapter 14

Humanity struggled for a time to pick up the pieces. SOR was expensive to manufacture and global scale production was going to take time, the result of which was that it was difficult for most to acquire. So, instead of life returning to the way it was completely, people learned to forego some of the extravagance that had come before. Anything in people's lives that required power was suddenly questioned, the value of its function weighed against the simple question everyone had come to face—survival.

In the meantime, the entertainment industry collapsed. Movies, music, and TV all went dark. The major sports stadiums sat unused like the monolith colosseums of past civilizations. People instead turned to stories told by candlelight as the reality of their new lives took hold.

But with SOR came opportunity as well and new industries grew with it. Transportation made major changes as alternative methods became popular—the biggest of which being the Electricycle. An electric, lightweight cousin to the motorcycle with great range on a single charge; the e-cycle quickly became the preferred method of getting from point A to point B.

James understood what SOR was—a band-aid to the real problem. But he didn't care. The whole world seemed like a bad daytime television show, just playing in the background as he withered away in his own pain.

In the time that he had spent tucked away in Vigo's gleaming tower, James had come to learn that he would never be allowed to leave without an escort. It seemed that Vigo had created an entire security team just to monitor one man.

And so, the yellow writing implement rolled back and forth; an endless cycle reflective of the man's days. Any desire James had for retribution had come and gone, replaced by a sincere depth of mourning. Sleep deprivation starved his mind as he couldn't close his eyes without flashes of his family haunting him. Being inside Vigo's dungeon had trapped James, even in his own mind. The brief relief he had experienced at the diner was the last. He couldn't even recall their smiles in this place, for fear of the hole it would leave in his consciousness.

James was meant to be working on an SOR convertor for a tank, but he wasn't motivated. He kind of liked the idea of no armies and no wars. The work wasn't difficult and most of it was completed by other engineers looking for a paycheck so they could acquire convertors for their own automobiles or lawn mowers—all so they could try and get back to the way things were.

James didn't care, he had already discovered that things could never be the same. Civilization was once again throwing itself at technology without understanding its effects. He had figured out how SOR worked and the realization worried him even more than oil and gas. SOR production required a tremendous amount of sugar. A material that was once considered the most abundantly sustainable resource on earth, but if SOR was going to replace oil, the amount of resources required would rapidly deplete the planet's ability to replenish itself if restraint wasn't used—a restraint he knew humanity didn't have. But sometimes he felt a brief reprieve from his grief when thinking about it, at least his family wouldn't have to be around to watch the earth go dormant. James believed it would be a time worse than any ice age that had come before it. Humanity believed itself capable of killing a planet, but quite the opposite was true. Life on earth would continue on as soon as it was rid of its biggest parasite.

Letting the pencil roll off onto the floor, James got up and went for the mail. Most of everything was electronic these days to save on transportation energy but some organizations still liked the old way of physical paper. Gathering the mail off his father's old desk, which Vigo had delivered to the lab as a token of good will, James thumbed through the usual interoffice pamphlets and bulletins until he stopped on a letter.

It was from the American Physical Society, apparently it was time again for the yearly conference. James had been a speaker the year before but he was sure the council hadn't asked him again this year due to the loss of his family.

Turning the envelope over in his hands, James studied the clean, crisp edges and previously opened flap. He would never be able to go without Vigo's henchmen tagging along. All of his mail was opened and examined, his internet access was monitored, and if he left his lab then his every step was watched by Vigo's security team. They had set up a prison for him in all but name.

James had only left the building once since being escorted inside that dark, cold night. He had been escorted, much to the churning of his stomach, by Vigo and Mondo to the funeral for his family. He couldn't remember many details from the ceremony.

He sighed; James couldn't face his colleagues in such a state. He could barely face himself in the oblong mirror of the lab's living quarter's bathroom. Slamming the envelope into the trashcan, a heat formed under his shirt collar. He stood staring at it, crumpled and creased. An envelope representing more than just a conference—the sum of his career turned to waste.

Thousands upon thousands of hours spent studying piled into the fist that James made. James couldn't take his eyes off the envelope. Something was there, causing rage to build in James' heart. There was nothing left for him but he couldn't bring himself to turn away from the trash. A dormant drive resurfaced, driving his hands downward, closer and closer to the discarded invite.

Touching it once again, the sharpness of its edges caused him to shutter. A spark of rebellion from deep inside him emerged. He placed all of his pent-up rage at his situation into the simple act of reading this letter. The act of defiance making him pick the thing up and tear it open with eagerness.

The contents were the usual spread. A pamphlet announcing the conference and the speaker lineup. James smiled at the sight of friendly names and revered peers. A visitor's guide to the host city was also included—Chicago. It could be possible for James to go, even with his brute entourage. Maybe some social interaction would be beneficial and give him a new perspective.

The colorful pages were accompanied by an invitation letter. It had the standard information, dates and times, as well as an assertion about how important their work was at this critical time in history. There always seemed to be some problem for the scientists of the world to solve.

James kept reading until the closing quote caught his attention.

> "If you want your children to live, read them fairy tales. If you want them to be alive, read them more fairy tales." - Albert Einstein

James' head spun. They screwed up the quote and he should know, he used it in his presentation at the conference the year before. The quote should have been:

> "If you want your children to be intelligent, read them fairy tales. If you want them to be more intelligent, read them more fairy tales." - Albert Einstein

Something happened— the words— the intention of it… an ember buried deep in the pit of his stomach had a light breeze suddenly stoke it. With new life, it glowed in a desperation that iced his veins. *If you want them to be alive… YOUR CHILDREN…* it couldn't be true, but for the first time in six months, the corner of Doctor James Stevenson's mouth quivered upward ever so slightly. He was going to that conference, no matter the cost.

*****

New hat pulled tight onto his head and fresh shirt slung over his shoulder, Owen entered the historic hall with Walt not far behind. The pair stood in astonishment at the space, seemingly endless in its detail and expanse with only the two of them to fill its walls. Owen didn't know where to start looking for his father's hidden note but he was sure it was in here or the bar downstairs. Since Owen thought it wasn't ideal to hide a note in a bar or take a kid there to form a special bond, then the next clue was most likely somewhere in the hall. But as he wandered around among the dimly lit venue, there wasn't anything that stirred in him—no memories, no recollection, just the faint smell of events gone by.

Owen studied the lines of architecture and soon noticed that there weren't really many places to hide a note. Everything was open and exposed to view from plenty of angles, maybe his instinct was off and they were in the wrong place. But, as he studied the unlit stage with its large velvet curtains hanging closed, the events of the night before came into his thoughts and the faint hint of his mother's song returned to his ears.

The melody swelled, filling his heart, distracting his mind just enough to slip in an idea.

"Walt, what do you think about this place?" he asked.

The man who was studying the ceiling lowered his gaze. "I really enjoy the opera boxes; they look like the best seats in the house."

Owen chuckled slightly, a smirk curling on the corner of his lips. Walt knew where the next clue was, but he wasn't going to let on unless asked a direct question. Owen was headed for the staircase to the opera boxes when he stopped. *Two Bohemians hang a right…* Owen turned and headed to the boxes on the right of the hall, the even numbered ones.

Scanning the ceiling of opera box two, Owen felt his heart sink. If there was a card sized manila envelope stuck up there then he wasn't finding it. He paced back and forth in the small space, turning over Walt's words.

'They look like the best seats in the house.' Then it hit him and Owen instantly began flipping over each of the eight chairs lined up in two neat rows in the box. He made it to the third one before he found it. The same size and style as the first note. His fingers fumbled about clumsily as he tore at the adhesive. Despite being named a terror suspect and being unsure of what each step might unfold, Owen had to admit—he was enjoying himself. His smile beamed, lighting up the room even before he read the hand written words on the page.

Owen,

Excellent work deciphering my shoddy riddle making. You are undoubtedly standing in the opera box at this very moment, reading these words. I wanted you to see this place because it is very special to me. It wasn't a connection between us but a connection between your mother and I.

As you know, being in academics doesn't really lend itself to a lavish lifestyle. But I needed this particular night to be special. I spent months saving up any money I could make doing odd jobs and tutoring. Hopefully you remember because it was one of her most ubiquitous characteristics and that is: your mother loved music. She would sing at any chance she could get and she loved to just wade into song and the freedom it brings.

Well, one of her favorite bands was coming to town, to this particular theater in fact, and I couldn't pass up the chance. My heart was already no longer my own, I lived and died by her every breath and I was pretty sure she felt the same, with whatever romantic metaphor for physics algorithms there may be.

I took all of my earnings and bought us two tickets and not just any two tickets, but seats in the opera box that has, as you can see, the most spectacular view in the whole hall. At the same time, I managed to acquire a piece of jade from a buddy in the geology department and I fashioned a ring after hours and hours at the university shop. Everything was set and I was ready.

The night came and I surprised her with the tickets. We ate a modest meal of bread, cheese, and cheap pinot noir before we went to the show. We sat down and the opening act began. As the music played the lights and sounds brought pure elation to your mother's face. I couldn't take my eyes off of her.

The chords rolled on and my knee became increasingly twitchy, my hands always brushing up against my pocket, just to verify that some supernatural force hadn't stolen the ring in the seconds since I touched it last. Finally, the opening act ended and the stage lit up to change bands. She turned to me and thanked me profusely. Her eyes beaming, she said that she understood how hard I worked to make this happen and she would never forget it.

I couldn't stand it anymore. The plan was for me to propose when we got to the downstairs bar after the show where our friends were waiting, but I couldn't wait. I had to ask. I fumbled in my pocket and the ring rolled out onto the floor. I caused a scene scrambling around to get it. But it was quite comical and did manage to bring me down to one knee. Your mom was no fool, she knew what was going on and would never admit it to me, but knew weeks before that something was afloat. (Some fatherly advice, it might not make sense until you get married yourself, but they know, they always know, and are always right.)

That being said, I can't say I even remember the rest of that concert. All I could hear was her ecstatic answer to the only question that ever mattered, "Yes!"

That night we were up until dawn celebrating with friends in that old basement bar. And our lives together were just a continuation of that celebration. I wanted to share that with you because I'm sure you have very few memories of her. You were so young when she was taken from us. I can't explain and I am certainly devastated that I have to write you these words. But I don't want you to have to suffer with false hope any longer than you should have to.

You should know the truth and the details will be revealed in time. But for now, just know, your mother was murdered in order to get to me. I never thought it could be possible and I have lived every moment since in anguish. You can hate me, I certainly understand. But know that she loved you, just as I do. I only ask that you use the anger and frustration to continue on this journey. Do it for her sake and for your sister's.

Dad

Under immense pressure, Higinbotham's hall outshines them all.

Owen knew it was true, even as he read it. Somehow, he had known it all this time. He couldn't believe that a mother's love could be kept at bay for so long without the most logical of explanations—she was gone. Even still, seeing the words written out, confirming it, they pressed against his heart, the lonely little boy inside curling up into his own ball of self-preservation.

He knew that she must have passed and that was the only reason that she didn't tear down every boarding school door on the planet until she was reunited with him once again. He could come to terms with it, reassured by the discovery of her song and the fact that now, it could be with him forever. He was also comforted in the revelation that he had a sister. She was living, breathing, and his family. He hadn't even considered the fact before. He had no recollection of her—no name calling, no teasing, no sibling rivalry... nothing. He felt worse about that fact than anything else.

Owen rubbed the back of his neck and smiled. He didn't know how to feel about his father, what it meant that his enemies had torn their family apart. Owen could only push that aside for the moment and focus on the fact that he may have lost a mother, but gained a sister. He had to find her. He had to warn her of what was going on, that their family was real and their father was in trouble. But then he realized, if their father had set up this elaborate maze of riddles for him then he must have taken precautions to protect her as well.

There was only one path forward, one path to his father, his sister, and whatever retribution could be found. The path lay straight ahead in the next clue... if only he had any idea what it meant.

*****

The musty Chicago air refreshingly stoked James' outlook. The smells flooded his thoughts with the warm embrace of the city he grew up in. Being cut off from the world, he hadn't realized how much the little things meant to him.

Vigo's large black car pulled up curbside and Mondo came around to let James in. Though he gave the appearance of a chauffeur, James knew the large henchman was only there to keep an eye on him. James smiled in forcing Vigo to give up his precious commodity for the day.

The city streets passed by as if they were a dream, the noise and energy of the landscape held at bay by the thick bullet proof windows. James observed quietly the thousands of people moving along the paths of their lives, their tiny fractions of existence compounding to form society as a whole. James wondered if his daughter and son were out there now, somehow nestled safely among the crowd, their little hands reaching out to him, calling for him to come and save them... to take them home.

Pulling up to the University, Mondo mumbled something about waiting just outside the doors for him. Apparently sitting in a physics conference wasn't high on his list of entertaining activities. James' didn't mind, he was happy he wouldn't have to explain why this big lug of a man was accompanying him.

Checking in, James received his welcome packet with his name tag and a schedule of events. It also included a special insert inviting him to sit in the balcony of the auditorium for the lecture on SOR power to weight characteristics. It seemed odd but he filed it away as he was quickly enveloped by smiling faces. The community of intellectuals may have been the most comfortable with Sci-fi and limited social interaction but when it came to their own, the awkwardness melted away.

James was hurriedly ushered into the conference amongst the chatter of equations and the politics of federal grants. Entering the doors however, James was aware of eyes burning a hole in the back of his skull. James turned. Mondo had moved inside and watched from a vantage point in the foyer.

James swallowed hard; his fist clenched with tension. Vigo's hired eyes passed beyond the auditorium doors as James entered and he released his breath. He was among his peers and he hadn't felt any form of kinship in longer than he could fathom. The interaction felt good. The laughs at shared stories of the past began to refill an empty emotional tank, lending a levity to the nagging voice in the back of his mind— would he find answers here?

As the conference moved along through the day's activities, James' levity recessed further and further. He couldn't focus on anything the presenters were saying, instead the inside of his mind was left to spiral among a chemical cocktail of emotion.

Finally, it was time for the keynote speaker, a young pioneer on the forefront of the SOR movement. James, now a nervous wreck, excused himself from his colleagues to head to the restroom. Once outside the auditorium he had to catch his breath, his thoughts daring not to dwindle too long on his small sliver of hope. A hope that maybe, just maybe, his children were alive.

Walking slowly up the stairs to the balcony, James gave his eyes time to adjust to the darkness of the area. The conference was all on the main floor so the lights were out over the balcony, however James instantly saw the silhouette of a man sitting in the back row. Creeping along slowly, James realized he was more afraid of what the man might say than the man himself.

Taking a seat with one chair in between himself and the mysterious man, James looked straight ahead and waited. His heart beat soundly in his chest with the silence, the gravity of the situation weighing heavily in his arms and legs.

A full minute passed before the man spoke, his voice calm and rehearsed.

"Dr. Stevenson," the man started. "I am so glad that you got my message. I'm afraid that I have something very important to tell you but you are constantly being watched. It seems that you have some very powerful enemies and I'm afraid that I fell victim to them as well."

"I'm sorry," James whispered, his mind racing to process every input. "I don't know who you are?"

"We haven't met," the man said before a long sigh. "My name is Ethan Abbott and I'm a Chicago police officer, or was... was a Chicago police officer."

James' eyes widened with the news. Was it possible law enforcement was onto Vigo? Was it possible they were planning to take him down? Or was this man fired from the force because of Vigo's influence?

Ethan continued from beneath a tightly pulled down baseball hat. "I am a gambling addict and I racked up some debt with the wrong people. They were going to take everything from me. My house, my job; everything. And that was when I was hired to do a job, given the promise that it would all just go away. But I should've known, I was played. They never paid up and even though sports are gone, the debt is still owed."

Ethan was sitting straight up, keeping his focus forward, never turning to face James. Even with the posture, James could sense his embarrassment.

"The job was simple, torch a car so that no evidence could be pulled from it. I had nowhere else to turn so I took it on. I was given a burner phone and told to wait for further instructions."

James' mind sped ahead; this man knew everything. His teeth clenched tightly with anticipation.

"The call came with a little over an hour to get to the location. I had the make and model of the car with the simple task of making sure it was destroyed. But… when I pulled up to the scene, what I found broke my heart. It was a family… your family, they had been hit head on. Your wife… I'm sorry, but she had already passed. But, looking in the backseat, your daughter and your son… they were alive."

James' heart burst open, gushing raw adrenaline that caused him to hyperventilate.

"I was a good detective once. I didn't know who exactly had hired me at the time, but I later put together who was involved when I ran the plates on your car. I knew that we had a mutual enemy and that he had staged this wreck. It was my job to destroy any evidence, so I did what I was hired to do. I understood that I couldn't mess with Amarth, but I couldn't just let those kids die."

At last, Ethan turned to James and looked him square in the eye, almost whispering the words that James so desperately wanted to hear. "Dr. Stevenson, your children are alive."

The tears poured out of their ducts in warm streaks of joy down the physicist's face. The ember of hope deep in his stomach had been real, pointing him to the truth.

"I pulled the kids from the car and loaded them in my cruiser. I'm sorry Doc, for your wife, I really am, but I torched the car. I remembered there were a few children that passed in a warehouse fire the week before. So, I made a few calls and cashed in a few favors to have two of them transferred to the hospital under the same case. It isn't unusual for bodies to come in at different times, so I was sure they wouldn't suspect anything. And as I figured, the medical examiner had been paid off to keep shut and declared the bodies your family without ever actually confirming it."

James could barely focus, his mind full of images of his daughter's blonde hair blowing in the wind and his son's enthusiastic smile at the promise of a new project. They were alive and well, breathing out there amongst the crowd, their lives still an infinite realm of possibility.

"Now that I had bought myself some time, I had to get the kids safe. In the moment, I didn't know who they were or why someone wanted them dead, but I knew they weren't safe with me. I was too close to it all and someone might come checking up on me.

"So, your daughter Clare was sent to live with my sister and her husband in Southern Illinois. They always wanted kids but it wasn't in the cards. They have a great place. It's a working dairy farm on almost a thousand acres. She will be safe.

"I figured it would be safest if the kids were split up. If there is one thing about that boss of yours, he is thorough. So, I created a new identity for your son and sent him to boarding school in Boston. It is one of the nicest with an emphasis on science and tech; I figured he took after the old man."

James sat in astonishment; he owed this man more than he could ever repay.

"Doc, I am telling you all of this because I have to disappear. They never intended on paying off my debt and instead exposed me to the police department. I came forward with the story excluding the detail about your children but I was ridiculed and lost my job. That wasn't the worst of it, however. My debt came due and they came to my house to collect. I managed to buy some time but I have to get out of town. My family is already on the move and I'm risking everything just to be back in the city. I just couldn't see any other way to contact you."

Ethan raised his head to the ceiling, his eyes glassy with tears. He handed James an envelope without looking at him. "Here. It is everything you need to know. New identities, locations, recent photos. It is the best I can do."

James reached over to take the envelope with one hand and clasp Ethan's shoulder with the other. "Ethan, you are a great man. I owe you a debt that I can never repay… thank you… thank you for saving my children."

The men locked eyes, their hearts beating in sync with the gentleness of kind fathers. A deep respect was there, one that would mean more to them than any words of gratitude.

James felt the heft of the envelope in his hand. A new resilience traveled through his wrist and churned along his elbow, rushing up his arm and into his chest, the feeling sweeping over him with determination. The dormant genius hiding behind his painful loss burst into the foreground of his thoughts.

"Ethan, give me the details on who you are in debt with. I can take care of that so that your family won't have to look over their shoulders."

Ethan cocked his head to the side with the sudden appearance of steel behind the doctor's eyes. He asked, "What are you going to do?"

The wide grin of a man on a mission spread across James' face. "Retribution… no matter how long it takes."

CHAPTER 15

The plain walls of his lab were oddly welcoming upon James' return. The remainder of the conference had been a short splash of faces and words that James would never remember. His mind now raced as he studied the empty space, designed to breed invention. James had a new purpose but the path forward was murky and fogged over.

Sitting down at his father's desk in the center of his immaculate lab, James stared longingly at the sealed envelope that Ethan had given him as it laid quietly in the corner. James had promised himself, *come up with a plan first, then you can open it.*

Ripping his concentration from theories about its contents, James set to work again at his computer. The first task was seeing what he was up against. He already knew that Vigo had security cameras all over the building monitoring his every move but what else was Vigo up to?

Quickly, James hacked his way into the security protocols for the company. Being inside the network worked in his favor, as most of the protections were designed to keep people out. Once he was in, he was free to roam around.

James discovered in a few strict confidentiality memos that Vigo's team was also watching everything that came into contact with him. All of his email, phone calls, conversations in the hallway, and internet searches; it all seemed to be an attempt at keeping Vigo apprised of any attempt James made to contact the outside world. James understood that if Vigo thought he controlled the door, then James would never be able to leave.

James went to work as a new man, his vigor and diligence returning once again. He easily set up encrypted drives to store his work. He forged multiple backdoors to the internet for his use and away from prying eyes. Once he was online, he decided he needed to repay a favor. James was still an employee and got paid with no costs to speak of—he had plenty of money to work with.

He managed to set up a bank account under a false name and filled it with the money Ethan owed on his gambling debt, plus interest. He then contacted a lawyer and offered to pay double the usual fee, to deliver the account information directly to the leader of the gambling ring. Once the lawyer had cleared Ethan's name, James would find a way to let Ethan know.

Satisfied that soon Ethan's family could live peacefully, James sat back to look around the room for inspiration. He needed an idea, something he could pull off from the confines of the pristine lab walls and that would take Vigo down without question.

There were all kinds of brand-new test equipment and tools, but nothing inspiring. He had a full wall made into a dry erase board and another on wheels that could travel between the four lab counters that formed a square with his father's desk at its head. There was a short hallway to living quarters. A treadmill, some workout equipment, the kitchenette and bunks; nothing of real interest there as well. Everything was so bright and white, no clutter, no remnants of past projects, nothing lending itself to trial and error—giving inspiration to the need.

James let his eyes wander once again to the envelope. If only he could open it, he was sure it would give him the push he needed, the contents providing the clarity of vision he needed to see the path forward—something worth fighting for. Strands of his own long brown hair passed through his fingers; James sighed deeply. He needed to see his children; he needed their bright faces to light up the darkness that had taken hold of his heart. Straightening up in his chair, he started to reach for the envelope…

The disturbing beep of the badge reader at his lab door and the metallic click of the lock startled the doctor, his hand froze mid-reach. Before he could even react, the door flew open and Mondo filled the void. Was it possible James had tripped an alarm on the computer and they were already onto him?

Holding the door open, Mondo stood aside for the appearance of the sharply dressed Vigo. His presence proceeded a blast of cold air into the room. A rigid tension crept down James' spine. What the hell was he doing here? The man hadn't set foot in this lab since the day they escorted James from the diner. What did he want?

Vigo walked slowly, taking his time to look around at all the test equipment and tools he would never understand. James sat frozen, only his eyes able to move while they tracked Vigo's movement.

With his characteristic, I'm-one-step-ahead grin, Vigo turned to face James. "So, I heard you had a little expedition, you have a good time?"

"Ye, ye, yeah," came the muffled response as James struggled to find his voice, uncomfortable with the amount of hatred filling his heart.

"Don't worry," Vigo's grin grew as he talked. "I think it's great. You need to be out there, staying in touch with the latest tech learning all you can about SOR. I'm glad you finally seem to be back on your feet. It's the reason I came to visit."

Vigo moved slowly, casually approaching James, who sat unmoving at his desk.

"I came down to discuss a new project with you. Something I think you will be very interested in." Vigo said as James suddenly caught sight of the envelope lying on his desk. He was such a fool, why hadn't he hidden it? Nobody had come to the lab until now but still he cursed himself, his face flushed with nerves.

"We need to automate SOR convertor production and distribution. We are getting too far behind in the market and I thought… I know just the man for the job," Vigo said, arriving on the opposite corner of the desk than the envelope, continuing to move slowly across in front of James. "I want you to start up a robotics division. As I recall that is your specialty. You will have full control and can task the engineers as you need. I'm thinking long term, the future, isn't that what you always said?"

Vigo's hand slid right onto the envelope, his fingers drumming lightly on its manila coating. James couldn't breathe with the nerves, his heart pounding out of his chest. "Anyway, three years to get something up and running, I think. I want to establish us as the go to source for these things, our government contracts are enabling us to undercut the commercially produced units. In a few years we may be the only player in the market and that's when I want to rake in the profits. What do you think? You have been working these convertors for a while now."

Vigo stopped talking and let his eyes cast down to the envelope beneath his fingers. He seemed curious and James could sense it as he blurted out, "Sounds smart! I can do it, no problem."

The hand pulled back from James' desk; Vigo seemed satisfied. "Excellent! You must begin right away." And with that, Vigo turned hard on his heel and walked rapidly out of the lab. Mondo let his eyes hover on James a moment longer, before closing the door to the lab.

James sank into a pile of exhaustion on the desk. His heart felt as if he had just outrun an enraged grizzly bear. The adrenaline of being confronted so quickly after discovering his children were alive coursed heavily in his veins. Quickly he snatched up the envelope and slid it into his desk drawer. Slamming the door shut he said, "SOR convertors, the future? What a waste…"

The clang of the desk drawer reverberated against the lab walls along with his thoughts. James' lips slowly moved, uttering barely a whisper.

"Wait a second… robotics, that's the key."

*****

The sun quietly slipped behind the western horizon as Clare pulled up to the old canning factory. Malcom had sent a text that Owen's phone had been off for almost a day but the last location was his apartment.

The news worried Clare as she dismounted her bike and made her way slowly down the sidewalk. There were plenty of people around the university campus for that time of day and so Clare had no problem blending in. The only thing Clare could think to do was search Owen's room. She hoped to find anything that would point her to where he might be or with any luck, run right into him.

Entering the building her nerves began to creep up in her throat. What would she say to him? Oh hello, I'm your long-lost sister and I am here to protect you. By the way, we are up against Vigo Amarth and his army of influence and power. Clare laughed at the ridiculousness of the thought. There was no way it wasn't going to be awkward or sound crazy when the words came out of her mouth, so she shouldn't worry about it.

In the foyer things suddenly became very real as the completely caught off guard feeling rushed right back in on Clare. She was storming in again, letting the past drive her without preparation. The same mentality had caused her to run straight into Vigo's bodyguard and left a bad night's memory on her jaw. Clare's cheeks started to flush as she scanned the hallway and stairs. She was fine. Nobody was looking for her, she just needed to be careful and keep her guard up.

More deliberately now, Clare bounded up the stairs to the second floor.

Finding the apartment, Clare tried the door and found it was still unlocked. Cautiously she pushed further into the entry, still unsure of what she would say if faced with her long-lost brother. She proceeded slowly, her senses tingling with anticipation, causing her hand to instinctively touch the knife tucked at the small of her back.

The door fully open, she found the loft apartment empty. Clare scanned the single room and saw the light was out in the bathroom diagonally across. She moved forward, unsure what she was looking for but believing there had to be something.

She searched the apartment haphazardly. Clare looked around but there were no signs of any struggle or leaving in a hurry other than the unlocked door. The apartment was as it had been before. It looked like Vigo's bodyguard hadn't disturbed anything.

Clare flipped through some papers on the desk. The crisp edges pressed on her fingertips as she watched equations as foreign as an alien language pass by. The disconnection between the life he had and her own made her think. Was this man really her brother? Could the names have been a coincidence? But then, why had she been hired to protect him?

Clare let the papers fall back into place. An odd sense of familiarity beyond her previous visit set in. She crept along the desk's edge, running her fingers slowly across its surface, trying to grasp what the recollection was. The feeling was faint, no real concrete connection; that was—until she saw it once again.

The black and white, hand-drawn print hung immaculately on the wall. Everything in the apartment looked well used except for the perfectly straight and spotlessly clean frame. Inside it were the familiar lines of a strong character Clare recognized. The same one she had connected with Malcom over, the one she knew but couldn't place until now. Hanging there on the wall was an original storyboard from the cartoon *Samurai Jack*.

She had connected with Malcom over the same show but she had blocked out why. Now she knew. The corners of

Clare's lips turned upward as a suppressed memory of hers came quickly rushing to the surface. She was a kid again and her younger brother moved in front of her. He was wielding a foam sword as he battled against her. She could hear herself laughing maniacally as the villain—hiding behind her black cape and shouting what creature she had just shape shifted into. Clare could see his face once again, the big curls of his hair, his large brown eyes, and she could hear his laugh, his beautiful, innocent, joyous laugh; there was no mistaking it… Owen was her brother.

Clare gazed at the picture as her grin melted into a stern jaw. She knew they weren't kids anymore and that Owen was a grown man. But there was a surge of responsibility for him inside Clare's chest. She didn't know if it was guilt for not protecting him before or for forgetting him for all these years. The pain and sadness were too much for a little girl, Clare thought. She had done what was natural and protected herself. Now she was grown and, in that moment, she decided she could no longer run from the fear of more loss.

There was nothing for her there at the apartment. Owen wasn't around and the top priority was finding him. She knew he was smart, his apartment told her that, but she was sure he wouldn't be able to handle Vigo on his own. For that matter, neither could she.

Clare pulled out her phone.

Apartment was a bust, nothing to go on. You got anything?

MTRex: I guess you haven't seen the news.

What does that mean?

MTRex: And we got a new note from our employer. I think we better meet.

Yeah. Two hours. Usual spot.

Clare tucked her phone away then backed out of Owen's apartment. As she closed the door, she hoped she'd be back again under different circumstances. Entering the foyer, she saw that it had started to rain. She smiled; Malcom always loved the car anyway. She'd take the bike over and switch on her way to meet him. Quickly she ran out of the building, letting the water land where it may. She hopped onto her EC 2600 and sped off.

*****

The envelope sat empty at the corner of his heirloom desk its contents spread out before James like a window into another life.

The imprisoned physicist couldn't keep the smile from hurting his face as his focus bounced back and forth between the two photos now clutched in his hands.

The first, a picture of his daughter Clare, capturing the smallest hint of a smile as she held a bucket of grain up to an eager heifer. The side of the feed container stamped with a label, Furmore Dairy, Towanda, Illinois. James chuckled at the sight of her overalls; she would certainly thrive on a farm.

The second, a picture of his son Owen, his face disgruntled, but the light in his eyes still there. He was sitting stoically for the yearbook photo with the emblem for Milton Academy stitched proudly on his sweater vest. James laughed softly, he knew that Owen would settle in nicely there, and although young to get started, he would soon blossom with the promise of fun and exciting projects.

The photos were reassuring, providing relief even from the confines of his imprisonment. James now knew that his

191

children were okay and that the promise their beautiful lives held still existed. Continuing to rifle thought the envelope's contents, the doctor found a letter from Ethan essentially saying what he had tried to convey at their covert balcony meeting. This included specific information about the children as well as the need for Owen's school to be paid for as Ethan hadn't quite figured that out. James made note to set up a recurring wire transfer to the school.

Carefully he packed the envelope back up and placed it in its hiding spot amongst the stacks of papers. It was time to begin his work. In the stunned minutes left in the wake of Vigo's surprise visit, James had come up with an idea. Vigo was going to get his automated factory and advanced robotics division, but at the same time it would be a cover. James was going to develop an assistant, a robotic helping hand. A machine that would be able to aide him in his quest to take down Vigo, something that could be trusted beyond doubt because it would be an extension of James himself.

Vigo had given James the keys to develop automation processes for their factories. It was Vigo's lack of oversight that led James to decide he could hide his own project among the development and enlist the help of the Amarth engineers. It would be up to him to dissect the pieces into unrecognizable chunks to give to the team and then reassemble them once again. The idea would take time, but now that he knew his children were alive and safe… time was merely a number on the wall.

The plan would be to make a fully functioning assistant, standing on two legs that could walk, talk and act almost human. A full-scale robot capable of moving about the building to gather any information James needed in his hunt for a weakness in Vigo's armor. If he was going to prove what Vigo had done and expose him to the world, then this was the only way he could do it without attracting attention to himself and in turn—possibly his children.

James had to believe it could be done, it was the only possibility of retribution that he had. His post-graduate work in automation and adaptive robotic processes gave him the foundation on which to build. A foundation that would provide his children and the world with a brighter future.

His mind turned to thoughts of his wife, the look from her deep loving eyes forever in his memory, the lines of her smile and the glow of her touch. He missed her. Her guiding force was always strong, loving and worth fighting for; he missed the strength he found in their everyday playful conversation and how there was never a problem too large for them to tackle. He knew that he would never love like that again, that hers was a once in a lifetime blossoming, their time together as magical as the universe itself.

She would do anything to protect her children and she trusted him to be her partner in raising them. He owed her everything. He had to see this through.

Vigo may have had control of the lock, but James was taking control of the key.

*****

The bus continued forward after another stop. Owen looked on as the streets were crammed with bodies. After Thalia Hall, Owen had no idea where the third clue led to next but once out on the street, he was suddenly very aware of his new status as Chicago's most wanted. The number of eyeballs that existed in a densely populated major metropolitan area gave him pause. Without a clear direction of where they needed to go, Owen just wanted to keep on the move. He seemed to believe standing still meant they would most certainly be caught. So, they had boarded the next available bus to buy some time to think.

Owen realized too late that they should have been more discerning with their choice as the bus headed further and further downtown. Every few minutes, the bus let more and more people on. Soon, Owen had his face completely turned to the window, his cap pulled low, unmistakably avoiding eye contact with the now overflowing aisle. He tried to keep the panic at bay, but he felt like a thousand eyes were questioning him, all ready to sound the alarm and bring an end to the hope swelling in his chest.

Closing his eyes, Owen desperately tried to calm his frayed nerves. He had to think; he had to take control. A deep breath filled his lungs, then released as he began silently chanting his favorite mantra.

"Observe, question, hypothesize, predict, test, and repeat." Over and over he repeated the scientific method as his quickened pulse slowed with each iteration. The chant was a practice he picked up in late grade school, when the task ahead weighed heavily in his stomach. The steady familiarity brought the calm of his academic self-confidence and methodical practice to the forefront of difficult emotional situations.

First, he had to observe. He braved a glance and noticed there wasn't anyone looking at him. Everyone on the bus was minding their own business, either concerned with the next stop or off in their own thoughts. Then he questioned, had the events of the last few days fueled his paranoia? Was it possible nobody saw the TV broadcast or cared enough to pay attention anyway?

Hypothesize: Owen's shoulders crept away from his ears, sometimes the best cover was no cover at all. Those after him were getting desperate, but he knew he could avoid capture if he stayed on the move and didn't draw attention to himself. Owen predicted that having Walt with him helped. They were looking for one man, not two. The pair of them looked more like casual colleagues about town than two men who barely knew each other on a city-crisscrossing scavenger hunt of self-discovery. Owen's gut told him that his father was out there, and that some greater plan was at work that would fully reveal itself soon. All he had to do was follow the clues.

Test and repeat: One thing he did know was that he couldn't go back to the life he had. He had gone from respected rising physics expert to a suspected terrorist on the run in only a matter of days. He had no idea how to clear his name and certainly wasn't going to turn himself in. There were people at work here that stayed in the shadows, full of dark, powerful secrets. They had already murdered his mother, what else were they capable of? Owen knew the only way out was to follow his father's plan. The man may have made some terrible decisions in the past, but he was still Owen's father. And Owen had to believe in that fact and trust the bond, even after years of separation, was enough. He had to solve the riddle.

"So, who is Higinbotham?" Owen asked of Walt who had sat quietly next to him, tucked into the aisle seat.

"I'm fairly certain that it is a reference to Harlow Higinbotham," Walt answered.

"Does he know my father?"

"Oh," Walt chuckled slightly. "I'm afraid that's impossible."

Owen frowned. "Care to share why?"

"Harlow Higinbotham passed away in 1919," Walt said as an obvious statement of fact.

Owen thought about it. He must not be asking the right questions. Walt was a lock box; Owen only needed the right key.

"What did Mr. Higinbotham do when he was alive?" Owen asked.

"He was President of the World's Columbian Exposition in 1893 and was instrumental in getting international participation for the event. He later purchased several of the collections from the Exposition to be donated in the creating of the Field Columbian Museum right here in Chicago. He influenced the plans and building of the museum as it is today, but was unfortunately unable to see its opening."

Owen gasped. "The Field Museum? In Chicago? In downtown Chicago? With security and guards protecting the halls of priceless exhibits?"

Walt simply nodded.

Under immense pressure, Higinbotham's hall outshines them all.

There must be something still in the museum from the original collection. Owen was stunned by how quickly they learned of the destination. Ask the right questions, Owen thought to himself; I'm getting good at this. He didn't hesitate to look up at the bus route plastered above the windows. The lamination curled in at the corners and the route colors faded, but Owen found what he needed to know. He wasn't sure how they were going to pull it off, but at least they had their next destination.

CHAPTER 16

The years passed and James worked in his lab imprisonment, becoming increasingly more and more motivated to simply hear his children's voices and to hug their fragile bodies. He worked night and day, an endless flow of trial and error, pushing the boundaries of what he thought possible. A once neat, pristine lab was now covered in papers, wire cuttings, soldering irons, and piled scraps on every surface.

James toiled endlessly. There was no time for cleanliness, James could only think of the next step. The sum of his steps leading to his goal.

As he had predicted, the energy crisis took on a new twist as the production of SOR peaked and then began to falter. The toll the vegetation and fermentation processes to generate SOR had taken on natural resources were too vast for any sort of recovery or continued production cycle. Every scientist on the planet concluded the same thing, the earth was beginning to fight back, battling an intelligent, self-serving parasite.

James watched as the world around began to change. The building across from his window, once bustling with activity, now shuddered for use only during the day. There were never any lights on at night. It sat, a dark, stoic monolith against an eerily moonlit cityscape. The new state of affairs led to conflict, and already deep social separation grew into chasms as the standard of living for those with and those without widened. With this conflict, Amarth Corporation prospered. James never went hungry, never had the lights out, and could set his thermostat however he liked. He kept it mildly uncomfortable as a physical reminder of what the world outside dealt with.

Vigo being the right cut-throat man for the times, was unrelenting in his pursuit of power. He had completely lost sight of their founding slogan, *To Pursue the Prosperity of All Humanity*, as he leaned fully into the SOR convertor business and acquired every new startup that had any promise.

James watched over the years in disgust but was in no place to make any objection. Instead, he used the plump research and development budget for his own attempt at keeping the company's motto, via his own project. An undertaking he formally designated as the Lab Assistant Humanoid Robot, or LAHR.

"Executing test number one thousand and forty-two," the physicist said aloud. He had taken to talking aloud more and more with each passing day. "LAHR, hand me that pencil."

The six-foot-tall wad of wires and electronics lumbered forward, moving as rigidly as a man with a pair of full leg casts. Stopping within inches of James, LAHR brought its claw like apparatus up to the same height as the hand James was holding out. Slowly it inched forward, carefully readjusting to the closing distance of its target. Finally, LAHR uncurled its pincher like grip on the pencil and James felt the weight of it drop into his hand. The doctor let out a dramatic sigh of relief. This was quite literally the first step in his plan to get revenge on Vigo—the simple act of delivering a pencil.

LAHR had to become so much more than just a robotic spy for his vengeance. LAHR had to be the way to save his children and their future—a future that looked more and more desperate with every cycle of the moon. For his children to have a future, it meant that James had to save civilization from its own destruction. Time continued to tick away, so he continued to work.

"LAHR, take note," James said, as he moved around his creation. "Get the engineers to work on the distance algorithm; movement is too slow. Also, the approach is rigid, seems flimsy and unstable," James said, thinking of the story he had told the engineers. He had said there was a need for an uneven terrain handling bi-ped carrier that resulted in a flat, smooth riding platform. They had developed a machine based exactly on what he had hoped—human legs. And for another team, he told them to work on a simple voice command interpretation and instruction output. James had been working on connecting the two for his own application in LAHR. Moving around to the back of the exposed mechanical exoskeleton, studying it, James nearly tripped on the power cord running from the device.

His gaze followed the large black cable from the connection in LAHR along the white floor. The coiled snake of an umbilical cord piled near the wall where it was plugged in. The simple act of using electricity a novelty.

Power. It was always about power. Not the self-serving pedestal that Vigo sought, but the backbone of the global economy ever since it was first harnessed in artificial light.

A renewable source had been the problem James had wanted to solve when he first discovered the end of fossil fuel. And it was the same obstacle that stared at him now.

SOR had proven that it wasn't the viable solution. And he was sure teams of the brightest minds on the planet were working to bring the next attempt. But none of them worked around the clock in a lab they never left. And none of them were fighting the battle in front of them from the heart. This task was his to fail, over and over; there was only the next iteration. James took solace in the fact that history was on his side. He thought of Edison and the search for a steady artificial light. Just as it had been an instrument to lead civilization out of darkness, James' invention had to do the same. Ingenuity changed the very fabric of society, the time before the lightbulb and the time after. And now it was the time of fossil fuels and then the time of... whatever came next. The thought was hard to fathom, like comprehending the vastness of space. So many things would change with too many variables to predict it. James could only believe in society at its core, that the years of destruction left in the wake of the Fuel Wars were a thing of the past. He hoped that this new age would be that of harmony, even though he knew he wouldn't live to see it.

With everything he needed at his disposal, James made his plans. He could task engineering teams to build anything he wanted. He was the sole voice for the technical direction of the company. And Vigo's new position on automation might have provided the perfect opportunity to take control of it all.

James would have to keep the project to himself. The design of it had to remain secret because its viability as a product was too large to calculate. And that was where the others would fail, they wouldn't think past the profitability. But James had no need for profit, no need for money and objects; he only cared to give his children a future, a chance to live and to love, a chance to have their own families or quite possibly, travel the world. James smiled. They could see where their mother was born, where she was from. He had to give them that. The need fused with his every fiber of being. To do that, he would have to fix it all.

The protruding darkness of the plug powering LAHR burned deep into James' stare. Something was there, a hint of an idea he had always known was there but was afraid to chase… and in that moment he decided it was time.

"LAHR, make a note," James said, a smile spreading wide across his unkempt beard. "This one is for me… solve the power issue."

*****

"Impossible," Owen stated, on alert again now that they were out in the open. "There is no way we are getting in there."

The pair had found a vacant bench in the park adjacent to the Field Museum. They sat with the sun warming their skin as they studied the entrance from afar. They were precariously stuck right in the heart of one of the busiest spots in all of Chicago. Owen looked down the path that ended at the steps leading up to the large doors, the stone pillars on either side looming down on him, barricading him from continuing his journey.

"It's the museum. How am I supposed to walk past all of the security when I am currently at the top of Chicago's most wanted?" Owen asked in hushed tones. He was certain the museum was the next stop, but it seemed so odd that his father would put him in such a crowded location with security around the clock.

Walt however, seemed to be enjoying the kiss of a breeze and chatter of birds arguing over a scrap of food. He didn't react to Owen's question and certainly didn't offer any answers. Another frustrating interaction with the man for Owen as the sun sank lower on the horizon. Harlow Higinbotham founded the museum and there must still be an exhibit hall bearing his name. They had to get inside. What they would look for once there, Owen had no idea, but he was hoping for the same memory trigger as before. Then his past could lead him to his future.

But before any of that, they still had the little problem of actually getting into the building.

"So, no suggestions then as to how we get in?" Owen asked, again.

Walt just looked out at the scenes of the park and the dark blue lake beyond it. His eyes remained distant as he said, "Act normal, like you belong—out for a day of culture."

"And what in the hell does that mean?"

"Smile, make eye contact, keep your hands visible and relaxed; don't close yourself off with crossed arms or hands in your pockets."

Was Walt some kind of body language expert? Or just someone who knew about sneaking into places lined with armed guards? Owen studied him, the man's expression remained unchanged; he was serious. Walt's eyes followed a bird as it caught an updraft and a tiny bit of doubt chipped away in Owen. It was enough for him to admit—maybe they had a chance.

"Okay, we need a plan," Owen said, an unsure tremble in his voice.

Walt simply nodded. But then again, he wasn't the one on the run and wanted for terrorism. He had the luxury of relaxation.

"So," Owen started. "We wait until within one hour of close, which is soon. Everyone will be ready to end their shift and nobody will suspect me to walk right in with my face plastered on the news. We then have to be quick to find the next clue and get out of there before raising suspicion."

Walt nodded in understanding and confirmation.

So, the clue was in there. The way Walt responded so rapidly confirmed it for Owen. He thought about it and decided to press the subject. "You know. It would be a whole lot quicker if you just told me exactly where it was."

"I can only guide you. You must make the discovery for yourself."

The delivery was as if Owen had said it himself, he was so sure of the response. But its predictability could still be infuriating.

"Even if it gets me caught?"

"I believe that it a question you have to ask yourself," Walt answered, his gaze still unwavering from the activities in the park all around.

Owen knew that there were singular moments that could shape an entire life. He could go into hiding and fight with his regret for the rest of his days. He had been there, walked that path, boarding school room after boarding school room; he knew what that felt like—it made the decision easy.

"Alright then, let's do this." Owen said. The pair of them looked at each other for a brief moment, then turned towards the entrance. Owen took care not to walk too fast, or too slow.

Entering the building, Owen stepped up to the ticket counter as Walt remained a few feet behind.

"Two please," Owen said to the young lady working the counter.

She looked at him curiously, her eyes focused on him as her head tilted to the side. The voice in Owen's head screamed and it took everything he had to focus. He touched his hand to his pocket. The crisp line of folded notes from his father reassured him.

"You know we close in one hour?" The lady finally asked, her focus returning to her work station.

"Yes ma'am," Owen replied. "My colleague and I have some time to kill and he's never been here."

Owen nodded his head toward Walt and the lady looked up to glare at him for a moment as well. Walt stood plainly with his hands at his sides, looking around the room with his own type of curiosity. Owen smirked; Walt looked like a tourist.

Owen paid and the lady handed over their tickets. Taking a deep breath, Owen tried to steady his nerve. If instant dread was how he reacted to a look from her, how would he react to the security guards?

If he got caught, he could be thrown in jail for the rest of his life. If the forces after him were big enough to frame him for terrorism then they were surely big enough to have him locked up without any kind of trial.

He handed Walt his ticket and they moved towards the entrance. The criminal justice system had become something of a joke in the years since the Fuel Wars. Owen knew the facts and almost every major crime statistic was triple that of before. He assumed that meant corruption within the system was even worse.

Owen tried to focus on something else but his mind wouldn't quit. He quickly counted three guards and a custodian. One worked the entrance and two more standing in reserve, chatting with the man leaning on a mop handle.

Moving in front of Walt, Owen handed over his ticket.

"Empty your pockets," The guard said, holding a plastic dish for the contents.

Owen hurried to cooperate, tearing at his pockets with a fervor that could shred everything but denim. Was this worth the risk? The notes and his wallet spilled into the bin. He had spent his entire life until that point wanting to belong and now, he had to take a leap of faith to find out where the trail led?

"Come on through," the guard said, waving Owen to move through the metal detector. His legs felt foreign but they walked on to the other side with the sheer luck of autopilot.

The guard held out Owen's ticket. The slim printout dangled from the end of his hand. Owen reached for it timidly.

"Stop right there!" The guard said. Owen froze, his hand only inches from the ticket. This was it. No Higginbotham, no clues, no long-lost father; Owen's journey ended here. A two-bit museum cop had spotted him.

The ticket moved away from Owen as the guard spun in his chair. Owen couldn't breathe, all he saw was the space the slip had once occupied. Then his ears got through to his brain.

"No, Capstone isn't about pure strength or stamina; it takes accuracy and finesse," the guard said, waving Owen's ticket at the other guard.

Owen's understanding rushed to catch up. They were discussing last night's Capstone match. Owen let his arm drop to his side and tried to get oxygen to his crying muscles. They were discussing the latest sport to rise out of the ashes of the big five. Capstone was a relatively cheap sport that played like a mashup of obstacle course racing and ultimate frisbee. The ability to play it in abandoned buildings or almost anywhere made it inexpensive and exciting. The popularity of local teams from different boroughs had filled the void left by the overpriced sporting events from years prior. Owen was thankful for it, as there were no long glares or second glances at him. The guards were too preoccupied with their discussion of the Chicago final.

Finally able to take his ticket, Owen moved directly away from the men. Walt went second, encountering even less of a delay.

Out of the view of the main entrance, Owen's strides grew in length and pace. He studied the brochure's map as he walked, searching for a flash of an H in the listings. He checked twice, but was quickly disappointed. There wasn't an entry for former founder, Harlow Higinbotham. Now standing in the center of the main hall, he spun around, taking in the exhibit wings leading in all directions. The halls spread out away from him with too many to search in the time they had. He had to stop and make an educated guess. Walt, ever on his heel, pulled up beside him, patiently matching his every move.

"I don't understand. No exhibit dedicated to the founder of this whole place? Why?"

Stanley Field Hall, Holleb, Levin, Webber, Africa, Mammals, Birds, and Reptiles. He didn't see anything that sparked an idea. Ancient Egypt, Regenstien, a Maori Meeting House and Cyrus Tang Hall of China. Galleries, discovery centers, geology and the Grainger Hall of Gems... wait.

Owen looked at the words for a moment Grainger Hall of Gems. A tickle danced on his nose. He slowly rotated towards the exhibit. He saw the ornate letters in a geology-based font above the door on the second floor. He could feel the folds of paper in his pant pockets pulling him that direction.

Under immense pressure...

Owen dashed to the right as fast as he could without drawing attention. He found the stairs and bounded two at a time to the upper level of the museum. He paused momentarily outside the exhibit to catch his breath, letting the surprisingly fit Walt come to stand beside him.

"Gemstones, Wal," Owen said between breaths. "They're formed by years of constant intense pressure; this is the right place."

Here goes—he thought while entering, studying everything his eyes came to rest on. He gazed eagerly at the history of the hall informational display. It explained that the Grainger Foundation was now the sponsor of the exhibit but most of the stones seen were purchased from Tiffany and Co.'s captivating collection at the 1893 World's Expo and donated to the museum by Harlow Higinbotham. Owen smiled and turned to tell Walt that they had found it, but instead Owen saw that Walt had taken a wide circle around the exhibit, letting Owen browse by himself.

Reassured he would find the next clue, Owen moved on, making his way between the glass cases. The displays were stunning. An entire spectrum of color and craftsmanship caught his eye, but Owen didn't have much time. He kept going, only giving each item a glance for as long as he believed it would take to stir a memory.

Then a raw, unpolished piece mounted with a full 360-degree view caught his attention. He approached it slowly, the depths of it went for miles beyond the coarse limestone the gem was protruding from. The edges were jagged with purple, blue, and a fragmented hint of the earth's soul, timeless in its beauty. His eyes studied the hard crisp edges formed over the ages, they were as strong and sharp as his resolve needed to be. Owen was captivated, completely losing track of what he was there for in the first place.

"We have to go," Walt said, pulling Owen's attention from his internal journey through time and space.

"What do you mean? We still have plenty of time," Owen said, unsure how long he had actually been mesmerized.

"That is not what I mean."

Straightening up, Owen was suddenly very aware of the eerie quiet in the room. There wasn't anyone else around and there were no voices floating around from nearby exhibits. A chill crept up Owen's spine—the security cameras.

"Facial recognition?"

"Don't know," Walt responded, moving toward the door.

Owen moved to follow but stopped. His eye caught something on the display that he had been staring at, except what he saw wasn't in the display… it was on it. There was a reflection interrupting the blank black background behind him. He spun rapidly to look in the direction it was coming from but nothing was there. He turned back to the case— the reflection remained; his brain motored forward. They did special things with the lights in there, so the displays were never in shadow. His hand flew up to cover the reflection, trying every angle in order to find where it was coming from.

Once he had it, he traced his hand backward until he was pointing where he should look. He went to the wall and found what he was hoping for. Taped high in the corner, only visible from a few select angles, was the small envelope. It wasn't easy to see and someone would have to really be looking in order to find it. Owen sighed with relief as he approached the wall. But it was too high for him to reach. How did it get up there? He didn't have a moment to ask however as his sixth sense told him to get a move on it.

He hissed at Walt, "Give me a boost, and hurry up."

"No need," Walt replied.

Owen watched in dismay as the man walked over and leapt effortlessly up to retrieve the note. Owen was sure he had never seen anyone jump that high but he'd read such feats used to occur in one of the forgotten sports.

Walt handed Owen the note. That was when they heard the unmistakable sound of approaching feet, several of them, walking strong and deliberate.

"This way," Walt said, turning to the door opposite the ominous sound.

They made their way out of the room and out of sight. Owen glanced back to see a large figure fill the doorframe leading into the hall of gems. It was the same man that he had seen at his apartment. The man was fully clad in his custom business suit and looked like he could turn any of the stones in there to nothing but dust with his iron grip. Owen didn't hesitate and picked up his speed.

They moved silently down the corridor. Owen wasn't sure how they could get out, but Walt seemed to have a plan.

Walt suddenly stopped.

"What are you doing?" Owen whispered in a panic. "How are we going to get out of here?"

Walt didn't respond. Instead, he turned in front of a poster for the debut of a new exhibit. Owen was furious with the lack of response. Then, with an uncanny swiftness, Walt slid aside the poster and punched in a code on the newly revealed keypad. Owen was confused. How had Walt known to do that? Who was this guy? The intensity crept up the back of his neck. Their pursuers were getting closer. What was Walt doing?

A door etched seamlessly into the hallway popped open. Owen stared blankly at Walt and the newly discovered door. They didn't have time for words. The footsteps were now approaching from both sides, closing in. The pair entered and closed the door behind them. They stood deathly quiet and awaited their fate.

*****

Was it possible?

Had he done it?

"LAHR, readings?" James asked, his voice trembling.

"Eight thousand five hundred twenty-sec and one point seven," came the response in the robotic voice of his lab assistant.

The excitement emanated from the physicist. The two hundred and seventeenth iteration of his device was spinning, and for the last half hour—holding steady. James couldn't believe it. He was challenging all he had ever known about the laws of physics. But, as he had reminded himself over-and-over again in the walls of his prison, some things are only the way they are because they have yet to be proven otherwise.

"LAHR, readings?" James asked once again after five more minutes had passed.

The metallic tone announced the same findings once again. It was the response to a simple command that LAHR had been programmed with. It would read the revolutions per minutes and power output from the newly built device every time it was prompted to. James certainly had a lot of work to do on the user interface of LAHR, but his mind had latched on to the idea for a new generator and his work on LAHR had taken a back seat. So they sat, the finished device on the table and his hope spread out beside it.

The hours passed with the same result, and the inventor began to let himself have more belief than doubt. There were still hundreds of tests to run and he would have to figure out how to scale the device, but the concept was proving to be sound.

"LAHR? Do you realize what we've done?" James asked, the robot and himself the only ones in the room. "I did it. This device… it is going to change humanity… it is going to save the planet…"

James allowed himself to smile; a lifetime of long hours and struggle were finally going to pay off. A swarming happiness filled his chest with a burning that he hadn't felt in too long to remember. His career, his life, his work; he had finally done it. His chest puffed up in pride and he felt like screaming the news from every rooftop for all the world to hear. SOR and the rapid, methodical killing of humanity— it would all end, the solution right in front of him. The device of their deliverance gladly spinning, content in its role to play for a thousand years.

"I did it LAHR, did you hear me? I did it!" James' voice rose to bellow out from his lips. The sound of his triumph filling the cavernous space of his solitary lab. "I did it! I did it! I did it! Can't you see? I saved the planet—my kids will have something to inherit after all. My kids…"

The words spilled from his heart and shattered his victorious mood. The thought of his children reminded him of loss… and that he was alone. There was no one there with which to share his success, no one there to raise a glass or give him a firm handshake. There was only the empty space and his own creations. His tears of joy faded into tears of pain, he wanted desperately to share this with his children, his wife, but he couldn't. The gut-wrenching desire to see their smiles was as strong as it was on that day in the medical examiner's office. The stabbing hurt of their disconnection was as real in his moment of achievement as it had been in his lowest moments of despair. He realized that there truly wasn't anything greater than them… no achievement, no invention; it was always them. And even as the echoes of his voice settled into the walls, James recoiled back into his shell of hiding. The thoughts of his children, protecting them, brought forth the understanding that Vigo still lurked outside the door, his eyes and ears everywhere.

There was still so much work to do. He may have found the answer for civilization, but what about an answer for the uncivilized? Clare would be sixteen soon, and Owen almost fourteen. James had a few years until they would be old enough to take over, but could society hold out? The weight of responsibility settled back onto his shoulders, the temporary relief provided by his invention coming to reality faded away.

James knew two things for certain. He would never let this get in the hands of Vigo, and there was still much to do—certainly still very much to do.

CHAPTER 17

The lines in the parking lot were almost non-existent but there were a few places big enough for her car. Clare pulled in facing the dimly lit windows of the 24-hour diner. The wipers stopped. Drops of rain gradually blurred her view to the outside world through the windshield.

Her stomach growled, but Clare paid no attention to it. She wanted to have this conversation in a familiar place.

Smiling, Clare's thoughts turned to the eight cylinders of muscle now sitting quietly. She had grown up with the car and it had always sat in the same spot of the Furmore Dairy barn. She worked on it with Big Tom, changing fluids, cleaning gaskets, polishing chrome, and rubbing conditioner into the leather. Clare learned every inch of that automobile, even installing a SOR convertor herself when it was time to fire it up once again.

She learned pride while taking care of that car, not only because it was something she bonded over with her adoptive father, but because it was something built long ago and it needed to be cherished—just like the handful of memories she had of her family.

On her sixteenth birthday, she learned the true origin of the turquoise beauty. After a small soiree featuring Malcom and a couple teammates from judo, Big Tom had led Clare out to the barn. He opened the door to reveal the car sitting where it had always been except now, a red bow was stuck to the hood.

Clare had watched as the soft glisten of sentiment welled in the corners of his eyes. He held up the keys as he said, "The car is yours—it always has been. It showed up here about six months after you came to us. It belonged to your grandfather and then your father. He wanted you to have it on your sixteenth birthday. Apparently, they dubbed it 'Emeritus' based on the stamp in the door panel leather… I think that is fitting given that it is being passed on to you. I know he would be so very proud of you, just as I am."

Clare didn't have any notes, any photos, any keepsakes from her parents; only faint memories and that car—she would be buried in that car.

The rain slowed as she heard another car splash up next to hers. The door clicked open and Malcom slid into the passenger seat. He smelled like Cheerios.

"Hey," he said.

"Hey," she replied.

Malcom looked out the front as he settled into the seat. The soft crinkle of the leather as his breath went in and out brought Clare comfort. She was really glad to see him.

"I guess you didn't hear the news?" He asked.

"No, needed to think."

"Well Owen is in a bit of trouble. The news is calling him a terrorist."

"A terrorist?" Clare asked, mind racing.

"Yeah, everyone is looking for him. The cops. Everybody. I can't find any reason for it. The news said suspected bomb threat but it doesn't make sense. Either he hides his tracks incredibly well or something else is going on, because he seems like a pretty normal guy. I think there is only one man in this town with the kind of power to get an innocent man declared a terrorist."

"Someone that wants to find Owen in a hurry," Clare replied.

"Yeah. A certain business tycoon that could stand to make a lot of money off whatever Owen has gotten into."

"So, how do we beat Vigo at his own game?" Clare asked.

"Well, I'm already tapped in to the police network. If they get wind of something, then I'll know as well. It already turned up a false alarm at the Field Museum."

"False alarm? At the Field Museum?"

"The police responded to a security flag from the cameras at the museum. The facial recognition algorithm tagged a suspect but they didn't find him. There was apparently an error or he managed to disappear into thin air. Either way, Owen is still on the run."

"Why would he go to the Field Museum? That makes no sense."

"Yeah," Malcom said. "If I was at the top of Chicago's most wanted, I'd probably be leaving the city."

Clare paused, her thoughts jumping between logic and emotion. She didn't know where to start. "I blocked him out

Malcom. I erased my own brother from my mind," she heard herself say. "I just want to meet him. I want that chance."

Malcom nodded. They sat in silence for a moment.

He turned to look at her. "Clare, you didn't fail your brother."

"Thanks," she replied.

"You were six years old and someone tried to murder your family. It is a wonder that you're a functioning human. Well, loose definition of functioning, but at least you're one of the good guys."

Clare smiled. "Wouldn't be anywhere without you."

"You're going to make me blush."

"I have been thinking," she said. "Who could possibly know that Owen and I are related? I mean, that's why I was hired to protect him, right?"

"I think you know," Malcom replied.

A light sprinkle of rain refreshed the windshield with haze. Clare's hand curled slightly, trying to recall how his hand had felt holding hers. She whispered.

"My father."

"Yes, I have something for you. I got about three lines in before I realized what it was. I printed it out because I knew you would want to read it for yourself."

Malcom produced a neatly folded sheet of paper from his pocket and handed it to her. She opened it carefully, unsure what he meant:

Clare,

I am so proud of you, every aspect. You have your mother's sense of community and I know she would love the dojo just as much as I do. It is amazing to see you giving back with such passion. I am so proud of the woman you have become even if some of your methods are a bit unorthodox. I want you to know that I know, I have always known. Watching you from afar has been the hardest thing I have ever done but I had to do it for you and your brother's protection.

I admire you. The way you take a stand against the evils of this world. I wish I had your bravery—it is definitely from your mother's side. I may not agree with your need to take justice into your own hands, but I understand it. Our system is broken and ideologies aside, I'm glad you are out there correcting the balance.

You have always been this way. I remember the time your mother and I got called to your kindergarten. You had taken on playground injustice by yourself and punished a schoolyard bully. To the principal, I offered apologies and agreement that such behavior shouldn't be tolerated. But inside, inside I was as puffed up as any father has ever been or will ever be.

Unfortunately, there is another bully that must be taken care of and I let him grow out of control. You know who I am talking about, by now you have put the pieces together. Vigo Amarth murdered your mother and imprisoned me in my lab. I have stayed quiet because he believed you and your brother were dead, but it is time to right the wrong and end the rule of his oppression. I have set it up so that he will be out in the open where it all began. All you have to do is be there, remembering that there is more to retribution than an endless cycle of violence.

I want you to know, that it was actually the kindergarten incident that gave me the idea to introduce you to martial arts. We went to a demonstration the week after and you have been dedicated to it ever since. Do you remember what we saw there? And do you recall what I said to you when you asked if it was possible to break sixteen boards?

You are ready.

I am with you.

Love always,
Your Father
Cleveland and Washington Avenue. Monday. 4 o'clock.

The rain was falling steady again. The drops plopped here and there, coating the windshield in a sheet of water, their movement the only thing registering in Clare's eyes. For her, there were no more tears. All she could feel was a sense of belonging. Like her brother, her father was alive and out there. He had been out there the whole time, watching her, protecting her, the mysterious man behind the curtain. She had so many questions but they quickly settled in the back of her mind, there would be time for that later. She had to keep her wit despite the rage that stormed inside her. Focus. Discipline. Respect.

"Malcom," Clare said. "Where is Cleveland and Washington Avenue?"

"I checked. It's just a regular old intersection in the Mid-North district, just west of the old zoo."

Clare smiled. "He'll be there."

"Who?" Malcom asked.

"Owen, Vigo, my father," Clare replied, her eyes trained on the note.

"What do we do?"

"You said something about cameras? At the museum?"

"Yeah."

"Malcom, I'm going to need your help… and we don't have much time."

*****

After an hour of nervous tension in the dark, Walt finally found a light switch, revealing quite a large room. As his eyes adjusted, Owen moved quietly among the shelves. There were spray bottles, levels, hand tools, and what had to be a thousand brushes of different sizes and bristle counts. They found themselves in a curator's room, an area near the exhibits where the museum kept the equipment necessary for upkeep of the exhibits and to store off rotation displays. How had Walt known it was there? And the code to get in? Owen brimmed with thoughts to discuss but until he felt they were really in the clear, he was going to explore in silence.

At least now he could use the light to read the latest message from his father. The last hour since finding it had been agony. The fear of being caught and hauled off added to the anticipation, while images of the note being left to stay sealed in its envelope, the next clue unfound, plagued his vision. Now that he could, Owen wasted no time in tearing the small envelope open.

Owen,

You always were a clever boy, even at an early age (a chip off the old block). You are no doubt standing next to the gem that was your sister's favorite. We used to bring her here all the time because she loved it so much. She was fascinated with geology and loved the deep purple of this stone. It was a special place for us and actually, it was standing there that your mother told me we were pregnant with you… and not a day has gone by where I haven't thought about you since.

I have always associated that gem with you even though it was your sister's special place. You came to us, and were like the final piece of stone needed to complete our little family. And your sister, she was so protective and gracious with you. She would peer over the stroller and whisper to you all of the fun facts about geodes and crystalline structures. It is a proud moment for a parent, to see his children caring for each other.

And now, you have that same opportunity; I'm afraid that your sister is older than you and has memories of the events that split our family apart. She is very smart, resilient, and has put the small fractions of clues together to discover the truth. But, because of that, hate has taken root in her heart. She is fierce, brave, and resourceful, but I'm afraid that the path she is traveling will eventually lead to her demise. That is where you come in. She needs your help. She needs your hope to counter her anger. You are the only family you each have left and you will need each other more now than ever.

The next clue will lead you to the end. In its solution you will find my identity and the final pieces will fall into place. You are on the path of great things, but it will take courage, cunning, and most of all—staying true to yourself.

Dad

You need only to look up to Fermi and the term will end after all.

The clue hit Owen like an anvil from the sky. He looked up from the sheet, a confident smile on his face. "Enrico Fermi," he said. "Do you know who he is?"

"Nobel prize winning physicist," Walt replied.

"The architect of nuclear physics and the atomic bomb," Owen replied. "One of only sixteen scientists with an element named after them."

"Lived and worked in Chicago," Walt added.

Owen slapped the man on the shoulder. "Lived and worked in Chicago indeed. Walt, for the first time on this crazy journey, I know exactly where we need to go."

*****

A company memo came to James' desk. Vigo was being featured in a magazine and the human resources department thought it might be good for everyone to see. The lonely physicist sighed—he could remember long before they ever had a need for a human resources department.

The piece was the cover story but not in the traditional sense. Magazines and newspapers only survived a few months after the collapse, everything that managed to stick around was now online. Even books took a huge hit, and only the biggest, most popular names could be found in new print. The once beautiful and inviting bookstores had to convert to the resale and exchange business.

So, when James opened his browser to the magazine's website, he was taken aback by the large shot of Vigo standing with his stylish leather shoe propped on top of a globe. The title of the article couldn't have done much better for his ego, *Amarth Corporation and the Man Behind the Meteoric Rise of an Empire.*

The distraught co-founder and actual product inventor standing up the pillars of the multi-billion-dollar company could only shake his head in disgust. Opening the article and casually scanning the lines, he wondered if Vigo was happy now. But James knew the man wasn't, that Vigo could never stop. His goal wasn't power itself but the seizing of it, like the fresh taste of a new addiction, where the only thing that can satisfy it is the chase, the seeking of something sparkling, novel, and just out of reach. Vigo had become an animal, his prey anyone that would stand in the way of his next venture. The article didn't say it, but it was written right there, for all to see between the lines.

James browsed through the exposé containing the usual information until he came to something interesting, something that struck a chord.

The author of the story had asked Vigo how Amarth had grown in the wake of the Fuel Wars and what it was about himself that allowed Vigo to lead the company forward.

Vigo's response stunned his old friend, breathing life to a memory dormant and collecting dust. Vigo said that it was his perseverance, his refusal to get knocked down and not get back up. It drove the company forward, to press when others would fold and that dedication had paid off... the article continued but James lost focus on the words. All the man could see, even locked away in his solitary lab, was the boy he knew. The boy who refused to give up. The boy who refused to let the bullies win. James had admired it then but now—he wasn't sure. Had the world taken something good and twisted it? How had Vigo gotten this way? They were so full of hope and honesty and trust when they opened those doors, declaring Amarth Corporation ready for business. Had he somehow driven Vigo to this? Did he set the hound on the scent? Was this all somehow by his own doing, yielding gasoline to a tiny flame that was always burning inside Vigo until it grew out of control?

James tore his eyes from the screen, leaving the article to whomever might care to read it. This wasn't his fault. He was never going to control Vigo and he shouldn't have had to. They were partners, building this company together from the ground up. Vigo had made the decision to take things too far. He had made the decision to try and control his partner for the sake of the chase for power—no matter the cost.

Vigo had sacrificed his morals instead of listening to reason, being willing to compromise and understand what his partner had to say. A flaw in Vigo's character that James never saw coming was magnified by his success. The same resilience to stand up to those bullies, somehow twisted his motivation until Vigo had become the very bully he had forgotten how to fight.

James swallowed hard. He missed his family so much. They were all he ever really thought about. Replaying the events in his mind, wondering if there was something he could have done different—some way he could have stopped Vigo.

But the path of self-pity always ended the same way, back where he was to begin with. The only course of action was to keep moving forward, just as Vigo had told that journalist with a grin and evil hiding behind his eyes. James would have to use that, use his own experience to take back control of what Amarth Corporation had set out to be in the first place. While Vigo glad-handed with the shallow influencers of power, James quietly built a company underneath that would someday topple its very head. A plan to seize control because if there was one thing the two founders had in common—it was that they refused to stay down and be controlled.

*****

"The Fermi Institute at the University of Chicago," Owen stated plainly after three hours had passed. They hadn't heard anything other than their own cautious footsteps in a long time, so they talked openly. "That is where we are going next."

"The next clue?" Walt asked from his perch on an empty tabletop.

"Yeah, it all comes full circle."

"And what about the institute? Isn't it quite a large place?"

Owen nodded solemnly. He was thoroughly familiar. That was where he taught, where he studied, and where he shared an office with three other post-graduates. There was no way he was getting in there without being noticed. Surely the campus was in an upheaval at the news of his suspected terrorist plot and every faculty member, student, and campus cop would be on the lookout.

"Yeah," Owen finally said. "It's a big place, and quite busy. I won't get within five hundred feet of the building."

Walt slid off the table and began looking around the room with deliberation. "Well, I guess it is a good thing we are stuck in this room for the night."

Owen looked around, catching on. "Yep. Could be something useful here to help with a disguise."

The two of them began looking for anything they could use.

They found chemicals including bleach and dyes. They found knives, brushes, creams, and minerals that could be used for dusting. They found latex gloves, work shirts, and even a small bathroom with a sink they could use to make the transformation.

Owen got to work mixing a bleach solution that would turn his dark brown hair into a sandy beach blonde. It took multiple tries to get it right, but finally after the fourth rinse of his hair, it was a completely different color. Owen had been careful to also color the short beard he had acquired and the look was even through every follicle.

Owen then set out to shave the extra stubble from his neck and make his facial hair look intentional. As he soaped up his face and worked slowly, Walt began to ask him questions.

"Have you had time to develop a plan yet?"

Continuing the short knife strokes just fractions of an inch from his carotid artery, Owen answered, "Well… tomorrow is Monday. We need to get out of here first thing and leave the museum a little after it opens—I assume you know a side exit." Walt nodded. "Then we will need to get to campus while classes are in session to cut down on the foot traffic and possibility of being spotted. On Monday, Wednesday, and Friday, classes are an hour and a half with fifteen-minute transitions. So, the best time to be there is after 9:45 and get back out by 11:15."

Walt added, "Museum opens at 8."

"Right. We could walk out a half hour after that and take an e-cab to campus," Owen said. "Maybe get out a few blocks away and approach on foot. I know a much less traveled route into the back of the institute."

Walt nodded agreement, as was becoming his custom.

Owen rinsed his face and winced at the makeshift razor. "Really wish I had some aftershave or moisturizer. Hand me the modeling clay maybe that will help a little."

Walt hesitated at the shelf; unsure what Owen was referring to. Owen noticed the struggle and added, "The gray metal tin on the shelf, second from the top." Walt seemed to pause mid-step, his brain shorted out, unable to keep up. Owen thought it was odd but just brushed past him and grabbed it himself, shrugging it off as Walt stuck mid-thought.

To reanimate his friend, Owen said, "The longer we are there, the more likely it is we are spotted. But I have been thinking. I have spent the last two years practically living in that building and I have no idea where to look. It seems like it would be ridiculously hard to hide an envelope where I could find it but nobody else would. I mean I keep my desk locked, so I doubt it is in there… I just don't know."

Owen grunted in frustration and began to wipe off the clay from his neck, it hadn't helped soothe his shave. Now his skin was on fire and their possibilities of success seemed miniscule—dark alleyways felt more inviting.

"What do you think about the man chasing us? The man that showed up at your apartment?" Walt asked, broaching the subject that he had been avoiding the entire time since the two of them met.

Owen shook his head. "You're supposed to know and I bet you do know but you aren't telling me who he is or who is after me."

"Have you seen him before?"

"No."

Owen's response was quick, but his thoughts lingered. Walt had been direct and to the point so far in their journey. Although it felt like the man was dancing around a subject, his comments were always purposeful. So, what was Walt getting at? He was trying to show Owen where to focus but what was it about the enormous enforcer following them that Owen should recognize? A slight eeriness of recollection crept up on him. This had all started when Owen had first laid eyes on the beast. Or was it something about the car, the large black one, which stirred the depths of his memory?

"It isn't the man, it's the car." Owen whispered softly, his eyes cast down, his only sight on images from the past. "I've seen it before."

Owen looked up to meet Walt's eyes, but the plain man simply stared back, expressionless.

Rolling through memories as they flashed quickly in his consciousness, Owen frustratingly tried to untangle the cobwebs of time's passing. He remembered seeing the car on campus, but it wasn't outside his apartment like the other day; it was somewhere else. Where had it been… Owen tried to think. He tried to focus on events that were ordinary at the time but now had significance. His subconscious had been working on the problem, but still, bringing it to the forefront took clarity and concentration on the problem.

The day hadn't been an ordinary day. There had been an event. There was a large gathering at the Fermi Institute. And it was that day, and that car, that Owen was suddenly remembering.

His pulse quickened; the event was a dedication—for a new lab. Owen's face went ghost white as the blocks fell into place. The lab had been sponsored by… Amarth Corporation. They owned the car, they were after him, and they were one of the most powerful companies in the world.

Owen reached out to grasp the table's edge and steady himself. What had he gotten himself into? Or better yet, what had his father gotten into? The room swirled with thoughts as Owen hurried to take ahold of what he knew. Aided by the Fuel Wars and their government contracts, Amarth had risen to power meteorically in an amazingly short amount of time. Owen knew that it wasn't beyond their capability to hunt him down and operate outside of the law. While he had understood he was dealing with something big, he couldn't have imagined it was this huge. Whatever was going to come next, he was on his own, just him and Walt…

Owen was suddenly very aware of Walt's blank face and the anger boiled over into his words.

"Amarth Corporation! Amarth Corporation is after me!" He yelled, forgetting all about the fact they were hidden inside a museum.

Walt wasn't fazed, he appeared to almost expect the outburst. His voice pressed Owen calmly. "Amarth Corporation is not after you. Think again about when you saw that man."

Owen was fuming at Walt's indirect nature but the question triggered his rational, logical side. He forced himself back to that day and with clenched fists, he could finally see it.

The construction had finished in late spring and the day he remembered was the ribbon cutting ceremony. The new building was a state-of-the-art physics lab built with sponsorship by Amarth Corporation. They would provide the funding; the university and its young nimble minds would provide the research. The arrangement wasn't uncommon in the academic realm and Amarth was practically their neighbor, with the headquarters only blocks from the University of Chicago's campus.

Owen thought about the proceedings and how it seemed like the entire physics department was in attendance. Everyone clamoring for a chance to meet... founder and CEO Vigo Amarth. And all the while, right by his side, was the absurdly large man with his ever-vigilant eyes.

"He's a bodyguard... for Vigo Amarth," Owen whispered, giving fear to only a name. "Vigo Amarth is after me for some reason, but why?"

Walt nodded slightly, his expression urging Owen to pull the thread.

Owen remembered being disgusted with everyone that day, with all their self-promoting and misplaced reverence for the titan of industry. Owen had taken one look at the man and felt nothing but loathing. The entire department had rolled out the red carpet for a chance at the scraps from his table but they had completely forgotten one of their own.

Suddenly, Owen couldn't move. An intense, paralyzing heat rose in his chest as his feet sank deep into the earth, his core shaking with turmoil at the revelation. The crowd, the ones he had called colleagues, they had forgotten Dr. Stevenson, an accomplished and respected graduate from the very halls they roamed. He had been lost to history, left to the yearbooks and the footnotes of great feats of physicists.

"Dr. Stevenson…" Owen said. "This is about Dr. Stevenson."

"What do you know about him?" Walt asked.

His mind spun, Owen could only utter random phrases. "On campus the man was a myth… a once revered pioneer that had suddenly gone quiet. The stories were as varied as they were outrageous. Some believed he worked on top secret government projects but had somehow released a virus in his lab, forcing him to confinement.

"Others believed that he had attempted to solve the energy crisis so as to end all of the war and bloodshed. But, while doing so he had inadvertently torn open space-time and fragmented reality, thus he now existed in two planes of existence: our world and some reality stretching across natural history. Now however, he was plagued with knowing humanity's demise and thus relocated himself to the solitude of his lab to attempt feebly at a course correction."

Owen paused, he had never really considered the doctor beyond his physics department legend. Owen had never thought about what it meant that the man had disappeared so early in his career and life. He had simply respected Dr. Stevenson for his selflessness and bold trailblazing in a field of study they shared. But what did it mean if Owen considered him to be the human being behind the title, a person and not just a list of accomplishments? What if Owen thought of Dr. Stevenson as not only a role-model, but just like himself? A man with hopes, dreams, likes, dislikes, friends, and a family that he loved. What if Owen put himself in those shoes, of a man who hadn't been seen or heard from in over a decade? Did he suffer from the same loneliness that haunted Owen?

Had Owen known it back then? Was that why he had gotten so upset on that day? When Vigo Amarth came down from his self-absorbed tower to dedicate a lab that should bear a different name… the name of his father… Dr. James Stevenson.

"He's my father." Owen spoke. "He disappeared from the public eye years ago… around the same time I entered boarding school. I think… I think I may have always known. Or at least, have hoped… never able to confirm or truly believe."

Owen's heart unburdened itself with the words as his search unearthed yet another truth. Owen looked at Walt for any kind of acknowledgement. Walt, like all great teachers whose students discover the lesson for themselves, simply nodded.

With the revelation, the tumblers locked into place for Owen. He felt a sudden clarity, as if a cloud of haze had been removed from his mind. He now knew his mother, Mairéad, and his father, James, and his sister's name…

His sister's name was Clare.

He could finally remember that very small, yet very significant detail. The simple realization was so invigorating. Owen spent all those years searching for the family name Bradley and his connection, but he had been looking in the wrong direction. His past had been hidden from him but now he was pulling back the sheet and taking charge of what lay ahead.

With a look of resolve solidifying on his face, Owen asked, "My father, he's being held against his will, isn't he?"

"He has been," Walt responded. "He has been for a very long time. But you, and your sister are going to set him free."

Walt held up the last piece of the disguise. A simple pair of lab glasses, surprisingly trimmed in a modern look. Owen took them slowly in his hands, feeling calm somehow, ready.

"You know him, don't you?" He asked.

Walt said with a solemn face, "We worked closely together for many years. He was more than just a mentor and friend—I owe him my life."

"When this is all over, I would very much like to hear that story," Owen said as he turned the final piece of the disguise over in his hands, studying them. They were only protective glasses, but they could pass for prescription. Would the disguise be enough for him to sneak onto campus undetected and get the final clue? Would it be enough for him to see this to the finish and free his father? Owen took a deep breath and slid the final piece onto his face. Opening his eyes, even he barely recognized himself in the mirror—maybe this would work after all.

They both agreed to get some rest and Owen laid down near some storage cabinets despite the low rumble of hunger in his stomach. Walt found a place in the opposite corner. Very little airflow added to the already warm room. Owen guessed that rocks and old stuffed animal pelts didn't require very much ventilation and since energy was at a premium these days, they only got what they absolutely needed. The night was going to be uncomfortable but Owen didn't mind. Through the sweat and turmoil of the last few days, he was finally getting some answers. Real. Concrete answers. With a lab coat bundled under his head, his mind was at ease when he drifted off to sleep, a slight smile of belonging resting on his face.

CHAPTER 18

"Functioning one hundred percent," LAHR reported with varied inflection.

James grunted, unsatisfied. "Not real enough, that voice will draw attention."

He paused for a moment, running his fingers across the uncharacteristic stubble on his chin. "Let's try this," he said. "LAHR, in what city do little bears wear white socks?"

"The Windy City."

"Perfect, your logic is working," James replied. He turned to a notebook and made a quick annotation. "Well, I've got a mountain of patent paperwork to fill out. I probably shouldn't have waited until now to start. Doesn't matter though, there's still a major part of the plan that I have yet to figure out."

"What is that?" LAHR asked.

James grinned. "Very intuitive LAHR, your conversation programming is working well."

"Thank you."

"The issue is, LAHR, that Vigo is untouchable. We need to find a way to lure him out, to expose a vulnerability. We can't just go to the FBI or Chicago P.D. He probably owns the entire force. That is if his brute Mondo Bot doesn't catch us before we make it to the sidewalk. No, it needs to be swift and something that he never sees coming. It is the only way we'll keep him from buying his way out of it. And at the same time, we have to teach Owen and Clare the truth."

James walked casually to the window, interlocking gears of thought slowly turning. He did notice that LAHR's eyes followed him, the tracking algorithm working flawlessly.

"The only thing Vigo cares about is the next stepping stone…"

Three beeps sounded in the lab as red lights began to flash.

James spun away from the window. The beeps repeated themselves. He hesitated only a moment.

"Quick, LAHR, return to storage. Someone is coming!"

James rushed over to the desk. He pressed the red button under his main computer monitor to suppress the proximity alert. At a normal pace, his system would catch someone coming down the hall to his lab with about a twenty second warning.

No one had been to his lab in months, maybe even a year. James scrambled around, shoving things into drawers, intentionally adding to an already overwhelming mess. He needed to make sure the work he had been doing wasn't easy to figure out among the scattered items.

Time moved quickly. James looked over his shoulder to check that LAHR was put away just as the door to his lab opened. James reached something solid to brace himself as the imposing figure of Mondo entered the room. James' hands and feet went cold as he watched the brute of a bodyguard hold the door open for his boss.

Vigo entered the room like a man that owned everything his eyes set upon. He wore a full suit and gave off an air of impatience despite only just arriving of his own volition.

James swayed slightly as his knuckles turned white along the desk's edge. The cold surface was nothing compared to the ice coursing through his veins. He hadn't been in a room with Vigo for over a decade. Now that he was so close his retribution, he couldn't stomach that thought that his secrets had been discovered.

Vigo came ten feet into the room and stopped. The man's gaze scanned the room as James could only watch, planted to the spot in fear.

"James, is this really how you keep your lab? It's a disgrace."

"I've umm, been very busy," James replied.

"I can see that," Vigo said, picking up a wiring harness that laid on the bench next to him. James recognized the first attempt at LAHR's shoulder joint and gulped.

Vigo let the device fall back to the pile and wiped his hands together like a man that found even the air around him to be disgusting.

"You know why I'm here, don't you?" Vigo asked.

"Can't say that I do," James replied.

Vigo started to walk in a slow arc around the room, kicking things out of his way as he went. James could only watch, the anticipation pounding in his thoughts.

"Its SOR," Vigo said. "Phoenix is producing less and less of it. Only a matter of time now before it collapses. But I bet you knew that already, didn't you?"

James shrugged and thought to himself: So, someone outside has been paying attention.

"I want Amarth Corporation to be at the forefront of a solution and I thought, I know just the man for the job."

James' eyes searched the floor, shaking his head to buy time. "If Phoenix hasn't found another way, then I doubt one exists."

"The value is beyond comprehension. Just look at what they made on SOR. A new solution could be worth so much more. Who would we be if we didn't try?"

A flash of an idea swam into the back of James' mind. A glimmer of a way to solve his own problem. The fresh jolt of creativity turning his fear into resolve.

"I seem to recall telling you that once," James said.

Vigo stopped moving, his eyes pulled together to glare at James. The physicist stood firm. He understood that Vigo didn't know what he was up to in that lab. Vigo had simply come to prod his most prized cow.

The businessman's look settled down as he rolled his shoulders. "Very good James, I see your point. I admit you were right about the Fuel Wars. Could we have stopped it? Probably not. But you wanted to fix it so badly back then and here is your chance now."

James' teeth mashed together, the sound of enamel grinding burrowed into his ears. He thought, I have to keep it together. Breath, just breathe; there's a plan, stick to it.

"I'll see what I can do," James replied. "I'm not the man I once was."

A venomous grin spread across Vigo's face. "I don't believe excuses are in your vocabulary, Dr. Stevenson." With that, Vigo turned and made a straight line for the door. Reaching the frame, he called over his shoulder, "And James, I expect results."

Mondo closed the door with more force than was necessary. The air rushed out of James as his body gave way and he slumped to the floor. The smooth surface of the floor embraced him as his back found the side of his desk. He brought his hands up to look at them. He expected them to be shaking but instead, they were as steady as a surgeon's.

"LAHR?" James called. "LAHR my friend, we have a new plan, but I'm not certain what it means will happen to me."

*****

The morning snapped at Owen with pain down his neck and left arm. He had slept, but stiffly. As he rose and attempted to loosen his muscles and get blood flowing, Owen noticed Walt was already up. The traveling companion was standing near a shelf, gazing off into the distance.

"What time is it?" Owen asked.

"Seven A.M.," Walt replied.

Owen's mind quickly began firing on all cylinders despite the physical exhaustion. His journey over the last seventy-two hours was taking its toll, only to be compounded by the hard surface he slept on the night before. Still adjusting to the idea of his actual surname, Owen tried to gather as much information as he could.

"What do you know about my father?" Owen asked of Walt. "I mean, what should I know about him? I don't know much more than his academic accomplishments and his impact in the first few years after co-founding Amarth. But I want to know who he was, what was he like?"

The small room smelled of cleaning solution. The odor stirred up as Walt turned from his trance to face Owen.

"Your father was a good man. He was regimented and hard working. All I know is that he worked every moment of every day for you and your sister, to build a better future and to attempt to undo his mistakes. He loved you and talked about you often. He had hoped that you would one day take up the mantle as well."

"And what mantle is that?" Owen asked, confused.

"That one, I honestly don't know," Walt replied with a slight grin. "Your father only said that it would be revealed in due time."

"Is that what Vigo wants? To take control of some sort of secret project?"

Walt didn't have an answer.

"Is that why this is all happening now? Is that why he choose to initiate this whole run around the city scheme? Vigo had somehow caught on to him and he needed help?"

Once again, Walt didn't have an answer. Owen ran his finger along the edge of glass jar while he thought. The cotton balls on the inside looked like puffy clouds of his own ideas floating in his head. He knew Walt didn't have the answers or wouldn't give them up freely.

"Don't suppose you found any food in this place?" Owen asked.

"I did not look," Walt replied.

"Are you hungry?"

"I'm not sure."

"You aren't sure?" Owen asked, his face contorting with doubt and confusion. Walt didn't respond so Owen shrugged. He couldn't worry about Walt. He had his own needs. Now that his arm began to feel better, his stomach had started barking. The realization that he had been too busy to even eat added to his understanding of what this journey meant to him. Never in his life had he been too busy to find something to quell his hunger. The years of late nights at school and marathon study sessions, he always ate.

"Let's get out of here," Owen said.

"Agreed."

The pair gathered the few items they carried with them. Owen returned his notes neatly to his pocket and rolled his hat up to put in his back pocket. He would return it to his head once outside.

Satisfied, they slipped out of the curator's room with a few minutes until the museum opened. Owen looked cautiously in both ways, there wasn't anyone lurking nearby to pounce. But then he thought, why would they be? If they knew he was in the room, why not just come in and get him?

The thought calmed Owen's nerves and his shoulders sank away from his ears.

"Let's go the other way, away from Higginbotham's Hall," Owen said, before he led the way.

They walked as casually as they could. Owen would stop at an exhibit and looked at the words on the plaque. He saw that they were in English but his focus remained on the periphery. The first person he saw besides Walt startled him. But the elementary school teacher was probably having a worse day than he was with fifteen kids in tow. Owen watched them head towards the natural history section then decided that was enough.

The breeze hit Owen's face like an unexpected twenty-dollar bill in his pocket. The next time he went back to the museum would bring back quite the memories, if he ever got the chance. Owen curled and uncurled his fingers. The street was busy, crammed full of people moving this way and that.

"Hat," Walt said, standing to Owen's left side.

Owen scrambled to pull the cap over his hair. He was in disguise, nothing to worry about. Owen reassured himself. If he was going to worry, he needed to direct that at what he was going to do when he got to the university.

They moved briskly to the street corner, so Owen could hail an e-cab. They didn't have to wait long. Soon the city was passing slowly by, the haze of morning still creeping between buildings.

"Well, do you at least think that we made it cleanly out of the museum, or is Vigo's big guy baiting us to see where we go next?"

"I don't think we were followed and no one appeared suspicious of us as we left," Walt answered, finally offering something to the conversation.

Owen nodded, satisfied with the answer. He instinctively touched the glasses now perched over his eyes and agreed with the assessment. No one had stopped them, no alarms were raised, and no one asked why they were leaving a museum that had been open for less than twenty minutes.

Traffic was stopped on the busy downtown streets and the e-cab's circulation fan sat idle, as it only spun when the wheels did. The growing swelter didn't bother Owen, as he was instead focused on his father's legacy. A legacy reduced to only whispers and a single line in the Amarth Corporation's annual filings. There at least, he was still listed as Chief Technology Officer, but his name was never associated with a press release on a new product or milestone from the company.

Owen thought about his father. What was he like? What was his life like? Did he feel as alone as he had all those years? Was it harder to know or not know that his family was out there? Owen thought he understood loneliness but this put things in perspective. The only feeling that Owen had always wanted to feel started to grow—love. His parents hadn't abandoned him and part of his family was still out there, this zig-zag journey across Chicago proved that his father was try-ing to reunite them. His chest swelled as Owen thought of all the things he wanted to share with his father. But then he wondered, what had his father been doing all this time? What had it been like to be locked away, afraid for yourself and your children? It must have been tough, but if Walt was truthful, then the solitude had only driven his father to work harder. Was it possible then, that Dr. Stevenson was living up to the legend bestowed upon him by the undergrads at his alma mater? Was he constantly working on something extraordinary, and when he finally had his breakthrough, he knew that he couldn't let it fall into the hands of Vigo? Is that what kicked this all off? Is that why it was time to come out of hiding?

The e-cab pulled up to their corner and they got out. Owen threw some cash at the driver and pulled his Thalia Hall cap tighter onto his newly colored hair. He could run into someone he knew at any minute and the longer they stayed in public, the more likely it was that he would get spotted. So, they got moving.

The two of them walked in silence the remaining few blocks to campus. Owen was careful never to look anyone directly in the eye and it made it difficult to act casual. Approaching from the east, the morning sun's rays of light from behind them brought an ominous feeling to the academic architecture.

"It will be less suspicious if you go the rest of the way alone," Walt said, sitting down at a bench two hundred yards from the building. "Just act natural," he finished as he seemed to relax and enjoy taking in the shade.

Owen didn't hesitate and kept moving steadily forward, his eyes trained on the side door to his once frequented building. Suddenly nervous, Owen became aware of how much of a comfort Walt's company had become. He was grateful for the man's presence even if he lacked a certain empathy for the magnitude of the situation. Owen got closer; his destination was the Amarth lab inside the Fermi Institute, but once inside, what then?

A lump grew inside his throat, Owen suddenly wanted to turn and head back to ask Walt for help but he knew what the man would say—he had to figure this one out on his own. The campus had pockets of students and faculty either engrossed in conversation or mesmerized by their own corner of the world. As he passed, Owen wasn't given a second thought. Every step he took without being recognized propelled him further forward. He slipped inside the building alongside a big group actively discussing the paradox of Schrodinger's cat and his senses intensified. The hallway lights developed a buzz, every shoe squeaked with each step, and a thousand frequencies of conversation flooded his ear.

He paused, somehow unfamiliar with the building he knew so well. A staircase unwound to his immediately left as a long hall leading to classrooms, offices, and labs of the first floor stretched out in front of him. The walls bent in and out of focus, almost like they belonged to a life long ago, even though he was teaching in them only three days prior. Still, with the muscle memory of hours spent in that very space, his feet traveled directly to the Amarth Lab. Classes had started while he walked and by the time he was outside the door, only a few stragglers remained to scurry hurriedly towards their destinations.

Stopping outside the door, Owen peered inside. Through the vertical sliver of a window in the door he could see a small group gathered around a lab bench, most of their backs to the door. There were about a dozen of them and they were on the opposite side of the room, but still, Owen needed a plan. He was certainly going to be suspicious when he burst into the room, so he had better know where he was looking.

Thinking back, he really wished that Walt had been a little more helpful—a clue, a hint, something. What was he going to do? He was already risking being hauled off to disappear like his father or worse, just by being on campus. The anxiety grew inside his stomach as the walls began to grow eyes, each one focused on him. He searched the recesses of his mind but couldn't come up with a memory to jar loose a hint of where to look for the next envelope.

Owen tried to breathe, letting himself imagine what his father would do. And with the thought of his father and a name he now knew, Owen wasn't alone as he stood awkwardly outside the lab door. He was filled with a confidence that his father was standing beside him, guiding him in the only way he could. The presence brought an idea—maybe his father had given him everything he needed, maybe his father really was guiding him home. The last clue, his mind replayed it.

You need only to look up to Fermi and the term will end after all.

Owen smiled, there it was… *look up*. Bending slightly, he peered back into the room and scanned the ceiling. Towards the center and directly over a lab bench sat a disturbed ceiling tile, slightly lifted in one corner. Only someone looking directly at it would notice, Owen knew the envelope had to be there.

Gathering his nerve, he opened the door calmly and walked briskly into the room. He grabbed a stool as he passed by it and slid it next to the lab bench. And within eight steps of entering the room, Owen was on top of the solid lab bench's surface. His feet brushed up against the sink in the center of it while he hoisted the ceiling tile with his left hand. Shooting his right up and into the darkness of the ceiling—Owen began to feel around.

Concentrating all of his senses into the touch receptors on the fingertips of his right hand, Owen glazed over as his eyes rose to look at the gathered class. The chatter had ceased and they could only stare at the unapologetic stranger who came so abruptly to disturb their discussion of Newtonian physics. The simple yet complex subject of gravity.

Owen continued to feel around but it wasn't long before he started to feel the social awkwardness. The amount of time that the situation allowed for silence became increasingly short and Owen's fear of their attention began to fry his nerves. Just as their eyes began to turn from inquisitive to worried, Owen's index finger brushed a sturdy edge. He exhaled dramatically as his hand closed around something flat and approximately the size of a credit card.

Pulling the envelope from its perch, Owen brought it to his lips and kissed it. He had found the final clue. Realizing that twenty-four eyeballs were still unwaveringly focused on him, Owen turned to them and said, "Girlfriend set up a scavenger hunt… I was beginning to get a bit worried she had gotten the best of me."

The class erupted in laughter as Owen saluted his audience with the envelope and hopped off the table. Clutching the envelope in his hand as he exited, Owen's smile couldn't have been brighter.

CHAPTER 19

James hit stop on the voice recording and stood up straight, his lip quivering with fear and remorse. The path had been set, now he must walk it.

Another eight months had passed since Vigo descended upon his lab, demanding an energy solution to replace SOR. James already had a solution and it beat proudly inside LAHR's chest. He spent the time however, finalizing his plan to strike down the wolf that had haunted him for almost two decades. The hunger and desperation for power that foamed at his mouth, revealing the weakness to exploit. The plan was complete and James looked again at the recent photos of his kids that LAHR had taken when out doing surveillance.

There was Clare, her tight ponytail frozen in time as she walked the street that ran alongside her dojo. James couldn't believe how much she looked like her mother. They shared the same infectious smile that hid cool, calculating eyes.

There was Owen, face scrunched up with deep thought as he exited the physics building of their shared Alma Mater. James had read and re-read every paper his son had published. James knew that Owen was ready to take up the mantle where he left off. The new, promising technology would be in good hands.

James' gaze slowly rose and took in the room around him. Had it really been seventeen years? He didn't want to leave any traces behind so he cleaned up. Thus, the lab appeared almost as it had on his first day, some new equipment here and there but nothing major. The walls of his makeshift prison constant against the outside world's unrelenting change. Looking at it all now, was he crazy to think that his plan would work? Had the loneliness and pain driven him insane?

He laughed, a choked, half-hearted laugh. There was nothing he could do now except trust in his work.

"LAHR?" He said, his voice half cracking in fear.

"Yes, sir," came the response, believably human if James hadn't been the one who spent countless months perfecting it.

"Everything is in place? The museum, the observatory, the school?" James asked as his voice trembled with the weight of the moment, his hands busy with final checks and preparations.

"Yes, sir."

"You know what you have to do now, correct?" James asked.

"Yes, sir," came the response again, only slightly more emphatic. James really did do a good job programming LAHR.

"That's good… that's good," James said, his voice trailing off once again deep in thought. "Because I am trusting you with everything."

They stood facing each other in collective silence at the words. James concentrated on LAHR and his uniqueness. Recalling in his mind what powered the robot and the secret quietly humming inside. The world needed the answer, to shed light on the darkness he had been living with for seventeen solemn years.

The red light above the door was suddenly ablaze as the auditory proximity alert sounded.

James turned to the monitors showing the halls leading to his lab. The large shadow of Vigo's dog approached.

"Quickly LAHR," he said. "Tell me again what you are going to do."

"I am going to exit and proceed to the University of Chicago. Once there, I will make contact with Owen Bradley."

"Very good, keep going," James said, packing up several papers and other items on the desk into a metallic tube.

"I am not to interfere with Owen's journey, only provide guidance. I am to ensure that he remains on the path and will arrive at the designated spot on time."

"Good. Now promise, no matter what, you won't interfere with anything that happens in that warehouse," James said, stopping to stare directly into LAHR's eyes.

"I promise," LAHR replied, the rules of his programming governing his actions so the exchange was just a reassurance for its creator.

James nodded, motioning for LAHR to open the compartment on the left arm. Sliding the tube now full of notes, pictures, and blueprints into the space, he said, "When Owen and Clare are reunited, you send the footage of the warehouse to every law enforcement agency and news outlet in your contacts list. When the time is right, play the recording and give them this tube. Understood?"

"Yes sir," came the same response in the last five minutes but in a third iteration of tone.

James smiled at his work and felt an odd sense of peace. He knew that stomping down the hallway towards his door was certain death, but what he left behind was beautiful and life-saving. He hadn't been there for his kids; he hadn't had the courage to defeat Vigo at the time, but over the last desolate years of his life—he may have finally found it.

"LAHR, there is something that I never got around to doing," James said, taking LAHR firmly by the shoulders and looking directly into the robotic lifelike eyes. "LAHR, I never gave you a proper name."

LAHR's head tilted, puzzled.

"LAHR, there once were two boys, long ago. They were the very best of friends. And even though they were bullied and picked on, they grew up with a sense of duty and purpose. Together they swore to work hard to make the world a better place. I know that sounds naïve, but they were young and idealistic. They really believed that they could make a difference, that they could invoke change.

"The years passed and the two boys grew apart. One became overwhelmed with power and greed while the other lost his stomach for the fight, never finding his voice to root out his old friend and find common ground.

"LAHR... you have to be that voice now; you have to be that fight. I have built you to the best of my ability and what drives you will save us all. There is no hope for those two young boys, the chasm is simply too wide and too deep. But, for the next generation, for Clare and Owen, there is still a chance. So for that, and in honor of that bright-eyed boy who was my best friend, the one who gave me strength to be myself, taught me the value of friendship, and encouraged me to seek out the impossible... you will now be known as Walt."

James looked at his invention, taken aback in wonder and awe of it. But all he really saw was his greatest creation, the eyes of his daughter, the jawline of his son, the nose of them both and the presence of their love.

"Walt. I like that," came the response as they both smiled.

"It is time, you must hurry. Thanks for helping me right all the wrongs I was too weak to correct otherwise."

Walt simply nodded in understanding, the cyborg's programming of human nature and subtle mannerisms almost perfect.

A peaceful air passed between them, an air of understanding of old friends, beyond what was written in Walt's code.

James smiled, sure of his destiny. He took the ring his father gave him off the hand it had rested on for decades. Turning it over in his hand he remembered the words inscribed there and the story behind them; the purpose the next generation will carry on. The thought of his father and how much Owen was like him as well, brought a resounding joy to his heart.

Handing the ring to Walt he said, "We have no more time, Vigo is desperate once again and has come for something that he will never find. It is up to you now Walt."

A look of understanding flashed over Walt's eyes, almost as if he knew this would be the last time they spoke. But the programming took over and the nimble android moved quickly out of the lab.

The door closed behind Walt with a resounding thud, the sound of it leaving the lab in silence. James had grown to enjoy the robot's company and it would be missed. But events had been set in motion that couldn't be undone and

James knew his lack of cooperation would almost certainly result in his death. Vigo hadn't lost in any of the years since taking up that mantle. Any insolence from what he perceived to be his trained lab monkey wouldn't be tolerated. James hoped his calculations were incorrect but his plan didn't hinge on his own survival and for that he was thankful. All there was to do now was execute his part with dignity.

Placing shaking hands flat on the table that was his father's, James saw the monitor flash in the corner of his vision. Mondo's massive frame passed under the hall surveillance camera—he was moments away.

James had spent so long in the lab that by nature, he didn't want to leave. With every tick of the clock, the time grew shorter. James reviewed his plan, a singular moment from his past the lynchpin of it all. He let his mind wander over the event so that he was there once again, a flood of visions spewing forth.

A much younger James looked from the two lawyers on his left, to across the table at his co-founder and friend, Walter Vigo Amarth. James really knew him best as Walter and the legal documents laid out on the table felt like exactly what they were—a hope that maybe Vigo really was Walter, deep down. That the two boys from Chicago's Park West District would be able to truly make a difference in the world. And that James would have been right to suppress the growing suspicion that his old friend was lost forever.

"You sure this is what you want?" Vigo asked, grinning as he loomed over the documents to officially incorporate the Amarth business.

James could remember the moment like it was only hours before. It was a moment that he knew Vigo didn't recall, his focus at the time so clearly on power and fortune.

James could see it now, even as Mondo came to escort him somewhere that he was sure he would never leave.

The large conference room of the law firm the pair had hired to formalize everything had felt overwhelming in that moment. Taking a deep breath, James took up the pen. He knew he could do this, go into business with Vigo. He was smart and motivated; this was his best chance at a valuable career.

"It is," James had said, taking long strokes to sign his name on the founding document. "Just the one clause."

"I'm not sure if I should be offended or thankful." Vigo responded while accepting the papers slid to him by one of the lawyers. "We are old friends. You can trust me."

"I do, this is just business—to protect myself and my family," James had replied.

"Very well," Vigo answered, signing his full legal name as well. "I will be Chief Executive Officer and you will be Chief Technology Officer. Both of our names will be on the founding document, but I will be majority shareholder at fifty-five percent, and you will be given a fifteen percent stake with the rest to go to investors and such as we grow. Your clause is now in full effect and if either party should commit a crime against the other party in any means, then the perpetrator forfeits all stake in the company and transfers seventy-five percent of all their net worth to the victim's estate, regardless of how the worth was acquired. Agree?"

"Agreed."

Vigo turned to the lawyers and they both nodded. The process was complete. The two boys, Walter and James, who had met because of a street fight in the intersection of two avenues almost twenty years prior had now turned their company into a corporation.

James had remained seated as the lawyers left, letting the gravity of the moment settle in his mind. After Vigo thanked the firm's representatives and closed the door behind them, he turned to James.

"You know, you could have gotten more. We are in this together."

"I know. But it isn't about money. As long as my family is taken care of and I get to work on what I am passionate about, then it is worth it. I trust you to turn this company into the global force we always dreamed it would be—while I work behind the spotlight."

"I think that is a good idea," Vigo said. "You have always been a bit of an introvert. I've learned all too many times that if you want something, nobody is going to give it to you. You have to seize it with your own hands, by force if you have to. Then, you hold onto it… and claw for more."

James understood the words to be Vigo's and not his friend Walter's. They were of a businessman hell-bent on success, no matter the cost, the same characteristic that his wife feared in Vigo on the night of their engagement. After Vigo had swept in and stolen the show, she told him that if he went into business with that man, then he better ensure he had protection. She had seen a fire, something deep in Vigo's eye that screamed he would stop at nothing for success.

James hadn't wanted to believe it then and even now, as the very man's enforcer descended upon him to take him to a dark and abandoned warehouse. James had been so overjoyed at the sudden appearance of his lost friend that night, that he suppressed his own intuition of the man's new character. He hadn't known what Vigo was been capable of, the lengths he would go, but he had told himself he had to try. He thought that Vigo provided the best opportunity for him to continue his research and hopefully make a difference. He didn't know then the sacrifice that it would cost. To James, at the time the leap had been worth the risk, would he do it again? He couldn't make himself think about it—the toll was too great. He had known that deep down, inside that passion and fire that his wife had seen; there was a little boy named Walter. A spirit that refused to stay down in the face of his bullies and it was still there.

"To Amarth Corporation," James had said, extending his hand to Vigo across the conference room table.

"To the future," Vigo replied.

And they shook.

James' lips quivered as he watched the past fade. He tried to remain strong as he looked longingly over his children's photographs. He studied their features so he would be able to focus on them in the hours to come. With no more time, he slid them back into the drawer and a veil of determination slid onto the great man's face. He had set the path; now he must walk it.

The air shifted with the change of pressure as the door opened to reveal the shadow of destruction cast in his doorway.

Mondo Bot stood as wide as the framing. He didn't speak, he simply stared dark holes of promised suffering into James and James simply stared back, his own fire of promised retribution filling his eyes.

Vigo had sent his messenger of destruction. James knew where Mondo would take him, he knew what awaited him there—he knew Vigo's every move. The man was predictable to those that were observant, and that would be his demise.

James looked at the man just hovering in the door frame. Then he scanned over his lab, his home for all these years. The secrets it held and the promise of a future beyond his own that it had created.

Sliding his fingers across the old desk one last time, James moved around to join Mondo at the door. He knew he likely walked towards his death. But like his grandfather's desk, it was about the legacy. He had to look to the future and take down the tyrant standing in the way. Vigo wanted an answer for SOR and James was going to give it to him.

His first steps were unsteady, but with every foot forward they found their place. The comforting laugh of his son returned to his ears, the sweet smell of his daughter's hair, and the tender touch of his wife's hand in his; they were there, with him… and he realized, they always had been.

*****

Owen slid onto the bench next to Walt. He knew they were still on campus and there was still the chance of him being recognized, but he didn't care. The thrill of the hunt across the city had given him new life and he knew now that nothing could take that knowledge away.

Walt only sat quietly, patiently waiting for Owen to open the next chapter in their journey. And as Owen tore into the final envelope, the space between them began to feel like friendship. There was trust there, as well as respect. Sliding the note out of its sleeve, Owen paused and took a deep breath.

"I couldn't have done this without you," he said in Walt's direction, barely above a whisper. "Thank you."

And in classic Walt fashion, he simply nodded. The subtle acknowledgement meant more than any words he could have spoken. Owen smiled, nodded back, and unfolded the paper with delicate precision.

Owen,

By now you must know the truth—your given name is Owen Stevenson. The name Owen Bradley is a cover for your protection so that you could grow up in relative peace. That peace was necessary because the man you know as Vigo Amarth murdered your mother and thinks that he murdered you and your sister as well. Vigo's greed and lust for power outgrew his already skewed sense of morality. He took our family away from us and locked me up in his monolith of a prison. Vigo is a very powerful man and you were only safe if you stayed a secret. Not a moment goes by where I don't long to sit around our dining table again and laugh with the three of you—not a single moment.

My inability to stand up to tyranny on the face of my oldest friend tore apart our family. I understand that you will want retribution. I understand that you will want recompense for the years lost. But I want you to know that I am always with you and have always been. I watched from afar as your explanation of how to increase solar panel efficiency won the national science fair. I listened from a distance as you gave your valedictorian speech to rival the great orators of all time. And although I am not there to shake your hand and wasn't there for you when you needed me all these years, I hope that someday you will forgive me.

Remember the sacred oath that you now wear on your finger. Remember the selfless love of your mother. Remember the longing you had for a family and embrace your sister. Do these things no matter what the coming days may bring. Set aside the anger and instead replace it with hope for the future.

I am proud to call you my son.

Love,
Dad
Monday, 4 p.m.
Corner of Washington and Cleveland Avenues

Owen turned from the page to face upward. The morning sun warmed his face. Years of solitude and abandonment erect powerful walls and at first, his temples flared with rage at the pitiful excuse for a man that murdered his family. He wanted vengeance, to tear apart Vigo limb from limb. Sure, he was only a scholar with barely any exercise to his name, but he wanted the satisfaction of feeling Vigo's jaw crunch under the weight of his fist, to watch as a powerful man cowered under the might of Owen's life of darkness.

The rage faded a little with every beat of Owen's heart. His thumb touched the ring which had now become natural to him, a piece of his body. Deep down he knew violence wasn't the answer. He had to trust his father had a plan. The plan had gotten him this far. Owen believed that he could trust it to see him through.

Owen watched the morning clouds move away from the building pierced sky. The anger turned into sorrow at the past his father had to endure before it turned to the future and hope—a hope for the life they could have out from underneath the boot of Amarth.

The curiosity and desire that drove him this far returned. Owen, who now confirmed himself to be the son of the mysteriously reclusive but undoubtedly brilliant physicist, Dr. Stevenson, took to his given name with all his heart.

Rising from the bench, the new man shot out his hand towards his traveling companion and friend. "Walt, I'm not sure we've been properly introduced. I'm Owen Stevenson."

And for the first time in all of their exchanges, Walt smiled. It was a big, full smile that made his eyes gleam. Standing, then shaking Owen's hand, he added, "Pleasure to meet you Mr. Owen Stevenson. I believe that there is somewhere we need to be."

Owen cocked his head to the side, an astonished grin on his face. "You knew the whole time, didn't you?"

"Sometimes it is the journey that outshines the destination."

Owen laughed. There were still a thousand unanswered questions roaming through his thoughts, but there was one thing he was sure of—whatever lay at the rendezvous, there were no longer doubts about his past—he was ready to take hold of his future.

*****

Echoes of fist meeting flesh filled the empty warehouse rafters. James took the pain as it came, every blow furthering his resolve. This was his plan and the violence paled in comparison to the years of solidarity and preparation it took to reach this point.

James sat in an old wooden chair in the center of the room. Thick fibers of a dusty rope wrapped around his arms and torso in a losing battle to keep the beaten pulp of his body propped up. The enforcer, Mondo, took a step back. Drops of the brute's sweat splashed into a pool of blood on the concrete floor.

The building hadn't seen electricity in over a decade. The only light in the room crept along the floor in a singular row coming through the shattered remains of windows along the ceiling's edge. Despite being in his late 50's, James kept his head held high. He wouldn't give in to the pain of the moment. Resolve blazed from behind his eyes among the swelling and matted tufts of his salt-n-pepper hair dangling in front of his face. James concentrated on Mondo's every move, the slow steps, crack of the knuckles, and grin of a bull that only saw red. The movement played out in front of

James like a brutal game of chess, black striking its blows against white, as white waited and drew its victim closer and closer to its snare. The only contrasting color to their match was Mondo's crimson knuckles as they shimmered in and out of the light—an honest display of a dishonest day's work.

A faraway door ground on its hinges, letting in a beam of daylight, forcing James to turn away from the brightness. The light dimmed as a large figure filled the opening. The new presence chilled the air, despite the scorching midday heat.

The steady tap of hard-soled shoes brought their owner closer to James, their pattern and pace efficient. James knew it was because their owner had spent years taking those very same steps. James had tracked the man's movements, studied his opponent and predicted his every action, right down to the very warehouse where the man's enemies went to disappear. The large open space had once supported an adjacent oil refinery until one day, the final drops of oil were sucked from the earth.

James listened to the footsteps approach and thought about the Fuel Wars. Society had torn itself apart but it wasn't desolation for all, there were still wolves among the sheep, profiting on the disarray and fear in the seventeen years since. James knew that even now, one such wolf had descended from his throne to pay his old business partner a final visit.

The footsteps stopped at the edge of the light. Mondo, dabbing at his hands with a small towel, moved to greet his boss—Vigo Amarth.

"The lab rat getting the best of you?" Vigo asked quietly.

James watched as Mondo's large shadow shrugged. The two pairs of eyes bore down on him in the eerie silence. James reminded himself that he wanted to be in that remote, godforsaken place on the outskirts of Chicago. Even if it meant it was the last place he saw, James had drawn the wolf out of his lair. So far, everything was going according to plan.

Vigo bent forward, his face sliding into the light. What James could see of a hazy outline was replaced by a tailored business suit and thick glasses. The dull brightness accented the man's weathered skin, cracked with deep, stern lines of a demeanor that hadn't been playful since grade school. Vigo's face was not the face James remembered. The years had changed them both but regardless of their age or time apart, James found himself looking at the man that had once been his best friend. The same man he had been plotting revenge against for almost two decades.

Vigo Amarth, CEO and co-founder of Amarth Corporation, had built on the back of James' ingenuity. Keeping James under his control by taking away everything James held dear. Vigo had established himself as one of the most powerful men on the planet and James knew Vigo wouldn't have spent time on anything unless he felt it could reinforce his supremacy.

Vigo bent further forward, his lifeless eyes scrutinizing the growing swelling of James' face. "James, still fighting the good fight, are we? The great physicist and inventor wearing his ideals like a shield of armor. All of your integrity and morals can't hide it from me. I know you. And we both want to find a solution to SOR." The CEO paused, studying James' bloody features in search of any reaction. "You've gone and done it haven't you? You solved the energy crisis."

James' ribs ached, his breaths growing more and more shallow. Yet, despite the burning in his throat for water, James gathered the strength to speak. This was the moment he had been waiting for; he needed to summon all of his courage and resolve. His voice stumbled at first, but his words were steady. "I should have left you on that street, when we were kids. I think about it often. I saw something admirable in you then, a resilience, a pride. But I showed you the power of technology and you saw only a way to control people. Now I've lived long enough to see you become the very evil we sought to stop."

Vigo revealed his teeth as a twinkle came to his eye. "There are only the weak and the strong, and I, my old friend, am not weak. To be successful in this world, you have to have focus and determination. You can't go walking around with ideals and clean fingernails; you have to get dirty."

"No matter how many heads of state you dine with or how many zeros are in your bank account, you will always be too power hungry to help the very world that has given you yours. But you can't escape the end of SOR, no one can. You will have to live out your life powerless to stop all of your comforts from falling away." James turned his head to the side, his hair flopping freely as the fresh taste of metal hit his tongue. He swallowed. "I have ensured it."

Vigo shook his head. "My world is your world and if it collapses, then so will yours. You think people are going to care about some two-bit scientist when they are starving and killing each other? You think you'll get an endless supply of anything you need like you have all these years without me? I'm the face of the company. I'm the man in charge, nobody even knows who you are anymore. I expect a little more gratitude and loyalty from you."

The ropes around James moaned against his expanding chest as he tried to rise out of his seat. "Loyalty! Gratitude! You wouldn't listen. You couldn't be reasoned with. I tried to leave and what did you do? You murdered my wife, my son, my daughter; you destroyed everything that ever meant anything to me and you talk about loyalty!"

"I gave you focus."

"You stole my life."

"No, I gave you a life. You were lost—a wanderer with no direction." The stout businessman's veins pulsed in his neck. "I gave you your lab. I've kept you going while the world burned and let you tinker away at your projects. And this is how you repay me? I saw your potential when you didn't!"

James stared at Vigo, knowing that the man would never apologize, never take responsibility and never admit he was wrong. James had known it was true but still held on to some tiny hope that Vigo could change. The white knuckles of Vigo's clenched fists told James that it was a lost cause.

Vigo took a step back to straighten his tie and run his hand through slick wisps of graying hair. "Now, we tore your lab apart and found nothing, so what did you do with it?"

"Vigo," the doctor said with a cough, his jaw pounding with pain, "thank you for coming down from your thirty-fourth-floor office to visit me personally—it's been too long. You are right, I have had a breakthrough. An invention that will provide clean energy for the entire world, not just yours. I will never tell you where it is, and you will never find it. My greatest creation will be right in front of you, but you lack the intellect to see it. I know every single one of your lies, but you never thought to look into mine."

Vigo's nostrils flared as his eyes grew smaller. James thought about all the years he'd spent as Vigo's prisoner and his spine straightened. His jaw set firmly with the memory of watching his children grow up from afar. Vigo didn't know they were out there. They were the reason he pressed on. The reason that he had to destroy Vigo. The one-track mind businessman thought he had won. And the fiery stare of Vigo told James that his plan was working. James poked the wolf. "See how you are always reacting and never thinking ahead, even now? I can see the wheels in your head turning as you continue to look out for yourself and never consider what you don't know. So… what don't you know?"

James laughed as best as he could, his mind working hard against the pain of his body. He was in control—this was all part of his plan—and as he coughed, he let a large wad of bloody spit fly from his mouth to the floor. Keeping his eyes trained on the pool of blood and sweat he said, "You think dining with the President makes you untouchable? You think influencing members of Congress makes you above the law? You think amassing enough wealth to buy a mid-sized country makes you invincible? You may be able to bend the rules for your own gain but, nobody is invincible. We are all human beings. You bleed just like the rest of us, even if you think that sheer violence makes you able to outsmart me?"

Looking up as well as he could into Vigo's eyes, James added, "My old friend."

Vigo Amarth smacked his knuckles together in front of his chest over and over like a prize fighter warming up. The pair stared one another down in the silence. It was the end of an era. Fate had brought them together; civilization had torn them apart.

Vigo moved, and James could only watch as the wolf began pacing at the edge of his darkening vision. James understood there wasn't a human alive that would cross Vigo, and that was why his plan was going to work. The time had come for James' family to emerge from the shadows and take back the corporation that was rightfully theirs. His son and daughter had grown into strong, steadfast people in a world full of every imaginable darkness. Their lives brought James to sit in defiance—even on death's door.

"It is my greatest failure," James started, "holding onto my past life, unable to let go. You were the sort of person who kept getting up in the face of oppression. I didn't realize what you had become until you resorted to murder. I guess it was all just misplaced hope that my friend was still in there."

Vigo stopped pacing, considering for a moment the conversation with furrowed brow. Then he said, "Let's not dwell on the past. You needed focus, and the company would have been lost without you." Vigo turned to look straight at James, it seemed he still had one card to play. "Who is Owen Bradley?"

James had known this was coming, and he brought his head slightly to the side and back again. He hoped it was enough for Vigo to bite.

Vigo smiled, "I found out you sent him something via private courier. And I know he's at your alma mater in the physics department. So, who is Owen Bradley?"

James let his head roll back. The light casting down revealed an intense grin that he knew would infuriate Vigo to his core.

Vigo pressed. "Is that why you chose him, some kind of sad, misplaced sentiment for the past? Did you somehow think he could save you and steal my company's property? Do I strike you as a man that would sit idly by and let that happen?"

James feigned concern, pulling his eyes open as wide as the swelling would allow.

Vigo smirked. "You didn't think I would find out? Even now you doubt the reach of my influence? Tell me what you sent him!"

James continued his defiant smile.

"Was it the blueprints for a machine? Was it the formula for a new form of SOR?" Vigo questioned with an air of sarcasm even though James knew that Vigo didn't for a second doubt his abilities.

"Vigo," James started, grunting against his restraints, "there was a time in our lives where I would have told you. In fact, you would have been there with me every step of the way. But now, you'll just have to settle for what your actions have brought you—loneliness in the place of true friendship."

The depth of Vigo Amarth's breath indicated he understood that this was the final stand of the great inventor, choosing this moment to defy him and what they had built. Smoothing his tie before flattening the lines of his suit against his body, Vigo said, "I am going to find where you've hidden the solution to the energy crisis. Then I am going to use it solidify my legacy, while you have already been forgotten."

"Same old Vigo," James replied. "Playing only as far as your fist can reach."

Vigo turned to Mondo, silently lurking in the shadows. "We already searched the lab so Owen Bradley must have it. He is the key. If this discovery really is a new energy source, then it is more valuable than the entirety of Amarth's product line and we must have it! This man dreamed of solving the energy crisis once, and now I think he has done it. Owen Bradley knows where it is. We don't need the doctor anymore; he served his purpose and has given us all he has to offer. Get what you can out of him and don't stop until his brains are all over the floor. No one will miss him anyway; he hasn't been more than a hushed rumor in years."

James smiled as Vigo turned and their eyes met once more. James no longer saw an industrial tycoon with his custom shoes and heavy lens glasses. Instead, he saw something familiar, something welcoming, something… he cherished deeply.

Whispering, James added, "Goodbye, Walter."

Vigo stepped back. He stood there, staring for several moments at the captive before him, each second appearing to weigh on his shoulders as if his suit were slowly turning to iron. James could see he had done it; Vigo understood the magnitude of the moment. Everything Vigo was, all of his power and fortune, was because of James. Now, his empire was as fragile as it had ever been. Neither of them spoke. Vigo turned on his heel and strode quickly to the warehouse door.

In the forty years James had known Vigo, he had never seen that look before. He knew that for the first time since Vigo ascended to his throne, the wolf was afraid. James knew his plan would work. In a matter of days, his children would learn their true parentage and Amarth Corporation would return to the rightful ownership of the Stevenson family. Vigo had every reason to be afraid because hidden among the deep-rooted stench of oil that permeated from the steel beams of the warehouse structure, was a camera—James was recording everything. A few more days and the world would learn the truth. Walt would make sure of it.

CHAPTER 20

Time had barely touched the intersection of West Webster and North Cleveland Avenues as it looked almost as it had forty years before. So much so, that when the sun shone bright and the breeze blew just right through the trees, one might think they had indeed traveled back in time.

As she waited for the appointed hour, Clare kept her distance from the parked, bullet proof luxury car—a ride easily recognized as Vigo's and not at all an oddity in his old neighborhood. For all of his greed, all of his hunger, Vigo could still be seen taking the time to pass through his old stomping grounds. He would say it was to feed that very hunger, to remind him from where he came so that he could continue to push forward. Others might say he felt the pain of nostalgia, given that he was too busy even to be present for his parents' final days.

Checking her phone, Clare had a message from Malcom.

All set up. Got every angle. I see the car… clever girl.

Closing her phone, she smiled. The note was Malcom's way of telling her to stay safe but that he knew she could handle herself. Whatever happened though, Malcom would be watching and could make sure the truth got out. With everything set, it was time for her to move into a better position. Crossing the street, she acted as casually as she could and headed up North Cleveland Avenue past Vigo's car. Twirling her arms about, she bobbed her head and mouthed words to songs that she recalled her parents singing to her as a child. Classic lullabies from her mother and 90's grunge from her father. She knew that her love of music came from them, the lyrics and rhythm somehow surviving the thinning of memory that is the passage of time. What little she knew of them, floated in and out with every chorus. Focusing on the melody was all she could do to keep moving forward, her thoughts focused on the songs and refraining from sneaking a glance at the matte black car with the occupants she knew were inside. She couldn't attract attention to herself until it was time but she had wanted to pass by the car. She needed the sight of it to steel her nerves before the confrontation.

Turning the corner to escape their view, she leaned up against the brick wall of an appliance store that was in its third generation of ownership. Looking up, she saw the small outline of two men approaching on West Webster.

Even from a distance, Clare could see a young man. It had to be her brother Owen—but he'd changed his hair? It was hard to tell from under the stiff, clean looking hat. He walked alongside another man she didn't recognize. Her heart fluttered—could it be possible? Was her father on his way to her at his very moment?

She hesitated in her preparation, the unfolding scene in front of her melted away as her focus was entirely on the pair striding towards her. Her eyes squinted to see, to catch a glimpse of what her heart had hoped for. She had only just learned the man was alive and it had torn into her chest deeper than she could admit. For so long there had been nothing but hatred, a desire for revenge, but now Clare had to face what she hadn't thought possible—she could know her family again.

As she watched, her pulse settled in along with the disappointment. The man with her brother was too young to be her father. He was simple and plain, nothing distinguishing about his features; if it hadn't been for the magnitude of the moment, she wouldn't have noticed him at all.

The pair were walking almost in lock step as they made their way towards the intersection. They looked more nervous than casual and cautiously kept their heads on a swivel. As they drew closer, Clare began to prepare herself for the retribution she had been waiting for since she was six years old.

*****

Owen didn't know what to expect up ahead, but he was glad Walt was there with him. The succinctly spoken man had grown to become his friend in only a way ducking into storage closets and camping out in prestigious museums could form.

"Remind me again," Owen asked of Walt. "Remind me again what we are expecting here."

Walt's demeanor had no noticeable change, he simply responded, "Your father, James, was a great inventor. I worked directly with him, and he told me to help you. He said that he had sent his greatest achievement to you, and that you would need my help because of the corrupt people that would want it."

Walt had always spoken in such sweeping vagueness and as they kept walking, Owen just looked at him longing for more. The last few days had been a whirlwind since they met. Owen felt like a new person and practically was. A complete part of his identity was unknown and yet now, it made sense. He had felt something, a calling all along—but why?

"And you don't know what it is? What it looks like? Anything?" Owen asked, using his thumb to roll his father's ring around on the finger it now resided on.

"Correct. I was not privy to the revelation. Your father told me it was for my own protection. He said that he had everything planned out and that I should trust him," Walt responded, his face contorting with his final phrase like he was trying to mimic someone.

"It is a rather pleasant day," Walt added after a moment of silence. "I believe that I would like to remember this."

The two continued the pace through the long tunnel of tree-lined canopy stretching before them. The air was full of songs whistled cheerfully by birds hidden among the branches. The path ahead was full of the promise that answers were growing near.

The leaves gave way to the sight of a large, black car. The looming presence of it sent a chill down Owen's spine. They continued forward; their destination was the corner where the two streets met.

Owen watched as the driver's door opened, then the passenger side rear door. Out of the car rose two men, their suits snapping slightly in the light breeze. Owen's feet came to a stop alongside Walt.

The two powerful men locked eyes with Owen. He watched them awkwardly, suddenly very aware of his hands and unsure what to do with them. They managed to find his pockets just as the businessmen came to within conversation distance.

The man Owen assumed was Vigo stopped, the other large man Owen had seen hung back, behind only a few steps. Owen looked at Vigo with all the gumption he could muster. Vigo smiled. Owen got the eerie feeling that the man enjoyed these kinds of encounters far too much.

"Alright Owen Bradley, you have what I am looking for?" Vigo asked, asserting his impatience.

Owen paused a moment, the name Owen Bradley felt peculiar to him now. Vigo had called him Bradley but Owen had already fully embraced Stevenson. The wheels turned quickly and Owen realized that Vigo didn't know his true identity. Owen knew that knowledge was the real power. He decided not to let on any information unless it was necessary.

Vigo chuckled, believing that in every situation he had the upper hand. "You were sent a package a few days ago. It's my property and you've come about it illegally. Now, hand it over."

Owen thought about what Vigo meant. The note? The one that started it all? Owen saw his father's plan unfolding before him. Owen's father had known Vigo would discover the courier and would then go on a wide chase after Owen, but why? Why risk the exposure? Owen didn't have the answers but he knew he needed to see this through. A few days ago, he would have been a blubbering fountain of information and acquiescence to every demand Vigo made.

But, Owen was now Owen Stevenson, and James Stevenson's son wasn't going to back down. The journey of figuring out that he belonged was all he needed in order to shore up his self-confidence. Touching his family's ring lightly with his thumb, Owen responded, "What I have can't be given."

Owen glanced from Vigo to the large brute standing just beyond his shoulder. He understood what the man's presence implied and that wasn't a fight he could win.

"You see, Mr. Amarth," Owen said. "What I was sent can't be given because it is different for everyone. It can't be taught. It can't be stolen. It can only be earned. What came for me was discovery, and that is something all of your money and power and influence could never take away."

Vigo brought his hands together and cracked his knuckles in front of his chest.

"The nerve on this kid," Vigo said, gesturing to his enforcer. "I don't know what it was. The package was fairly large, like a briefcase, so what was in it? A prototype? Plans for something? I'm going to get it kid, so might as well save yourself some pain."

Owen looked at Walt for a second. He didn't really know the man very well, but they stood side by side in that moment and somehow it felt like an extension of his father's own hand—it gave him confidence.

Owen fished the first clue from his pocket. The single sheet of paper was folded up tight.

Celestial bodies abound in close family heirlooms found.

Family heirlooms found, Owen thought, and so much more. Handing it over to Vigo, the businessman's eyes beamed with victory. Opening up the note, the grin quickly turned sour.

"Is this some sort of joke?"

"You asked for what I was sent, that's it," Owen replied.

"What are you trying to pull?"

"Like I said," Owen said, mustering every ounce of courage. "It can't be given; the discovery has to be earned."

"Very well then," Vigo said, the veins in his temple beginning to pop out with rage. "Teach him some respect!"

The command set Mondo moving forward towards Owen, the look in his eye that of an unmatched warrior, a man who had never met someone who could stand toe-to-toe with him physically.

"Vigo!" Came a shout from a third voice outside their confrontation. "Pick on someone your own size."

The two sharply dressed men turned to survey from where the bold exclamation came. Owen and Walt could only stare as a young woman focused the monster's wrath upon herself.

"And who are you?" Vigo asked. The man's face contorted with the confusion of being confronted by a petite young lady with long blonde hair pulled tightly back in a ponytail.

"I'm here to make you pay for your crime," Clare replied.

"Oh really?" Vigo questioned. The pair laughed with ease, saying all that needed to be said about how nonexistent the threat was to them.

The woman came to a stop in the middle of the intersection. Owen's eyes darted back and forth, his thoughts tumbling. The note. The meetup. The specific time. His father's plan—Clare. The girl was Clare, his long-lost sister. A new ache crept into Owen. His sister was real, and she was standing twenty feet away. He suddenly found himself wanting to be on a patio, a gentle breeze blowing, listening to her life's story away from danger.

The corner of Vigo's lip turned up in the ugliest of grins. "You'll have to be more specific Miss, there are so many crimes that I am guilty of." Vigo chuckled softly.

Owen watched as Clare shifted to stagger her stance and brought her fists up, ready to fight them both.

Vigo tilted his head to the side, curious. "The world is a dangerous and difficult place. I suggest you reconsider making threats on which you cannot deliver. Now leave. This business doesn't concern you."

"But it does," Clare added. "He's my brother."

"Your broth…" Vigo started, but was cut off.

"Vigo," Clare addressed him, her voice strong but ragged and coarse. "I am here to kill you."

"Really? Kill me? I'm sure whatever our differences, we can work something out. There's no need for bloodshed," Vigo replied, holding his hands up slightly in an expression of de-escalation.

Owen looked on as Vigo seemed to catch up.

"Your brother?" Vigo asked, looking between the two of them. "Are you hiding it then? Where's the real package? Is this some sort of plan to steal from me? I want what I'm owed."

"Then come and get it," Clare replied.

"I've had enough of these games," Vigo said, patting his enforcer on the back. "Break that pretty little face."

"No!" Owen exclaimed as he started to move in front to block them, but he was held back. Walt had shot an arm up to stop him in his tracks.

Walt finally spoke, addressing Clare. His words very clear and even among the heightened tension in the intersection. "Clare, both of these men are responsible for you losing your father. But remember that taking a life is the easiest and least rewarding path to retribution. It is no way to break all sixteen boards."

Owen stared at Walt in confusion at the sudden finding of a philosophical voice while the brute continued to lumber forward towards Clare.

*****

The words that were spoken met Clare's ears and penetrated the rage boiling inside. She heard him, and because of it, her nerves settled, her control returned and her body relaxed, confident in all of her training. What Owen's companion said sparked a thought in Clare's mind, allowing the memory of her past to trust that her path was destined to come to this. She had been given an opportunity and she had the choice of killing this man, or making him suffer.

Vigo's bodyguard made the same mistake as any thug of his size; he weighed physical presence higher than skill and cunning. Clare remained steady. She knew what she had to do and had to make it quick. The training kicked in: use your enemy's strength against them and strike before they catch on.

The big man arrived in front of her, taking no time before he acted. Clare saw his right shoulder sink slightly back, so she ducked and side-stepped to her left. She noticed that his hand was the size of her head as it swung viciously past, a blast of air fanning her in its wake. She understood immediately that she did not want to find herself on the receiving end of anything he had to dish out. So, shifting her momentum off her left foot, Clare brought her knee up, then dropped everything she had into her strike from her right heel. Landing straight on to the front of Mondo's kneecap. The big man was already off balance from missing his punch, and Clare's blow dropped him fully down to his right knee. With a grunt, the man landed hard, his eyeline now even with hers.

Instinctually he reached to grab her, Clare spun away from his hands and rolled across his muscular back. Landing on the opposite side of him, she planted her feet firmly. The next blow was meant to disable him, to knock him back and take the fight out of him. Squatting down, the screams of her young brother filled her ears once more. The scorching heat from the car wreck danced on her cheeks as hours of sweat soaked training propelled her launch. She left the ground, simultaneously bringing her left leg up to strike the big man directly in the side of his face. An audible crunch rang out amongst the calm, breezy day.

Mondo's left hand shot up quickly to support his face, while his right reached around for her. Now it was real for him, now anger surged into his veins. Clare patiently dodged his grasps, staying just out of reach until she had circled around in front of him again. Then she expertly clasped onto his wrist tightly and spun under his arm. The large man's eyes finally changed to shock when she fired the blow into his bound elbow—shattering it.

Crying out like a wounded bull, the large man's useless right arm went limp. Half kneeling there in the street, Clare saw the man's eyes flash fear. She wondered if he had ever felt it before. If, at that moment, his mind experienced a flood of understanding at what his victims had known over the years. Clare studied him as the wave passed and his focus turned once again to her.

Clare looked down at him through fiery eyes. The pain and hatred in her heart manifested by her stare. Struggling to rise, Mondo wouldn't accept defeat. He was going to force her hand. His left hand released his face, blood dripping from his fingers and chin. Closing it into a fist, he swung awkwardly at her, unable to gain traction with his other arm hanging disabled and an unstable knee.

Clare easily dodged his attempts, letting him tire out while she caught her breath. Once she was ready, she said to him, "You must pay for the crimes you have committed against my family and countless others…" Her hand slid over the hilt she kept closely to her low back. Rolling rapidly over the ground under his desperate attempts to catch her, she popped up at his side. Her blade, sharp as any, sliced right through the thick sinew of the man's Achilles; severing it in two. Then before the man could even react, she spun and delivered the same fate to the other leg.

Collapsing on the pavement, the man's screams spooked every cheerful bird for three blocks. The trees above the intersection were suddenly flush with the fleeing of dozens of wings. Clare paused to wipe her blade on the man's pant leg. Then standing up, she turned to face Vigo.

The man stood with pistol drawn, already holding her brother and his friend at gunpoint.

"Impressive," Vigo said. "Very impressive, but you didn't think I would come to this little rendezvous unprepared, did you?"

Clare studied the situation as she gathered herself, letting the pounding of her heart start to calm. Vigo thought he was in control, but he was simply giving Clare a chance to compose herself.

"Okay, you've got my attention. So who the hell are you anyway?" Vigo asked.

"Her name is Clare," came a reply from Owen, drawing Vigo's attention once again.

"That doesn't mean anything to me. Just another nobody, but she could be a queen with those skills," Vigo said. "Why don't you come work for me? Seems I'm in need of a new body guard."

Clare didn't answer. She only moved slowly away from her first victim while keeping her eyes trained on her second.

"Seems she's lost her tongue. I see you with that look. Why don't you go ahead and stop right there," Vigo said. "You see, your brother here has my property and if he would simply hand it over then I'll be on my way."

Nobody moved. Clare's hands grew more and more steady with each breath.

"Alright Owen Bradley, tell me where to find it," Vigo pressed. "End this game and no one else has to get hurt."

"His name isn't Owen Bradley," Clare answered. "His name is Owen Stevenson."

"What was that?" Vigo asked, confusion creeping into his words.

"Tell him!" Clare bellowed. "Tell James Stevenson's son the truth!"

The gun faltered slightly in Vigo's hand. Clare could see him questioning the truth of her statement. Clare knew it must have seemed impossible. For her, it had been only a small glimmer of guttural hope for decades. Now, everything she had dreamed was real. She watched as everything Vigo knew became surreal.

"You know it's true," Clare said. "All of your plans, your empire, built from the start on a simple lie. The Stevenson children didn't die that day. Now, they have returned for what is rightfully theirs."

"So that's why he sent it to you," Vigo said, turning his focus to Owen. "That's why you look so familiar. You are the traitor's son! It is almost impossible to believe, but here you are. He somehow found a way to save you, and was clever enough to hide you all this time."

"Tell him!" Clare screamed. "Tell him how you arranged the car wreck that killed his mother! Tell him that his father is actually alive and you have been keeping him as your prisoner!"

Her voice dropped to a growl; her chest heaved as chemicals poured through her every muscle. "Tell him the truth. You owe our father that much."

Owen's eyes darted back and forth between the two.

A crunching piece of gravel under Clare's foot brought Vigo back fully to the present.

"Stop right there," he said, waving the pistol towards Owen. "One more step and I'll shoot your brother."

Clare stopped, now twenty-five feet away and in perfect control.

"It's time you stepped down," Owen said. "Let our father go and we won't tell the world what you did."

"You can't prove anything," Vigo replied, defiance returning from his usual arsenal. "That was so long ago and there wasn't a police investigation. Drunk driver at the scene, case closed; nothing you can do about it."

"We'll see what our father has to say about that," Owen said.

"That's the thing…" Vigo started, his ugly, smug smile flashing across his face. "I hate to rain on the family reunion, but he's a little tied up at the moment."

"What?" Owen said as Clare's heart fluttered, a crack emerging in the fragile hope she carried there.

"Yeah, I'm afraid daddy isn't going to be able to make it."

"You have kept him prisoner long enough, where is he?" Clare shouted.

The gun still trained on Owen, Vigo turned his head to her and winked. The gesture tore apart all of her years of training, everything she had worked for and she lunged at the man.

*****

The shot rang out like a crack of thunder on a cloudless day. Owen could only flinch as he tried to process the adrenaline pressing his feet into the concrete. From somewhere afar, he sensed a shadowy figure pass before him but as it did, he instantly understood the ramifications.

The man that Owen had only known for three days jumped selflessly in front of Vigo's blast. His ability to determine the outcome of the situation inhuman. As Walt landed, Owen saw Clare spin and let loose of her knife. A shimmer flew through the air before it disappeared into the back of Vigo's hand. The man's grip buckled with the splitting of his flesh and he dropped the gun. The intersection filled once again with a surprised howl.

The gun fell in slow motion for Owen. The realization that his new friend had just jumped in front of a bullet for him was too much to process.

"You shot him!" Was all he could think to say as the shock set in. The words filled the surrounding streets as Owen turned to check on Walt. Clamoring to all fours, he peered over the man and what he saw, he could not comprehend.

Owen focused to try and make sense of Walt's condition. He was vaguely aware that Clare moved quickly towards them and scoped up the gun. Owen felt her standing there, between himself and Vigo. He turned to see what she would do next.

Blood dripped steadily onto the dusty gravel as Vigo let out a soft grunt upon pulling the blade from his hand. The sharply dressed businessman left his blood to stream from the wound as he studied the knife with the only working hand he had left.

The maniacal chuckle that arose from him sent waves of anger through Owen as he watched Clare get ready to fight once again.

Vigo's eyes left the blade and met Clare's; there was a look of recognition there. Owen saw that Vigo's gaze grow and turn stern once again as he accepted the truth—she was James Stevenson's daughter.

"You should have come to work for me," Vigo said, intrigued with the blade he kept turning over and over in his hand. "I could have made you a very rich woman."

"Retribution for the lives you have destroyed will have to be enough," Clare replied.

Vigo's head rolled back on his thick shoulders. "Well, the road is littered with those that tried to stop me."

Owen moved cautiously closer to Clare, his face red with anger and hate.

"There is only one that matters," Owen said, his voice strong. "The life of a man that trusted you and who you turned your back on, making a stepping stone of his loyalty for your own gain." Owen moved forward to stand just behind Clare's shoulder, the pair of them now facing Vigo as one. "A man that you kept prisoner… a man with more integrity than you ever had… our father."

Vigo looked at them both with a continued air of superiority. "James was pathetic. Look at what he did, spent almost 20 years locked away in his lab while his own children were forced to grow up orphans. What kind of man is that?"

Owen spoke up, "You are going to pay for what you did to our father and to Walt."

The name caused Vigo to take a step back, the ghosts of his past suddenly circling him; a white sheet of doubt spreading on his face, preying on his confidence. "Walt?"

Clare waved the gun at Vigo as Owen said, "Yeah! The man you just shot."

Vigo looked to the blade again; pausing to compose himself. "Well at least he stood up like a man and didn't beg for his life… like your so-called father."

Clare pulled the hammer back on the handgun and took aim. Raising his hands in mock protest, Vigo smiled at her. "I believe you'll be disappointed in the old man. He wasn't much more than a loyal dog."

A second shot tore through the quiet that had settled on the intersection. Vigo toppled over, clutching his right knee; Clare was deadly accurate with more than a knife.

Still the man held on to his self-indulgent mantle, despite the new pain; Vigo's smirk remained. Blood gushed through the gap between his clasped fingers, Vigo let his spiteful words fly. "Who do you think you are? I will bury you. I am powerful like you can't comprehend. Unlike that coward you call father, James. He just sulked in his lab and you two, his kids, were out here the whole time? He abandoned you, but don't worry… he won't be letting you down again anytime soon."

"What are you talking about?" Clare asked, her words strained.

"You're three days too late." Vigo laughed, blood pooling around where he sat on the ground. "I made him. I gave him purpose and drove him to any success he ever found. Then he betrayed me… I killed your insolent, washed-up old man and I'd do it again."

The siblings exchanged glances, the look betraying their understanding that the hope they shared was gone. The promise of being a family again, of holidays and traditions and some semblance of happiness… gone.

Owen's breath shortened, he was ten years old all over again; staring at a boarding school door, begging for the knob to turn and his loneliness to be over. He turned to the only comfort he knew…

*****

Clare's heart pounded, her pulse racing as it carried liquid fire to every fiber of her being. All the years of training, all of the kills that had come before, and yet she was utterly unprepared for loss. Clare raised the gun once again, aiming it squarely at Vigo's face; she turned to the only comfort she had ever known—violence.

She held steady in the opportunity she had dreamt of for years. Vigo was in her crosshairs and she could easily end him. Putting a stop to his reign of tyranny and avenging her father, setting her and her brother free. Her brother…

Owen was still there, humming something softly over her left shoulder. The melody was inviting, familiar. The notes fought against her desire to pull the trigger, the sweet sounds and promise of a life reunited with her brother wrestling with her need for satisfaction.

They all waited in suspended animation as Clare weighed her decision. Then, without warning, a voice from beyond the grave spoke to them…

"Vigo, my greatest creation will be standing right in front of you and you'll never know it."

Vigo's face turned white with worry. Clare lowered the weapon and turned along with her brother to see its source.

Walt was sitting upright on the ground. A blank expression on his face as his mouth stood open, the eyes blankly staring forward.

The reunited siblings turned to each with puzzled looks, then turned back to the being they couldn't explain.

"What the hell?" Clare muttered.

No blood erupted from the wound in Walt's chest, instead there was only the occasional spark. Wires and a clear ooze puddled near the entry area as Clare turned to face Owen. "Is he some kind of robot?"

"I don't know." Owen gasped, his hands starting to shake. "I only met him three days ago."

"A robot?" Vigo questioned.

"First things first," Clare stated calmly as she casually walked over and picked up her blade from Vigo's side. "Nice suit," Clare said as she wiped the blood from her knife on his pant leg. "Don't you go anywhere or I'll blow a hole in the other one."

Vigo was still clutching his leg as best as he could, grunting at her like a mad king unwilling to accept defeat. Clare made sure to keep the gun trained on him.

Satisfied, Clare turned to the amazed Owen and gestured toward Walt. "From the beginning."

"He just showed up at my apartment, said I was in danger and that our father sent him. I don't remember much about Dad…" Owen said, looking down at Walt. "His name is Walt. He had Dad's ring, so I had to find out for sure. I hadn't heard or seen anything from Dad since I was whisked away to boarding school. I had always thought he was dead."

"Did he tell you anything?" Clare asked. "Did he tell you anything about where we could find our father?"

Clare still hung on to some sort of hope. It was the same as she had done all the years since her parents were taken from her. She wanted to believe that Vigo lied; she knew he was good at it. But the quiver in her words betrayed her and for this, she was greeted with a deep heinous chuckle. It rose from the asphalt like hyenas on the fresh scent of a carcass.

"How touching, the prospect of a family reunited and the naïve hope you still carry. A ruthless killer with a soft side… you really should have worked for me. I am a very powerful man you know. I could have made you a goddess. I'm not sure your daddy would have approved but we can't ask him. I've lied about a great many things in my day, but this is the truth," Vigo said, chuckling at himself to shore up his blood-soaked ego.

Steel beams hot from an iron forge appeared in Clare's eyes, her heartbeat steady. Her heart was not to be toiled with. She took a wide arc to approach the downed Vigo, savoring every step. Casting her shadow over him once again, she let the disgust well up inside of her.

"He begged for his life you know," Vigo goaded her. "He pleaded with me like a…"

Bang. This time in the other knee. Vigo rolled violently in reaction, cursing her under his breath and swearing vengeance.

Just as Clare was raising the barrel to put another one in him, Walt spoke again. "It isn't true." His mouth was open, but his lips didn't move—reaffirming in a chilling manner that Walt was actually a machine.

She froze. Owen turned away from the violent scene to see if Walt had more to say. The lab assistant's eyes were animated once again with life as the occasional spark shot out of his chest.

"Your father was a great man and died bravely," Walt said, his robotic tone unable to capture the true nature of his words. "He told me to help Owen and that you Clare, would find your own way. He told me this would happen, that Vigo must be stopped. He told me to play this recording when you were reunited." Walt looked from Owen to Clare, then he froze.

Walt's voice changed, no longer his own. "Thank you Walt, you have been a trustworthy and noble friend."

Clare met Owen's gaze. They knew beyond a doubt that this was their father's voice. The memory of its rhythmic waves ingrained in their fondest memories.

"Clare… Owen… it has been my deepest regret that it has come to this, but I could see no other way. I am so sorry for what happened to you and your mother. I couldn't save her and almost lost you as well. I knew that I couldn't contact you or risk giving away your existence to Vigo. You see, it is true, the car wreck that took her away from us and tore apart our lives was no accident. Vigo arranged it all. Power hungry and willing to destroy anything in his path, Vigo hired a drug addict to crash into your car. He also paid off a cop with a gambling debt to torch the car and ensure no one made it out. What he couldn't plan for was something that he had lost touch with himself—human kindness. Despite the gambling debt and power of the man he was dealing with, the cop managed to save you two from the wreckage… but your mother was already gone. The cop replaced your bodies with some from the morgue to cover it up. He just couldn't go through with it when he saw you were kids. A soft spot that Vigo never considered. Then I am sure that Vigo paid off the medical examiner as well so your death certificates would be quick and official. To the rest of the world, you were all dead.

"Once I learned what Vigo had done, I knew that I had lost. I could never bring myself to the vicious and violent level that Vigo stooped, so I relinquished myself to my work. Vigo left me alone because my lab kept turning out product and his security goons reported that I never left the building. It was six months later before I learned that you survived. All I was given was that you were alive and more info would come. It took everything I had not to rush to your doors, just to see your faces, hear your laugh, and tousle your hair. But I knew we would never be safe with how powerful Vigo had become, so I instead decided to bury him and take away everything he loved—just as he did to me.

"I waited, patiently, for the briefest of glimpses into your lives that would come and could tell me about what you were doing. I never inquired or did anything to bring attention to you other than reading about you growing up without me. It wasn't enough. I couldn't bring myself to sleep, eat, live; that was when I had the idea for Walt. I needed an assistant. Someone who could execute my plan and be an extension of myself beyond my physical body.

"Clare, my darling. You have grown into such a beautiful young woman. There is so much of your mother in you. Strong and resilient, I know that you are a good person… vigilante and all. Take care of your brother, I already know that you can take care of yourself.

"Owen. Son. You are smarter and more brilliant than I ever could have believed. Even without my influence you came back to Chicago to study physics. On-track to be the next Dr. Stevenson before your twenty-second birthday. I am so proud of you and the research you are doing. Stay close with your sister, you guys are going to need each other in the months and years to come.

"My children, please meet Walt. His existence may be impressive but he is not my greatest creation… you are. However amazing and revolutionary he is, you are more. I have created him to battle the unchecked evil I see in Vigo. He must be stopped as none of my childhood friend remains. Walter Amarth was a hopeful, cheerful young boy and my best friend. In honor of that, I have named my assistant Walt, so that Vigo can know where he went wrong.

"Clare… Owen… I must now get to the important part. Before I tell you this, I want you to know, I love you with everything I am and everything I do. I hope that you will remember where you come from and to always seek kindness.

"Clare. Owen. Amarth Corporation is yours. You now have control over Vigo's majority shares as well as seventy-five percent of his estate. He won't need it while spending multiple lifetimes in jail, probably a cripple after Clare gets through with him."

An audible laugh came from the wounded Vigo, interrupting the recording for the first time with his hubris. "You stupid prick, they'll never see a cent!"

The recording continued, unable to respond to his outburst but doing so all the same. "When Amarth Corporation was set up, Vigo was made CEO and myself Chief of Technology. I left the business decisions up to him but I wanted protection. Your mother and her intuition had already warned me of the growing monster inside of him so I asked that a clause be added to the founding of our company. That clause stated that if either party committed a crime against the other then the offender would forfeit his shares and seventy-five percent of his estate to the victim. At the time, Vigo thought it was stupid and a poor business move on my part given that I could have asked for so much more. But that was all I needed. A beneficial salary that would keep us far from the poor house and that clause, to ensure that I would be protected if the monster inside of him grew out of control.

Vigo's eyes grew wide as he began to recall their history. "You can never prove anything; I'll tie you up in so many courts. Nothing will change, I know senators and judges, the board will never stand for this!"

The recording continued, with a lighter, almost gleeful tone. "The video of my death proving Vigo's involvement and enacting the clause is already on its way to every major news outlet and the FBI. Walt here was sworn to make the video but do nothing otherwise to intervene. Please do not be angry with him. He is only able to do what he was programmed to do.

"The next issue will be proving that you are who you are. The world does believe that you are dead after all. Your identity can be verified through a reputable blood bank that has had your DNA since both of your births. Vigo never found and destroyed it because he never thought it would matter. He was always terrible at chess.

"The Amarth Corporation board will back you on this. I have sent each of them letters of the situation and reminded them of where all of their money has come from. I assured them that the future with you will be far more lucrative than with Vigo—what with his being in prison and all. The company will be happy to usher in the long-lost children of one its founders in wake of the demise of their disgraced CEO.

"My final act is that I have left you with the keys to Walt so that you can decide his fate. Inside Walt is a power generation unit that I call: autonomous self-replicating energy core or ASREC. All of the patent and design details have been filed under a secret division I created within Amarth's umbrella. The ASREC is a near perfect alternating magnetic induction generator and can power Walt running non-stop at a full 27.8 mph sprint for five hundred years. Yes, I said years. A unit the size of Walt himself could power a city block for the same amount of time. ASREC is completely clean and safe. A baby could sleep on top of one and would never know it was there.

"ASREC is the answer to the energy crisis. This is what the world has been waiting for. Vigo had made big plans to set up a new plant to produce the replacement for SOR but I have gone behind his back and drawn the plans up to produce ASREC on a global scale. The ground breaks in a few weeks and now I must challenge you. Use this invention not for profit, not for greed, but instead give this technology to the world for free. Bring us out of this cataclysmic destruction that is our dependence on Earth's depleted resources. It will take a monumental sacrifice and selfless act to end the vicious cycle. Something beyond what anyone has been willing to do before. I know that you two are up to the job, knowing better than anyone that money doesn't buy what the heart truly needs. That is my charge to you and it is no small task, but I trust you. I am so very proud of you and will always be with you. I love you dearly. Now… go save the world."

Clare realized that their father had just entrusted them with the future of civilization. An entire planet's worth of people, each with their own lives, the future of which being determined on a single street corner. She looked at Owen with shared shock. Their father had sacrificed himself so that the world would have that chance. Her father really had been the man she dreamed of but because of it, she would never get to see him again.

It was a terrible thing to weigh the hurt from one against the hope of many but without even saying a word, the siblings nodded to each other in agreement that they would honor his legacy.

A low growl from just beyond their feet tore at the elation and remorse of the moment.

"You think any of that is true!" Vigo barked at them, his spit flying like a savage dog. The fear that had crept in from his old friend's final words reaching the surface. "You can't prove anything, I am Vigo Amarth. I built this company from the ground up and you'll never have it. And give away the greatest technology ever invented? Your father was a fool. I will bury you…"

Vigo kept up his act of defiance from his new found position on the pavement. The man couldn't walk, couldn't keep his company, and couldn't accept that he had been his own demise.

"What do you want to do about him?" Owen asked, all smiles.

Clare looked down the street as the sound of approaching sirens could be heard. Letting out a deep breath, she said, "They can have him. I have had enough retribution for one lifetime."

Throwing her arms around her brother's neck, they embraced. For the first time in seventeen years, she let the hate sink away. Her heart filled in reuniting with her brother and the realization that her father had really been out there—fighting for her all along.

They turned to see Walt nod at them in acknowledgement. They returned the gesture, unsure of the niceties in human cyborg interactions. Owen tilted his head Clare's direction and asked, "How are we going to explain what happened here?"

Clare beamed even brighter and motioned to the awning of the building closest to them, a security camera neatly tucked in the corner. "We've got a friend," she said and playfully punched her brother in the arm. Owen noticed the camera and chuckled while rubbing his arm—his sister sure was full of surprises.

They turned and walked arm in arm to a nearby bench to wait for the authorities. Leaving the intersection behind, the events still processing in their minds.

Vigo watched them turn their backs on him from his position of humility on the ground. His rant of defiance trailed off as an air of recognition of his surrounding took hold.

Owen was first to break the silence. "So, you ready to save the world?"

Clare sighed; it was a tall order but somehow, she felt confident that they could do it. That the boards were stacked sixteen deep and she had trained her whole life to break them.

"Yeah… for Mom and Dad."

"For Mom and Dad," Owen agreed, enjoying the fact that he could say that and know with confidence who they were. Owen looked at Clare, their loneliness fading. They were family now.

Clare surveyed the scene once-more, she was proud to be Clare Stevenson. Her father was a great man.

Owen chuckled softly. "I just have to ask… how the hell did you learn to take down a guy three times your size?"

"I'll tell you, but it's a long story," Clare said.

"No problem, I've got plenty of time."

Red and blue lights turned every corner, racing in their direction. The pair calmly took in the action.

"Honestly," Clare started. "I thought you would look different."

A big smile that looked strikingly like their father's, spread across Owen's face. He had completely forgot about his makeshift disguise and he slowly removed the glasses he didn't even need from his face.

"Let me just tell you what Dad had me doing these last few days…" The shared laughter broke out between them, not heard since they were both very young.

"I want to hear it and everything," Clare said, her words the verbalization from letting go of a lifetime of hate. "We certainly have a lot to talk about and big shoes to fill."

"Yeah, I have a feeling that all the stories about Dad are true. He's got quite the conspiracy legend on campus."

Clare smiled. "Speaking of conspiracy, are you a terrorist?"

Owen eyes widened with worry. "Wonder how long that will take to straighten out."

They chuckled in the irony. "We might need to lay low," Owen offered. "I know a great little place with some good music."

"Is that where you learned that song?" Clare asked.

"That is where it came back to me. It was Mom's."

"Yeah. I think it's all starting to come back now."

"Clare," Owen said, looking lovingly at his older sister. "I'm glad you're here."

Wrapping him up in a hug, Clare embraced her brother and felt the recognition of familiarity from many hugs long before. They eased apart and watched as the authorities tried to make sense of the scattered businessmen and apparent robot.

As the red and blue lights washed over their vision, they looked up from their little corner. They were standing under the sign for W. Webster and N. Cleveland Avenues. Owen studied it before he asked, "What do you suppose is the meaning behind this place? Everything I've just been through, every destination, it always had such purpose. So why here?"

They both paused and looked at each other with thoughtful silence, pondering the massive interlocking events that brought them there.

Owen looked to his sister; she could only shrug.

With the promise of a new era and looking to the future for the first time in their lives, the pair could ever so faintly hear in the branches above—robots battling monsters.

ACKNOWLEDGEMENTS:

I would like to thank my wife and two amazing kids. Without them, I wouldn't find a single word to fill these pages. They give me the strength to press on through every iteration of this novel.

I would also like to thank my family, the beta-readers, for their encouragement and support despite having to trudge through the early drafts of this book.

The book would also not be where it is without the amazing dedication and advice I received from my editors. From dev, to copy, to proof; over and over again, the encouragement and guidance brought this to the finish line as something that I am proud to put my name on. Along with my amazing interior and cover designers, I really had an amazing crew to work with.

Lastly, this novel is dedicated to my father. He is a man of quiet contemplation and hilarious anecdotes that I have only recently grown to appreciate upon becoming a father myself. When asked for advice by a group of graduating seniors he simply replied, "Buy low, sell high." He is truly a man of the mindset that if it can't be said simply, then don't say it at all.

My father was at every game, event, and activity I ever participated in. He worked, without complaint, to provide every opportunity I could ever want. I never heard a discouraging word from him growing up. And now that I have grown, I know it wasn't because he never had those moments, I know it is because he is the man that he is. The character of James is what that means to me.